Dear Readers:

Many years ago, when I was a kid, my father said to me, "Bill, it doesn't really matter what you do in life. What's important is to be the *best* William Johnstone you can be."

I've never forgotten those words. And now, many years and almost two hundred books later, I like to think that I am still trying to be the best William Johnstone I can be. Whether it's Ben Raines in the Ashes series, or Frank Morgan, the Last Gunfighter, or Smoke Jensen, our intrepid mountain man, or John Barrone and his hard-working crew keeping America safe from terrorist lowlifes in the Code Name series, I want to make each new book better than the last and deliver powerful storytelling.

Equally important, I try to create the kinds of believable characters that we can all identify with, real people who face tough challenges. When one of my creations blasts an enemy into the middle of next week, you can be damn sure he had a good reason.

As a storyteller, my job is to entertain you, my readers, and to make sure that you get plenty of enjoyment from my books for your hard-earned money. This is not a job I take lightly. And I greatly appreciate your feedback—you are my gold, and your opinions *do* count. So please keep the letters and e-mails coming.

Respectfully yours,
William W. Johnstone

WILLIAM W. JOHNSTONE

THE LAST GUNFIGHTER: MANHUNT

PINNACLE BOOKS
Kensington Publishing Corp.
http://www.kensingtonbooks.com

PINNACLE BOOKS are published by

Kensington Publishing Corp.
850 Third Avenue
New York, NY 10022

First Printing: October 2004

10 9 8 7 6 5 4 3 2 1

Printed in the United States of America

AUTHOR'S NOTE

In the 1800s, when cattlemen in Texas were spending a good deal of time, energy, and money trying to get their herds to market, the thought of a railroad spur and associated livestock yards in anyone's town could bring on a spirited debate—and even a fistfight or two. Though many cattle owners felt the railheads would be just the ticket to save time and help their fortunes grow, folks of a more temperate nature saw the cow towns as nothing but a magnet for drunken vice and other forms of debauchery.

When the good citizens of Parker County, Texas, faced the question of whether the railroad should put a major stockyard in their neck of the woods or in the small Texas town of Ft. Worth, people took sides and voiced strong opinions. It turned out to be a lively discussion.

Thankfully, it never rose to the level that follows.

1

"Dying ought to be something a man does in private," Frank Morgan said, his back propped up against three feather pillows. Most of the stuffing had long since worked its way out of the canvas ticking and it was bunched up behind him in a grimy wad.

Morgan stared, blank-faced, through the dusty window at the bleak world outside. A frigid wind had blown for weeks across the flat west Texas plain, with no more than a fence post and a few strands of wire to stop it. The wind rattled the rippled glass windowpane and sent a strong enough draft through the dingy hotel room to flicker the flame on the single beeswax candle at the bedside table.

The gunfighter watched as another tumbleweed piled its brittle gray skeleton against a dozen others along a fence row outside. He shook his head and let it fall to one side so he could look the young Texas Ranger in the eye.

"I'd be much obliged to you, Beaumont, if you'd just clear out of here and let me be alone when the time comes."

Beaumont groaned to his feet. It was a weary, bone-tired groan, much too old for a man like him.

He bit his lip and joined Frank in staring out the cheap glass of the filthy window.

"I heard yesterday that a pretty whore named Rita lived up here in this very room a few years back." He stood close, only inches from the window, talking more to it than to Frank. "They say she got so plumb sick and tired of tryin' to look out these stinkin' little windows that she rented her a room over at the Claremont instead." The stout little Texas Ranger turned slowly to look at Frank. When the gunfighter said nothing, he turned back toward the window. "Poor thing died of consumption last year, but at least she had a decent view toward the end. I reckon a whore spends enough time cooped up in her room she deserves a decent piece of glass."

"I reckon," Frank said. He let his eyes fall shut. "I think I'll take a nap for a while if it wouldn't disturb you too awful much."

Beaumont held a piece of heavy yellow paper rolled up in a tube in his hand. "Don't you even want to take a peek at what I brought?"

Morgan had to give the boy credit. He'd stuck by him for weeks, trying to cheer him up, trying to nursemaid him through the depths of despair that followed the confrontation with the killer Ephraim Swan. Frank could tell the poor Ranger was worried to the point of vexation—but he couldn't bring himself to care.

Beaumont read him the paper every day, but there was no news worth hearing. He tried to engage Morgan in card games, but even when Frank held a winning hand, he folded anyway. The exasperated Ranger even hired a girl to come in and sing. Sing she did, everything from beautiful arias to bawdy barroom ballads—but she'd reminded Morgan of Dixie's daughters.

Now the boy had some other notion of a surprise rolled up in his hand. Some little something or another he thought would salve Morgan's tormented soul and somehow make him forget about the brutal murder of his innocent wife, something that would set everything right in the world again.

Since Dixie's death, Frank Morgan had felt like little more than an empty husk of a man. If he walked outside, he knew he'd blow away like one of the passing tumbleweeds on the cold west Texas wind.

In the weeks since the standoff with Swan, Morgan had been slow to recover physically. He hardly ate more than a nibble, and spent all his waking hours gazing out the tiny window in his rented room.

The doctor insisted there was no reason why he shouldn't make a full recovery and regain his complete health, but Morgan knew he was only a shadow of his former self. The weeks turned into months, and though his body continued to mend, he knew the part of him that was really alive was slipping away with each passing day.

His long, dark hair had more silver to it than ever and it stuck out in all directions, depending on how he slept. He kept his pistol handy on a peg beside the bed, and threatened to shoot anyone who came near him with a comb. A heavy matted tangle of salt-and-pepper beard couldn't hide the hollows of his cheeks or the sunken crescents under his eyes. Frank Morgan looked and smelled of death.

The man who couldn't be beaten had simply given up.

Morgan's cracked lips barely parted when he spoke. "Velda was the only one with brains around here. She left when the gettin' was good." His once-piercing whisper was now no more than a careless mumble. "I wouldn't want to sit around and watch a used-up old gunfighter rot away any more than she did."

"Her leavin' had nothing to do with you, Frank. Velda just never could get used to settlin' down to a respectable life." Beaumont gave a shrug and chuckled. His lips pulled back forming an easy smile. He fell for women fast, but appeared to get over them with equal speed. "Last I heard she'd run off with a sassy gambler from Waco who had more money than he had good sense. Now, you quit with all this talk about rottin'. The doc says you're gettin' better in spite of your grumpy nature. A man like you is too tough to be done in by a little blood leakage."

Morgan scoffed, staring up at the leak-stained ceiling. "Son, the things you don't know about a man like me could fill a mighty big book."

Beaumont rolled the yellow paper tighter in his hands like a club and used it to point at Morgan. "I know plenty, you old cob. I grew up on Frank Morgan stories. My pa used to tell me all about your escapades when I was just a sprout. My only aim was to grow up to be just like Frank Morgan. I grew up idolizing you . . . and if you'd get up off your hind end I still would."

Frank waved away the compliment as if it were a

horsefly. "I don't much care to be emulated; it's too damned burdensome a responsibility."

The Ranger scooted his chair closer and shrugged off the comment. His face brimmed over with the enthusiasm of his normally positive nature—like a wide-eyed puppy, excited about everything. "Listen here, Morgan, the bubbles downstairs in Mrs. Pratt's weather-guessing glass say we can expect some clearing tomorrow and some warmer weather, I'd expect." He spread the paper flat out in front of him so Frank could read it. "I got something here that might be just the cure for what ails you."

Morgan scanned the yellow flier. A big drawing of two crossed Colt Peacemakers decorated the top third of the paper. It was tattered at the corners from hanging on a post in the screaming wind. He gave it a quick look and shook his head. "I don't care to enter any shooting contest." He lowered an eyebrow. "I been in enough of those for ten lifetimes."

"Don't have to enter it," Beaumont said. "Just come and watch me. Cheer me along while I shoot. It'd do you good to get out." For such a tough Texas lawman, the boy had eyes that pleaded as sadly as a puppy. "What do you say?"

Morgan took up the paper and read it over more thoroughly at arm's length. "Potter County spring shooting championship," he said under his breath. "Says here they have cash prizes. You thinking you might earn yourself a little grubstake and win Miss Velda back from that fool gambler?"

"Why don't you forget about her? She's gone," Beaumont said. He sat still, staring hard, waiting for an answer. "Come on, Morgan. What do you say?"

Frank folded the small poster in half lengthwise and handed it back. "Why are you still here?"

Beaumont slumped forward in his chair, all the breath going out of him at once. "I don't know myself, Morgan, the way you're actin'. There's at least three men in Amarillo who'd shoot you there in your bedclothes just to say they were the one who captured the honor of killing the great Frank Morgan. None of 'em give a tinker's damn whether you're asleep in your bed or facin' them on the street."

The Ranger got to his feet again and set his teeth in grim determination. "I figured that after what you did for me, I owed you a little watchin' over. You and my pa were friends—good friends from what he used to tell me." He rubbed a calloused hand over his boyish face. "I gotta tell you, though, I'm tuckered out, Frank, and I've got a long ton of other things I could be doin'. If you really do want me gone, then that's what I'll do."

Frank could see the young man had about given up. He knew he stood to watch the only friend he had for miles walk out the door. But the fact that he decided to get up and make a go of it had little to do with him being left alone. Morgan knew about loneliness and most times he relished it. It was something the boy had said that made Morgan pull himself up. It reached out and shook him is what it did.

"I suppose I could come and watch you show up a bunch of upstarts with your marksmanship," Morgan said softly. He managed a weak grin and motioned Beaumont closer with a flick of his hand. "But son, you'd better adjust your windage and elevation. Aimin' to be anything like me is what I'd call a misspent endeavor."

2

When Morgan scraped away his grizzled beard and trimmed back his wayward hair, he looked like he'd lost a tenth of his body weight. He was skinny as a picket rail. His faded blue shirt hung off his body like rags on a scarecrow. He pulled a heavy wool coat tight at the collar to keep the harsh Panhandle wind from going right through him.

Beaumont prattled on about the shooting contest, working off his nerves while Morgan got ready. His Peacemaker hung on a peg above the headboard of his bed. Morgan pulled the wide leather gun belt around his waist, and realized he'd need to punch another hole to keep it from ending up around his ankles.

Beaumont chuckled. "We got time to stop and get us some decent grub before the shootin' starts. Make sure you strap that gun on tight. There's a fierce wind a-blowin' out there and that pistol's liable to be the only thing anchoring you to the ground."

Morgan took his black felt hat off the wall peg and settled it down on his head. It felt good to have it on again—beyond that, it was the only piece of his former attire that still fit.

* * *

The short Texas Ranger hovered constantly, all the way to the café, wary of the half-dozen gunmen he said were waiting in the wings to challenge the infamous Frank Morgan. Beaumont made it clear with every word and gesture that even talking out loud about a challenge could earn a man a bullet.

Morgan took a seat near the back, facing the door. The waitress gave him an obligated grin and tapped her pencil on a piece of folded paper. She was pretty, but closer to Beaumont's age than Frank's. They ordered beefsteak and a pot of strong coffee. It wasn't long in coming.

"You're making me feel like a damned kid, lookin' after me this way." Morgan sucked in air through clenched teeth while he applied a liberal layer of black pepper to his slice of meat. "I been taking care of myself long enough to get a handle on how it's done, I reckon."

Beaumont's eyes softened and he leaned across the table, gesturing with his fork. "Look, Frank. You still got a ways to go before you're up to snuff again. I know of at least six desperados who are waiting for the opportunity to call you out. That don't count the dozen I ain't even heard about. You should sit back and take it easy."

"I might surprise you, youngster," Morgan said. "I been on my own for a good many years now—more than I care to count. . . ."

"I ain't sayin' you can't. I'm just sayin' you oughta be careful. You should . . ."

Morgan leaned back in his chair and stared into his cup. "Look, son, I appreciate everything you're doing for me. You've stuck by me and I know I'm acting the ass. You keep reminding me that I got so much to live for—but let me give you a little piece of advice. No matter how much you think you got to live for, don't try to hold on to it too tight. You're liable to wear yourself out just hangin' on. Sometimes you just gotta relax and take what comes at you."

Beaumont nodded, chewing on the thought along with a piece of beefsteak.

"Now, who are these men who'd like to face me while I'm on the mend?"

"Same story, different names." The Ranger gave a weary groan and nodded over his right shoulder. "See that broodin' kid over there by the bar with the withered right hand all drawed up like an eagle claw? He goes by the moniker of Lefty Cummins. Blames the whole world for his defect. He's been out of prison a grand total of three weeks for killing a poor sodbuster who looked at his crippled hand wrong. Did five years for manslaughter and the first thing he does as a free man is slide into Amarillo lookin' to brace you."

"Too bad." Frank pushed his plate away and smiled. He felt better than he had in months. To his surprise he'd eaten the entire steak, and even felt the urge to gnaw on the bone.

The front door to the café was propped open with a big chunk of flint, and a crisp spring breeze drifted in off the street. Morgan drew in a lungful and stood, slapping Beaumont on the back. Deep down he knew he was ready. He wasn't looking for a fight, but he was ready nonetheless. "I reckon he'll dog along after me for a little while yet," Morgan said under his breath.

Frank threw some coins on the table and started for the door—and Lefty Cummins.

"Be seein' you around, I reckon," Morgan said with a smile as he came up beside the would-be gunfighter. He paused at the bar a moment, looked into the kid's shifting eyes.

Morgan held another gold coin up between his thumb and forefinger so the bartender could see it, then placed it down on the scratched wooden counter with a snap.

"I'm buyin' him one more of whatever he's havin'." Morgan moved slowly toward the door, listening and waiting for the kid's next move.

Cummins turned and stared over his shoulder, but kept his gun hand wrapped around his glass, both elbows on the bar. He said nothing. This one still had a while to go yet before he was ripe enough to fall off the tree and get his self stomped.

"I wish I never would have shown you that damned handbill," Beaumont said an hour later, pulling his jacket up around his neck against a biting north wind.

Morgan gave him a taciturn smile. "That's just the old nerves talking, son. I think you're going to enjoy this."

"I'm not worried about the competition. That's gonna be fine. It's all the folks flittin' around there so well heeled that's got me thinkin'." Beaumont eyed two skinny boys in their early teens as they rushed past in the gangly-knees-and-elbows way boys that age were prone to move. One carried a forked peashooter with India rubber flippers. The other had a rusty Colt Dragoon as long as his thigh bone strapped to his side in an old Confederate holster with the flap cut off.

"Hell, Frank, even the kiddies are running around with horse pistols. Everybody and his brother wants to prove himself against Frank Morgan, and here we are aimin' to saunter in amongst 'em while they're hopped up on Prickly Ash Bitters and gunpowder fumes. I just now have you convinced to try and live. This may not have been the smartest notion that ever hit me in the head."

Morgan drew in a lungful of the sharp air and changed the subject. "Look how well these streets are laid out. Straight as a damned Comanche arrow."

"Yeah," Beaumont grumbled, still chewing on his problem at hand. He turned up his nose as though he'd smelled a skunk. "The country's so flat there was nothin' to get in the way while they were building the place—except maybe a longhorn cow."

It was impossible to escape the salt-sour smell of cattle on the wind. The rangy beasts were everywhere mooing and crowding and standing on mountains of their own crap. Frank had heard someone observe that the population of Amarillo was somewhere around five hundred human souls, half that many dogs, and fifteen thousand head of cattle.

The Potter County Spring Fair and Shooting Exposition was set up at the local grounds at the far edge of town adjacent to one of the many feedlots and holding pens.

It reminded Morgan of a Wild West show he'd seen once in Missouri, complete with sad-faced

Apache Indians wearing Cheyenne war bonnets and nimble young women doing cartwheels on horseback wearing puffy-legged bloomers.

Cigar and gun smoke mixed with the odor of burnt sugar, cooking meat, and the nearby feedlots. Some of the older folks wore buckskins and other costumes from their past, dressing as they had when they were young and trying to remind themselves that although Amarillo was relatively tame, the wild and woolly West was still only a few steps away.

White canvas tents billowed and popped against the wind while people hawked barbeque, sweet cakes, and liquor. A somber-looking woman in a green Mexican peasant dress told fortunes for two bits a pop by looking at her patrons' teeth.

Beaumont was right; everyone there was packing iron, and a good many of them threw Frank a challenging eye as he brushed by them in the crowd.

"I haven't seen this many folks in one place since the last hanging I happened onto in New Mexico," Frank said, tipping his hat to two passing girls about Beaumont's age. "Nasty old bandit drew a hell of a crowd. Everyone for miles came to see him dance at the gallows."

Beaumont had stopped listening and stood with a small group of men in front of a flapping canvas windbreak. His eyes locked fast on something out of Morgan's view, and his mouth hung open wide enough to show his back teeth.

Morgan drew up next to him to find out what had captured the young Ranger's attention so.

"That just might be the most handsome pistol I've ever set my eyes on." Beaumont snapped out of his stupor and nodded toward a nickel-plated Colt Bisley with black buffalo-horn grips and feathered engraving along the barrel and side plates.

"You like it, Ranger?" The jowly man behind the display table hooked a thumb behind the strap of his overalls and gave a condescending nod toward the handgun. "Go ahead and try it on for size."

Beaumont picked up the Colt and measured its heft and balance. He cocked it, sighted down the barrel, and let the hammer down with a slow, almost reverent click.

"What to you think, Frank? It would take me two months on Ranger pay just to afford the grips."

"It is a fine-looking piece, that's for certain. Have to wonder how it shoots, though. I seem to remember the Good Book talkin' about painted and prettied-up graves still having dead men's bones inside 'em."

The man in the overalls snorted. "Shoots like a dream, if the man behind it has the grit and know-how to use it."

"How many chests of gold doubloons would a gun like this here cost?" Beaumont looked starry-eyed and love-struck as he gazed into the bright finish on the revolver.

"Don't cost a penny on account of it ain't for sale," the man said, throwing a glance over his shoulder at the poster behind him. "You gotta win it. It's the grand prize in the pistol match this afternoon."

* * *

"I'm a pretty fair marksman," Beaumont said later as they watched a rifle competition where the contestants took turns shooting at playing cards at a hundred paces. The object of the game was to have the best poker hand after five shots.

The Ranger fidgeted and danced like he had a rock in his boot. The thought of the new pistol had obviously been eating a hole in his head. "Maybe I ought to throw my name in and have a go at it. The two-dollar entry fee would be money well spent if I happened to win."

"What kind of contest is this supposed to be?" Frank asked. Though he appreciated a fine firearm, it took a little more than a shiny finish and fancy grips to pique Morgan's interest. It would be a hard thing indeed to beat his trusty Peacemaker when it came to function. To date, no one had.

"I'm not certain." Beaumont shrugged. "That surly old cob was awful tight-lipped about the whole thing—just said it would be a 'true test of your shootin' proficiency.' I reckon we'll know soon enough. It starts in about an hour, right after this long-gun stuff."

Morgan looked up and down the crowded rows of vendors and sniffed the air. "I say let's get a cup of coffee then, before the real shootin' starts. I'd like to find me a chair and rest my bones for a minute or two before I watch you win yourself a fancy new pistol."

Twenty minutes and two cups of coffee later, Morgan felt invigorated and rested. He leaned back in the little folding wooden chair, felt the sun against his face, and pulled the makings for a cigarette out of his vest pocket.

He'd about got the tobacco poured when a hefty boy who looked like a dipper gourd with freckles came running up with a tan envelope wadded in his dimpled fist. Morgan drew the cigarette paper close to him to keep from spilling everything, pulled the pouch shut with his teeth, and slipped it back into his pocket.

"Mr. Morgan," the boy said, inflating his round checks as if hc might cxplode if he didn't deliver his message soon. His neck looked too long and skinny to connect such a round head to a round body.

"Tommy Paris," Beaumont said. "How are things down at the telegraph office?" The boy was all of ten years old.

"Busy," Tommy said, blowing out excess air so it fluttered the curly bangs on his forehead. He wore no hat. Frank supposed that he would have a hard time keeping one on the way he bounced around. It was a wonder he was so chubby considering the nervous energy that sizzled in the air around him.

Morgan lit his cigarette and took a look at the jittery boy. "What can we do for you, Tommy? Ranger Beaumont here says everyone in these parts wants to challenge me to a gunfight." He winked. "You haven't come to call me out now, have you?"

"Oh, no, sir, I . . . well, no, I never . . ." the boy stammered.

"I'm joshing with you, Tommy." Frank motioned at the empty chair beside him. "Have a seat and I'll buy you a sweet cake."

Tommy gave an audible sigh of relief and shook his head. "No, thank you, Mr. Morgan. I gotta be getting on back." He stood transfixed, staring at the famous gunfighter.

"Well, suit yourself then," Morgan said. "I can see you're a busy man."

Tommy grinned and turned to go until Beaumont touched him on the arm. "Aren't you forgetting something?"

The boy looked at him blank-faced for a moment, then chuckled, holding out the envelope. "I'm awful sorry. My ma says I'm a knot-head most of the time, and I reckon she's right on that account."

"You're no knot-head, son," Frank said fishing two bits out of his pocket and handing it over to the boy. "Now you go on and buy yourself a piece of sweet cake or some other such candy treat and enjoy it out of the sight of us needlin' adults."

"You got yourself a missive," Beaumont said as Morgan thumbed open the envelope and pulled out the telegraph flimsy.

"That I do," Morgan said under his breath as he read. He read it over again, then closed his eyes and sighed. "That I do." He folded the telegram and stuffed it in his vest pocket. He felt a knot low in his gut as the true meaning of the words sank in.

Beaumont caught his sudden change in mood and cocked back his hat. "Are you going to tell me who it's from?"

Frank shrugged. "You wouldn't know 'em." He threw what was left of his cigarette in the dirt and stood, suddenly desperate for more air.

3

Mercy Monfore tied her buggy to the iron ring on one of the upright wooden posts in front of Witherspoon's Hardware and Mercantile. She was a creature of habit and Tuesday had been laundry day for as long as she could remember. She had a strong notion that her mother, and likely her grandmother before her, had done laundry on Tuesday mornings as well.

The judge was particular about his shirts and insisted that they be sparkling white. When Mercy found she was out of Mrs. Stewart's Bluing, she decided to put off the chore until later that afternoon. Farnsworth's Notion Store was only four blocks from her home, but they didn't carry Mrs. Stewart's and the judge would surely notice if she used an imitation brand. He was funny that way.

Her plan was to pick up the bluing before meeting her husband for lunch. Witherspoon's store was situated on the wide town square directly across from Parker County's beautiful limestone courthouse. She would be able to run her quick errand, and then leave her buggy parked where it was while she took the covered basket of fried chicken and biscuits across to her husband's chambers.

Isaiah had a healthy appetite and loved it when she brought him a home-cooked meal for lunch. He often said no one could cook chicken as good as she did. She loved to make him happy.

Mercy liked the spring, when there was plenty of open space around the square. In the late summer, when melons and peaches were in full harvest, it would be difficult to find a place to tie up a pony, much less a four-wheeled buggy.

As a child, she had loved climbing in and out of all the wagons on trade day, sliding with her little friends over slick, ripe melons, and dodging the teams with her friends as if they were invincible. Now, the pressing crowds of people and animals made her nervous. When summer was at its peak and the square was packed wheel to wheel with row after row of wagons, Mercy consigned herself to her house away from all the hubbub. Then and only then, she let the judge fend for himself for lunch and eat other people's fried chicken.

Mercy pulled the slipknot snug on the tie rope and gave her Cleveland bay mare a pat on the forehead. The day was turning out to be warm for early spring, and the little brown mare swished her tail back and forth to chase off a green-backed fly. Mercy smoothed the front of her yellow dress and turned to fetch her shopping bag from the buggy. She wasn't very tall, and had to stand on tiptoe to reach the bag on the far seat.

A familiar voice cut the air behind her. She gave a little start and spun around, unwilling to be caught in such an unladylike position.

Nelson Ross, a prominent lawyer in town and a good friend of her husband, came out of the hardware store wearing a brown bowler hat and a grim look.

"You'd best get on out of the way, Mercy." The lawyer wore a gun belt. The tail of his pinstriped suit coat was pulled back to expose his side arm. He had a pale sandy complexion that looked out of place in the outdoors—as if the bright sun might do him harm.

"Mr. Ross," she said in a syrup-sweet Southern drawl that she never heard but everyone else accused her of. "Is there something the matter?" Mercy pulled the canvas shopping bag up in front of her chest and retreated a step back toward her buggy. "What's happening here?" Even as she asked, she knew the answer. With county elections coming up, tempers ran high. Petty disagreements and feuds that had merely simmered for years suddenly boiled over on a daily basis. The whole town seemed turned upside down.

Ross gave her an odd, almost pleading look. His eyes flitted back and forth between her and the hardware store. Before he could answer, the door creaked open again and Sheriff Rance Whitehead stepped out into the bright daylight.

"Please step back, Mrs. Monfore. The judge would have my hide if you got hurt in this matter." The tall lawman sounded sincere, but Mercy knew he made a living sounding like something he was not. The mere fact that he'd acted like he cared what the judge thought was a joke. Her husband never mentioned the sheriff's name without a spit and stream of vehement swearing. She was certain the lawman harbored the same feelings for her husband.

Whitehead was tall, with black hair slicked back under a dark felt hat. Everything about him, including his toothy white smile as his lips pulled back behind a thick mustache, seemed oily and fake. If he wasn't the sheriff, he would likely have sold snake oil. The judge often said the man's present job suited him better because it allowed him to lie and murder with relative impunity.

The sheriff was square-jawed and handsome. Had it not been for the overall air of guile that surrounded the man, he would have not been unpleasant to look at. As it was, Mercy felt herself shudder at having to occupy the same section of street.

The two men walked onto the deserted courthouse square and faced each other. They circled slowly, not ten yards apart. Their warnings to her given, they concentrated on each other and ignored Mercy altogether.

She could do nothing but stand by helplessly and watch.

"Since when did you start packin' a side arm, Ross?" Sheriff Whitehead sneered behind his curling mustache. "You know those damned things will only get you into trouble and grief. You got something on your mind that requires you to sport a pistol?"

Ross shook his head and let out an uneasy breath. His hand hovered uneasily above the butt of his gun. "You know the answer to that. A man's got a right to protect himself." The sallow lawyer was no gunfighter, but he did have a temper and a stubborn streak that wouldn't let him back away from a rabid dog.

"You seem all-fired ready to get yourself killed today." The sheriff advanced, pressing the other man. He talked like he wanted to avert the fight, but Mercy could see the hint of a smile in his eyes. He wanted Ross to draw. "Why don't we just go over to my office and talk about this." Even as he spoke of a truce, his sure fingers tapped the grip on his own pistol. He looked bored.

Ross's face twisted into a pink knot. He gave an irate shake of his head. "The things you're doing, Whitehead . . . everyone in the county knows what you and your boys are up to . . . we can all . . ." The lawyer rubbed sweat out of his eyes with the back of his hand, then held it out in front of him, warning the other man back. "You stay where you are, Sheriff. Any fool can see what's happening here."

Whitehead cocked his head to one side and raised an eyebrow. "Is that a fact?"

"Damn right it's a fact." Ross blinked his eyes and appeared to have a hard time seeing. "There are those of us who refuse to allow this to happen. . . ."

"Allow? Allow what to happen?" Whitehead's fingers continued to toy with the grip of his gun the same way he toyed with the sweating lawyer. "You've had your melon out in the sun too long. You're talking out of your head, Ross." Sheriff Whitehead's powerful neck bowed like an angry stud horse spoiling for a fight. He stepped forward, closing the distance between himself and his trembling opponent. He pressed, but his voice remained calm. "Easy there with that gun hand, mister."

Ross raised his left hand as if to ward off the advancing lawman. "All right, all right. Now you see here, Whitehead. . . ."

Mercy's breath caught in her throat as the fingers of Ross's right hand brushed across the wooden grips of his revolver.

The sheriff's pistol appeared to leap from his holster and spit fire and smoke. The wide-eyed lawyer now stood less than five feet away. He staggered forward, clutching at Whitehead's shoulder, clawing pitifully for a handhold to keep himself on his feet. The lawman shrugged him off.

Ross shuddered once, the color draining from his already pale face as a red stain bloomed across his chest. He opened his mouth to speak, but nothing came out. His gun had never cleared leather.

Mercy wasn't certain he'd ever even intended to draw. She clutched the canvas bag in front of her until her fingers turned white.

Whitehead turned slowly to her and shook his head. His face creased in the kind of false sympathy you might show a child when a pet grasshopper died. He reholstered and tipped his hat.

"I'm sorry you had to be a witness to such a tragedy, Mrs. Monfore, but you saw it. The fool left me no choice."

Mercy stood motionless, hardly daring to breath. The lump in her throat bound her voice and she could not speak. With a man like Whitehead, it was probably just as well. Right or wrong, he was a dangerous foe.

The speed with which he'd gunned down poor Nelson Ross was nothing short of phenomenal. Had the man really wanted to fight, it wouldn't have mattered.

Though it was well settled, Parker County was only just on the verge of becoming truly civilized.

Mercy had been witness to more than her share of bloody gunfights. In all those fights, she'd only seen one man as fast as Rance Whitehead with a gun.

But that was so many years ago . . . when that man was young and she loved him more than she ever thought she could love anyone.

Mercy looked meekly at the sheriff and gave a wan smile. She prayed that man would arrive soon.

4

Beaumont looked a little on the fidgety side for the tough-minded Texas Ranger Morgan knew him to be. He kept rubbing his chin as if to smooth the beard he couldn't quite grow. The broad little Ranger paid his two dollars and signed the entry book. He looked back at Morgan.

"Why don't you enter, Frank? I wouldn't mind so much losing to you."

A tall youth in tight pinstripe trousers snickered in the line behind them. "Don't worry, you'll be losing to me anyhow. It won't matter who else enters."

The kid wore a flashy, blue bib-front shirt and a mousy large-brimmed Stetson with a slight dip in the front. He was barely edging up to his mid-twenties if that. His blond hair hung in loose curls and reached his shoulders in the shade of the wide hat. A few wisps of golden beard and mustache adorned his chin and upper lip. He was every inch the dandy.

"Why, Mr. Custer." Morgan thrust out a hand. "I always did want to meet you. Must have my history all wrong. Thought you were killed on the Little Big Horn." He eyed the kid with an interested smile. Sometimes, dandies were the best shots off the line. They cared enough about their image to put in countless hours of practice. In his experience, though, most didn't hold up under pressure.

The dandy returned the smile and shook the offered hand. He had a strong enough grip to be a competent gunman. "Very funny. I suppose if I wasn't askin' for it, I might take offense." He let go of Frank's hand and tipped his hat. "The name's Ferguson. Chas Ferguson."

"As in the Ferguson Rifle?"

The dandy's mouth grinned, but his eyes gave Morgan a thorough once-over—sizing up an opponent for a fight. "Only a distant relative."

"Distant or not, it was hell of a revolutionary long gun. You got genius in your blood. Pleasure to meet you Mr. Ferguson. Frank Morgan."

The dandy's eyes brightened as if his suspicions were confirmed. "The Frank Morgan?"

"I don't know about *the,* but I'm definitely *a* Frank Morgan."

Ferguson took off his hat. "Forgive me, sir, but I heard you'd passed away."

"Not by a long shot, he hasn't." Beaumont stuck out his hand and stepped between the two men. "Tyler Beaumont, Texas Rangers. Are you plannin' to enter?"

Before he could answer, Morgan shook his head and mused. "There are still a few renegades that would consider your flaxen scalp to be a hell of a trophy."

"That'll be the day." Ferguson settled the hat back over his yellow locks. "I've already paid my fee. I'd be glad to pay your fee as well, Mr. Morgan, if you'd care to try your skill against me." He tossed a gold piece in the air.

Frank's hand snaked out and snatched the spinning coin. He placed it back in Ferguson's open palm. "Mighty kind of you, but I can pay my own way, thank you." Frank fished the entry fee out of his pocket and signed the book. He looked at Beaumont and grinned. "I'm feeling better. Maybe if I don't shoot my foot off, you'll relax and stop lordin' over me like a mother hen."

A half an hour later Morgan stood in a line of other shooters, listening to a heavyset man from the cattlemen's association explain the rules of the contest.

"All right, all right, gentlemen. Listen here now." He held out both hands to shush the crowd. "My name is Harry Lofton. I'll be the line judge and my rulings will be final. Any problems you have with my decisions you may take up with my associates." The self-important man in the bib overalls waved with thick fingers toward two men carrying double-barreled coach guns who stood at either end of the firing line on raised platforms.

A row of twenty-eight contestants toed the white chalk line. Four others had backed out of the competition without a refund when they saw Morgan was a contestant, but stayed in the crowd to watch him shoot.

"On my mark you will all fire one elimination round of six shots at the targets before you." Lofton jerked a stubby thumb over his shoulder toward a row of ringed paper targets some twenty paces away. "The best ten of you will move on to the next round of competition." He eyed the motley line of shooters with a mixture of scorn and pity. "Take as long as you like—up to one minute. Is everyone ready?"

"We will be if you'd get your fat ass out of our way," a gangly rounder said before spitting a slick stream of tobacco juice at his feet.

The line judge gave the man a pinched smile and stepped out of the way, drawing his own pistol from an absurd-looking *buscadero* rig cinched around the bulging girth of his bib overalls.

Frank had taken up a position with Beaumont to his immediate right and Ferguson to his left. A grizzle-faced cowboy in a dusty black hat stood in between him and the blond dandy.

The targets weren't that far away, considering the distances he'd shot before, but Morgan wasn't accustomed to having so much time on his hands. In a sure-enough, all-out gun battle, a minute was generally enough time to do his business, go get the undertaker, and maybe even roll a smoke. When the line judge fired his gun to start the countdown, Frank held his peace and watched.

Beaumont was quick out of the holster and concentrating so hard on the target, he didn't appear to notice Frank wasn't shooting. Others in the line took differing lengths of time, some using two hands and squinting down the barrels and leaning way back like they were scared the guns might explode in their hands. The smart-mouthed rounder with the cud full of chewing tobacco had his tongue out to one side while he fired.

When he looked to his left, Frank realized

Ferguson was standing with his hands folded at his belt, watching, looking up the line at him. Morgan suddenly knew what the herd bull must feel like when he first learns one of the young upstarts is making up his mind to try to cut in on the action.

The dandy looked at him warily. There was a challenge in the narrow, pale eyes. Both would wait until the last possible moment to take their shots. Only then would the contest really begin.

Guns fired intermittently as the seconds ticked by and men finished up their last few rounds. A cloud of gray and white smoke drifted down the line on the breeze. For a short moment Morgan drifted with it to his time during the war—the time when the same sort of smoke burned his eyes and whistling lead flew by from the Union lines not a stone's throw away. He could almost hear the cries for help as the shots tore into the soldiers all around him, but for some reason passed him by. . . .

The shooting began to peter out and he shook his head to clear it. He didn't have time for such useless reminiscing.

Frank knew the minute was drawing tight. He'd been subconsciously counting it down from the first pistol shot by the steady throb of pulse in his head.

Beaumont finished and looked over at him as he let out half a deep breath.

"Damn, Morgan," the Ranger whispered, sliding his pistol back into his the holster. "I never even heard you shoot."

"I haven't yet."

Morgan slipped his Peacemaker from the holster by his side in a fluid motion. He was faintly aware of the potshots still going on around him as the rest of the line finished up. The whiskered-jowled cowboy next to him squinted downrange as he fired his last.

Morgan's Colt barked six times in rapid succession, each round following closely on the heels of the one before it. The hammer snapped on the last round, and he slid the gun easily into his holster just as the line judge yelled: "Time."

"You nearly gave me heart failure—waitin' like that." Beaumont's face was all smiles as he spoke. All six of the Ranger's rounds were well within the center ring. He'd shot nearly as well as Frank—good enough to make the first cut, along with Ferguson, the tobacco-chewing cowboy who'd stuck his tongue out while he shot, and a ragtag group of others vying for the nickel-plated Colt.

"Keep showin' off like that and I might just beat you, Morgan." Beaumont took out his pistol and began to reload it as he spoke. "You are just gettin' over a lengthy illness."

"That's fine," Frank lied. "I'm just in on this escapade for the entertainment value."

"All right, boys." The line judge nodded at the surviving ten shooters on the line. "That was the easy part. From here on out it gets a might trickier."

Ferguson tipped back his fancy Stetson and peered around the tongue-chewer at Morgan. "I certainly hope so."

The next round of fire had each contestant shooting at a swinging gourd-squash suspended from a wooden cross-timber twenty yards away. The four men with the least amount of squash still on the tether after six rounds were declared the winners. Morgan, Beaumont, Ferguson, and a rawboned farm boy named Hackenmueller moved to the next round when they each shot the strings holding up their targets.

In the next event each contestant shot six rounds at fist-sized clay balls on top of wooden posts stuck in the ground starting some twenty-five paces away at staggered distances. Mr. Lofton, the line judge, put his hand on his own pistol while he explained that only shooters who hit every clay target would move on to the next round. If no one succeeded, no one would get the prize. That bit of news drew a rumble of angry murmurs from the crowd. It explained the reason for the assistants with shotguns.

Beaumont missed his last target by a hair, bring his total to five. Hackenmueller got four. Morgan and Ferguson advanced.

The young Ranger took off his hat and hung his head. "Don't know why I thought I could shoot well enough to win anything."

Morgan put a hand on his shoulder. "Shooting for sport and shooting for survival are as different as thunder and lightning—they might be related but they're a completely different animal. I've seen you send lead downrange when it counted. I'd want you next to me when bandits were about, and that's for certain."

A gruff voice from the crowd behind him jerked at Morgan's attention.

"Well, bless my ever-lovin' soul, if it isn't Frank Morgan." The gravel voice belonged to Bog Swenson, a ruddy-faced Swede with a bulbous nose that always looked like it had been stung by a swarm of two dozen angry wasps. Swenson was particular about his nose. He was known to get violent when anyone stared at the prominent feature. The problem was, it covered so much of the real estate that made up his face, it was impossible to talk to the man without spending at least a moment wondering what made his nose so red and swollen.

Morgan had given the muscular Swede a sound thrashing three years before in a saloon near Lincoln, Nebraska. At the time, a good whipping seemed preferable to killing the loudmouthed bully. Now, Frank wondered if he might have made a bad choice in not finishing the job.

"Fancy meetin' up with you all the way down here in Texas," Swenson said from twenty feet away. "I been lookin' for you for a long time. Yes sir, I have at that. I don't aim to let you get away so easy this time. No man whips me and gets away with it."

The pistol competition had drawn a large crowd. People were bunched tightly together to get a look at the contest, and now they were having a difficult time getting out of the way. Many such fairs staged mock events like this for the entertainment of the public, and it was likely many in attendance thought this was just such a stunt.

Morgan looked beyond Swenson's gargantuan beak and into his smoldering eyes. This was no stunt.

"Bog," Morgan said, squaring off with a slight nod of his head. His Peacemaker was empty from the last round of contest fire. He was sure his challenger knew it—likely he'd waited for the moment so he could exploit the weakness. Beaumont hadn't had time to reload either.

"You're looking well as can be expected," Morgan said.

"I ought to give you the thumpin' of your sorry life," Swenson sneered from behind his nose. "But I hear you been sick and it wouldn't be much fun breaking your brittle old bones. No, I reckon we'll handle it this way." The Swede's hand hovered above the wooden grip of his pistol.

"Hold on there, Bog." Morgan stood completely still. "We got too many innocent folks around here that might get hurt if we go at it. Let's let them step aside."

People in the crowd began to cheer them on. "Draw, boys!" The high-pitched voice of a woman came from Morgan's right. An old man directly behind him shouted: "Quit talkin' and earn your money. Give us a damn good show."

The onlookers managed to get crowded together enough to form a narrow alleyway between the two gunmen, eager to watch what they thought was playacting. A pimple-faced boy in his teens wearing an old cap-and-ball Walker Colt stood, hemmed in by the press of people, at Frank's left elbow. He was close enough to tell the men were serious.

"Don't move and you won't get hurt," Morgan spoke in a whispered hiss. He could almost hear the boy's knees knocking.

"Wh . . .What?" the boy stammered.

"Stay where you are," Frank said from the corner of his mouth. "If you move he's liable to shoot at you instead of me."

Bog Swenson would not normally have been much of a threat. In an honest gunfight, he'd be lucky to get the hammer thumbed back. But this time Morgan knew he was in a bit of a predicament.

He could easily outdraw the big-nosed outlaw, but that didn't do him much good with an empty gun.

Frank grinned at the quaking boy beside him to set him at ease, but kept a watchful eye on Swenson. The ugly Swede was moments away from jerking his pistol.

"That hogleg loaded?" Morgan whispered to the boy next to him.

Bog Swenson had finally worked up enough courage to draw on an unarmed man. "Adios, Morgan, you no-account son of a bitch."

"S . . . sh . . . sure it's l . . . loa . . ." the wide-eyed boy stammered.

"Good."

Bog Swenson's shoulder dropped and his hand reached for the gun at his hip. He was confident and didn't rush. Morgan used his left hand to snatch the heavy Dragoon from the quaking boy's holster beside him. He muttered a short prayer in the instant it took for him to bring the gun up and on target, hoping the kid knew how to load the old percussion pistol.

Bog's eyes got bigger than his swollen nose when he saw what Morgan had done.

A deafening boom drove the crowd back as Morgan pulled the trigger. Bog Swenson looked down at the gun he'd never had the chance to fire, then at the growing stain of blood low across his belly.

A woman near the dying bully screamed at the sight of his wound. The boy beside Frank swayed on his feet like he might pass out. A murmur ran through the mass of people when they began to realize what had just occurred.

"Thought I had it figured." Bog dropped his pistol and fell to his knees. He stared at the smoking horse pistol in Morgan's left hand. "I never figured on that," he moaned.

Frank had worried about the big .44 ball passing all the way through the grumpy outlaw, and aimed low hoping the big bones in his hip would slow it down. No one behind the Swede fell over, so it must have worked.

When he was certain Swenson was no longer a threat, Morgan turned and handed the rattling Walker back to the wide-eyed boy he'd borrowed it from. "Much obliged for the loan of the pistol, son. I'd reload it quickly if I were you. I'm about to do the same with my own."

The boy's mouth hung open. He looked at the fallen man, the man who'd been killed with his Dragoon. He turned back to Frank and shook his head emphatically.

"N . . . no, sir," the boy said. "I don't reckon I'll load it. I believe I'll just take it home and put it back in my pa's closet where I found it."

Morgan put a hand on the boy's shoulder after he'd slid the last fresh round in his Peacemaker. "That's a good plan, son. But I have to say, I'm mighty glad you were around when you were."

He fished a twenty-dollar gold piece out of his pocket and gave it to the boy. "I reckon my life is worth almost that much."

5

"Well, now." Lofton clapped his fat hands together and rubbed them in front of him like a housefly once his assistants dragged Bog Swenson's body away from the crowd. "You need a few minutes to calm your nerves?"

Morgan raised an eyebrow and gave the line judge a hard look. His voice was calm as a windless lake. "Do I look nervous?"

"All right then," Lofton said. He eyed Morgan and the dandy. "You two *pistoleros* are about to test your skill and provide some entertainment for the crowd at the same time." He turned for the first time and addressed the gathered crowd. "Both of these men have proven they're better-than-average shooters; now let's see what they're really made of." The line judge gave a nod to two men on the sidelines, and they carried two draped boxes downrange fifteen paces. The boxes were flat, no more than a foot high and two feet long.

"That's not far enough to be much of an effort," Ferguson said, grinning at Morgan. "I don't reckon either of us would have much trouble hitting a wooden box."

Lofton ignored the remark. "Inside those

enclosures are twelve bobwhite quail—six for each of you. We'll jerk the top off and you plug as many of the little beggars as you can before they fly out of range. My helpers in the tower will act as spotters for each of you. The winner of the fine Colt Bisley is the one who gets the most quail. But, I'm givin' you both fair warning. You gotta get at least one or nobody gets the prize."

Beaumont stood a few steps behind Morgan. "At least one? You'd think he'd never seen you shoot."

Frank just nodded and studied the box downrange.

"Care to put a little added wager on this round?" Ferguson tapped his holster with a slender forefinger and twirled at the end of his wispy gold mustache with his pale left hand.

"I don't believe I do," Frank said.

"Suit yourself." The dandy shrugged. "Just trying to earn a little extra gambling money."

Lofton's men moved off to the left and picked up a long cord that was attached to the lids of both quail boxes so they'd both come off at the same time. "Mind the crowd and careful where you're shootin', boys," the line judge barked. "Ready?"

Each man focused his attention on the box in front of him. Each gave a slow, deliberate nod.

On Lofton's command, the two assistants tugged on the cord and the flat lids slid off the two boxes.

Frank watched a half-dozen quail explode out of the box on his side with a drumming flurry of beating wings.

His Peacemaker was out of the holster before the last bird cleared the box. He cut down two as they flew up and away from the cheering crowd. Another hapless bird tried to zip straight up in the air. Morgan sent him tumbling back into the box he came out of. One of the quail locked its wings and glided toward Lofton. Frank pulled up to keep from winging more than the bird. By the time he was able to get back on target the other two birds were safely out of range.

Frank shrugged and returned his Colt to the holster. He'd been concentrating so intently on his own targets he had no idea how his competition had done.

"I let three get away." Morgan watched the remaining birds lock their wings and glide away until they were nothing more than dark specks on the prairie.

"Three birds on the wing with a pistol." Beaumont slapped him on the shoulder. "That's some fancy shootin'"

Morgan tapped the butt of his Colt in frustration. "I still let three slip away."

"So did he." Beaumont hooked a thumb at the dandy. "And you put one back in the box."

Ferguson tipped his fancy hat. The boy's cheeks were flushed from excitement. His narrow eyes had the gloat of youth. "You are a remarkable shootist, Mr. Morgan, but from the looks of things we may have to cut the prize in half. The great Drifter may have finally met his match. It seems I may be equally as good."

"You may be at that." Morgan shrugged.

Lofton sauntered up to the line in front of Frank. He had the quail boxes stacked in his hands, resting against the belly of his overalls over his gun belt. He didn't look happy to give up his prize pistol, but he was clearly impressed with the shooting display. "I gotta say, I'm surprised. But it appears we got us a winner, folks," he yelled at the crowd.

"What do you mean a winner?" Ferguson jerked off his hat and balled up his fists like a spoiled kid. "We both got three birds. I'd call that flat even."

Lofton took a few steps over to the dandy. "That you did, son." He reached into Ferguson's box and scooped out three tattered bobwhites and tossed them at the young dandy's feet. The huge forty-five caliber balls of lead had reduced the bodies to ragged bits of bloody skin and brown feathers. He moved back over to Frank and counted the birds out of his box in front of him.

"You both got three birds." Lofton grinned at the pressing crowd, shaking his head in disbelief. "But this feller left his edible."

Each of Frank's quail lay at his feet intact, the heads neatly clipped from the bodies. Ferguson strode over, crushing his hat in his hands while he studied the quail.

The dandy stood and replaced his hat, staring daggers at Morgan and the line judge. "This is an insult. You never said a word about this in the rules. It's a draw, damn you." His hand tapped the handle of his pistol.

Frank raised an eyebrow and got ready. He'd hoped it wouldn't come to this.

Lofton shook his head and raised a thick hand. "Boy, you listen to me. It's obvious who the better shooter is. And I told you from the get-go, all my decisions are final." The fat man's eyes grew dark. "Now, you listen here, youngster. You done good—better than almost every man here. Be happy about that. If you push this you're liable to end up all shot up like those birds of yours. Got it?"

Morgan shot a glance at the shotgun-wielding men in the tower. Each had his weapon trained at Ferguson. It didn't seem to occur to them that at that range, the blasts would kill or maim half-a-dozen bystanders as well. Frank studied the sneering men more closely and decided they just didn't care.

Ferguson's chest heaved with barely penned anger. Black eyes flitted back and forth while he worked out his options. At length he spit on the ground at Lofton's feet.

"This isn't the end of it," he hissed, catching Morgan's eye as well. "Not by a long shot it's not." A moment later, he pushed his way into the crowd without a backward glance.

"I didn't figure him for a fool," Lofton said as he watched the dandy go. "They always gotta say something tough like that, don't they?"

Frank shrugged. "I reckon they generally do. But I think this one means it."

Later, Tyler Beaumont looked on while Morgan packed the fancy new pistol in a scrap of oilcloth and stuffed it in his saddlebags. "That Ferguson boy was giving you some mighty strong stink-eye before he disappeared. I'd watch him if I were you." The Ranger scratched his forehead. "How'd you do that, Frank?"

"I aimed for the eyes. It's the same as flock-shootin' for ducks. If you aim at all of them, you're more than likely to hit nothing but air. When you go to face a man, put that front sight on a button or a pocket watch—not the whole caboodle. You won't miss by much. I aimed at the eye and got lucky and hit the head. Ferguson just aimed at the bird."

"You are feelin' better."

Frank smiled. "As a matter of fact, I feel right and fit as a fiddle. But I'm smart enough to know I've only got so many years left in me. A bandit can only cheat the gallows so many times, and so it goes with a gunman and a bullet."

"Morgan, I do believe you're gettin' poetic in your old age."

"I reckon dyin' twice will do that to a man." He slapped Beaumont on the back and handed him the folded telegram. "Take a look at this."

The Ranger took off his hat and held the paper out so he could read it in the failing light.

TO: FRANK MORGAN, AMARILLO, TEXAS

FROM: MERCY MONFORE, WEATHERFORD, TEXAS

DEAR FRANKIE STOP NEED YOUR HELP STOP KNOW YOU'VE BEEN SICK BUT PLEASE COME HOME AS SOON AS YOU ARE ABLE STOP FEAR MY FAMILY IS IN JEAPORDY STOP WATCH YOURSELF STOP THINGS ALL MIXED UP HERE STOP WANT YOU TO MEET MY DAUGHTER STOP SHE HAS YOUR TEMPER END

"Whew!" Beaumont handed him back the telegram. "Who is this Mercy Monfore?"

"A girl." Frank paused, remembering. "A woman I knew years ago."

"What do you aim to do?"

Morgan stared off at the low sun and took a deep breath. The wind was dying down a little with the evening and he found he could think a little clearer without it whirring against his ears. He was just deciding for sure himself. "I'm going to Parker County and check this out," he finally said. "If you're comin', you best get a saddle on that mean little beast you call a horse."

6

Two days after they crossed the Red River, Beaumont noticed a loose shoe on his bay's hind foot. It was late afternoon, and a gentle breeze rustled the dark leaves on the thick stands of post oak along the old wagon road. The air had warmed considerably after they left the open country around Amarillo, and tiny bugs floated in thick swarms along the road. Tiny brown tweet-birds flitted and chattered in the thick tangles of briars and new spring underbrush.

Morgan stood in the stirrups and stretched, scanning the rolling hills around him. The miles had been hard on his old bones, but he could feel the life coming back to his muscles. A half a mile ahead, a cloud of several hundred red-winged black birds rose in unison like a dark wave from the green canopy of trees only to settle back a few seconds later. Their chirps and fluttering wings carried on the light wind.

Morgan studied the spot. Someone else was on the road ahead of them. He couldn't tell if they were coming or going, but something, or more likely someone, had disturbed the flock of birds. He glanced around for Dog, but the cur was nowhere to be found. Probably hot on the trail of some rabbit or green-tailed lizard. That was the trouble with Dog. He was fiercely loyal when he happened to be around, but he led his own life and went where his old nose took him. Morgan couldn't fault him for that; it was a quality they both shared.

"I'm still thinkin' a nice bed at a good hotel would be the way to go," Beaumont mumbled, stooping under his horse with a mouth full of horseshoe nails. "I never did cotton much to sleeping on the ground."

"Know what you mean," Morgan said. He popped his neck to one side and then the other, still keeping a watchful eye on the road ahead. "But I'd prefer to steer clear of towns for a few days while I get my legs back under me. I'd like to ease into things."

Beaumont cleaned the hoof, replaced the loose shoe, and tapped the nails in one by one, ringing the sharp ends off as he went with the claw of his hammer.

"You're pretty good at that." Morgan nodded his approval at the shoeing job. "Ever think of taking up the profession? It's not near as dangerous as this lawman stuff."

Beaumont set the clinches on all eight nails and set the foot back down, rolling his shoulders to relax them from the recent effort. "You think horseshoeing is safe?" He pulled back his shirt collar to show a jagged white scar shaped like a six-inch smile, just below his neck. "My granddaddy told me horseshoeing was good business for a short man like me." Beaumont walked around the bay and picked up each foot in turn, checking the shoes while he had his tools out. "So, I took him at his word. I was shoeing a big sorrel mare that belonged to an old widow woman outside of Kerrville. The widow woman wasn't the nicest person I ever come across, and the mare took all her personality from the old bag. Damned horse picked me up with her teeth and threw me across the barn. Nearly took my head off. I told that widow woman right there I would have to shoot the horse between the eyes to get her shod." He smiled and patted his bay on the rump. "But then, I told her, I could guarantee the shoes would stay on for eight weeks."

Morgan chuckled. "I see your point."

Beaumont stuffed the hammer and clinch block back in his saddlebag. "No, sir, Frank, I don't mind tellin' you, I'd as soon be in a runnin' gun battle with a dozen Mexican bandits as shoe someone else's horse anymore. It just ain't worth . . ."

Frank raised an open hand. "Just an observation. Didn't know I'd stirred up a hornet's nest on the subject." He dismounted and dug around in his saddlebags for a small pot. They'd forgone the use of a packhorse, wanting to make better time, so he didn't have room for a proper coffeepot. Instead he'd settled for a small pan that held no more than three cups of water.

"What do you say we have us a cup or two?" Morgan held up the little pot. "I find that a good cup of coffee will generally chase most unpleasantness out of my head—even thoughts about horseshoeing."

Both men loosened the girths on their mounts to give the animals a little breather.

Beaumont gathered some small oak branches for a fire while Morgan got the water ready to boil. The fire was just beginning to burn well when four horsemen came ambling up the road toward them at a slow walk. Morgan cut his eyes to Beaumont and both men stood to watch as the newcomers approached.

"If it ain't the Four Horsemen of the Apocalypse," the Ranger said under his breath as the men drew closer.

Morgan spit on the ground beside him and nodded slowly at the comment. "Apocalypse maybe, but I'll show 'em Hell if they interrupt my coffee with anything shady."

The four men approached tentatively, scanning the road ahead of them, turning often to check their back trail. All carried their hands loosely at their sides, but each had a pistol at his hip and a rifle or shotgun in the scabbard at his side. The leader had a short-barreled coach gun in a wallet holster across the pommel of his saddle. It was canted at such an angle that if it happened to go off at the wrong moment, it might hit his own mount in the neck.

The men were obviously saddle tramps. Their ragged clothes were cobbled together from whatever they could beg or steal. The leader, or at least the man who rode point, straddled a flea-bitten gray bag of bones that looked as though it hadn't seen an oat or speck of corn in months. Ribs stuck out like slats on a feed bunk, and the poor animal's hip bones jutted out to show oozing sores. A swarm of flies buzzed around the horse's rheumy eyes and bent, Roman nose.

The lead rider wore a gray homespun jacket with a huge tear along the left side where a pocket used to be. A wilted hat with a matching rip in the brim covered a nest of matted brown locks. In fact, every inch of clothing the man wore was torn or damaged in some fashion or another. Even the sole of his right boot had separated from the boot itself and flapped absurdly at the stirrup as he rode. Morgan decided to call this one Rip, no matter what his name was. The way he and the others were eyeing Stormy and the bay, there was bound to be some trouble.

"Evening, gents." Rip tipped his torn hat and crossed his hands across the saddle horn. The leather wrap around the horn had come loose, and hung like a lazy snake in a loose coil between the shotgun wallet and the scuffed pommel. "You fixin' to make some coffee?"

"We were at that," Morgan said. These men were looking for something to take offense at; Morgan couldn't see any reason to waste time giving something. "My pot's a little on the small side, I'm afraid, so, you boys'll have to wet your whistles elsewhere. We only got enough for two."

Rip's face darkened. He sat up straighter in the saddle. "Well, that's might un-neighborly of you, mister."

"Just statin' a fact," Morgan said, nodding at the small pot. "I've never been much of one to tiptoe around the point. I'd be much obliged if you would just state your business straight out. That way me and my friend here don't have to go guessin' at it." Morgan's hand hovered above his Colt. He didn't have to look to know Beaumont had adopted the same posture.

Rip grinned, showing a mouth half full of yellowed teeth, and threw a glance over his shoulder at his compatriots. "This beats it all, don't it, boys. We ain't gonna be able to pull one over on these two, that's for shore." The three others nodded and laughed behind him. One, who was just as filthy and tattered, but looked as though he wasn't a day over fourteen, rolled one eye and giggled like a maniac until Rip gave him a withering stare. "Shut the hell up, Boudreaux."

Rip turned back to Morgan and shrugged. "You guessed right, partner. We want your clothes and your horses. As you can see, ours are plumb worn out." The three outlaws behind him suddenly fanned out to make themselves more difficult targets. "Now, both of you, take it easy with those shooters of yours. Get them hands up high. There's six of us and two of you. That ain't very good odds."

"Six?" Beaumont said, raising his hands even with his ears. "My eyes must be goin'."

Rip's lips pulled back in a victorious smirk and he shook his head back and forth. "Of course you don't see six, you stupid bastard. That's 'cause two of my men are hiding in the bushes yonder with rifles pointed at your brain buckets right this very minute."

"That a fact?" Morgan said.

"Damn right it's a fact. Now both of you step out of them clothes. I fancy that nice blue shirt you got on there, boy." Rip nodded at the *cinco-peso* Ranger badge. "That little trinket might come in handy down the road. Them short-legged britches of yourn will likely fit Boudreaux. Hurry up and shuck 'em off."

"Yeah." Boudreaux began to giggle again like a

crazed bird. "Hurry up and shuck off them britches."

"I told you to shut your mouth, Boudy," Rip snapped. "Can't you see I'm workin' here?"

Neither Morgan or Beaumont moved a muscle.

"You boys got mud in your ears or sumthin'?" Rip swelled up like a filthy toad. "I said shuck off them clothes."

"Don't believe I will," Morgan said. His voice was soft but piercing. "I want to give you fair warning, mister. Any of you make a move for your guns and I'll cut you down where you sit."

"Now see here," Rip stammered. "I told you, I got men in the trees there keepin' an eye on you. If you want to live, you best do what I say."

Dog came bounding out of the bushes with a long black snake in his jaws. He trotted over to Morgan and dropped the dead prize at his feet, growling low in his throat at the mounted men.

A smile spread across Morgan's face, and he let his hands fall slowly toward his side. "Keep your hands where I can see 'em, boys."

"You think Dog woulda noticed if there were men hiding in the bushes, don't you, Morgan?" Beaumont slowly lowered his hands has well.

"Not much gets by Dog." Morgan shrugged. He stared hard at Rip. "It was a decent plan; you just picked the wrong men to try it on."

Rip chewed on his lip and glared. The men behind him, including Boudy, squirmed in their saddles. "So? So what if it was just us? They's four of us against only two of you."

"What do you think, Frank? I'm not of a mind to give up my clothes."

"Me either," Morgan said.

"You smart-mouthed bastards. I ain't leavin' here without them clothes," Rip hissed. His dropped for his gun and the others behind him followed suit.

Morgan's first shot sent Rip tumbling back out of the saddle into Boudy, who accidentally shot him again in the thigh. Beaumont silenced the maniacal kid and one of the others while Morgan fished off the last one, easily beating the outlaw to the draw.

Rip lay bleeding on the ground, blinking up against the low sun. "What did you have to go and do that for?" He swallowed and struggled to get air.

"You called the shots, mister, not me," Morgan said.

"What do you think, Morgan?" I reckon we'll have to bury 'em now. That's gonna set us back considerable," Beaumont said while he reloaded.

"Morgan, you say?" Rip sighed, letting his face fall to the dirt. "Are you Frank Morgan?"

"I am," Frank said.

"Damn my luck," Rip cursed, beating his head against the ground now. "My first job outta prison and I gotta pick Frank Morgan to rob." His voice trailed off into a whisper. "I never had no damned luck at all. . . ."

7

"Victoria, pass the chops, please." Judge Isaiah Monfore picked his teeth with a sweet-gum twig while he waited for his second pork chop of the evening to come his way. He had the dignified air of a seasoned barrister and the pudgy jowls of a man who'd eaten a few more than his share of pork chops. He kept his thick silver hair combed straight back like a wood duck and sported a matching beard with no mustache so he looked like a graying, well-fed President Lincoln.

Mercy touched a cloth napkin to her lips and smiled. She liked to watch her husband eat. It pleased her when she could give him things he enjoyed. She recognized she was the flighty type, prone to fits of panic that rendered her incapable of rational thought. Isaiah was the stable force in her life, the rock-steady anchor to all her unsteadiness. She owed him more than he would ever know—more than he could possibly understand—and earnestly strove to make his life as easy and comfortable as a woman like her could.

It had turned out to be such a perfect evening. Isaiah hadn't had any trials, and he was content to sit and chat about mundane things—until Victoria decided to try her hand at a political debate.

"Papa." She handed over the plate of breaded chops, and followed it with a dish of applesauce without being asked. "Would you mind telling me why are you so against the stockyards coming in to Parker County?" Victoria batted her dark eyes with an air of contrived innocence and tossed her head so her long black hair flowed over her shoulders. She had a way of posing a question that let you know right away that she was absolutely positive your answer was going to be in error.

The judge began to saw on the thick slab of pork with his silver-handled knife. His gold and ebony ring glinted in the lamplight. He spoke without looking up. "Mercy, we have got to get this girl married off. She should be giving us grandchildren instead of talking politics at the supper table. She's on the backside of her twenties and very near to looking thirty in the eye if I do my math right."

Victoria flushed at the comment about her age. "I know perfectly well how old I am, Father. That has nothing to do with my question, which, by the way, you have yet to answer."

Monfore chewed thoughtfully for a moment, then pushed his unfinished plate away from him as if he didn't want to contaminate his meal with any of this particular conversation.

Mercy slumped in her chair. A resigned sigh escaped her lips. "Can't this wait until after dinner?" She hated talking politics at any time, but dinner was the worst. She'd watched the sheriff gun down Nelson Ross like a mad dog over this same issue only a few weeks before. "This has to be horrible for the digestion."

The judge held up a beefy hand. "It's all right, Mercy." He dabbed at his beard with a linen napkin. "We've raised her up to be headstrong. I suppose I must shoulder the lion's share of the responsibility for her willful ways." He shot a wink at Victoria.

This was the way it always went. He'd act tired and put out only to take the full blame for any indiscretion the girl might commit. "Maybe we should have sent her off to a convent years ago," he said.

Victoria kept her eyes glued to her father. "We're Presbyterians, Papa."

"Drowned you then, that's it, drowned you as a pup—or whatever it is we Presbyterians do with insolent daughters."

He pulled the plate back, unwilling to let a good chop go to waste just to make a point. "Well, my dear, if you are so set on discussing this; it's because of the type of people it would bring in—rowdies, gunmen, and swindlers."

"What about the jobs and the opportunities for the town—the whole county—to grow?"

"There are those who think the stockyards would be the type of growth we need." Monfore nodded and took a drink of buttermilk. "I happen to disagree—and so do a lot of other intelligent people. Weatherford is a fine little town and it will grow into a fine little city someday—all in due course, stockyards or no."

Victoria crossed her silverware at the edge of her empty plate. She was slender, but her appetite was almost as great as her father's. "Reed says the yards would help the economy in more ways than one."

Mercy's mouth hung open in horror. "What are you doing speaking to Reed Whitehead?" She could feel the familiar flutter in her chest—as if a thousand bees buzzed inside her, swarming around her heart. The back of her throat burned.

Victoria looked genuinely bewildered. "I should think you'd be happy. You and Papa are always after me to get married and give you grandchildren. Reed's a fine man. He's intelligent with a bright future. For pity's sake, Mother, his father's the sheriff."

Mercy wanted to scream that the sheriff was no better than a cold-blooded killer. It broke her heart that her only daughter was getting mixed up with the likes of the Whitehead family. She knew how difficult it was to be a young woman in love, but this was too much to take. "The sheriff is a hard man—coarse and full of meanness. I don't know how he ever got elected."

Isaiah had started back in on his chop. "I'll tell you how he got elected. He got elected because his rich financiers, the Crowders, bought him the job." The judge gestured with his fork, which was festooned with a large bite of fried pork. "I have to agree with your mother on this, my dear. You have to look at the whole situation in things such as this. It's touchy and more convoluted than you can imagine. Old Silas Crowder stands to make a bundle if he can sell this worthless parcel of his land to the railroad for the stockyards. He as good as owns the Whiteheads. Any of them are bound to say whatever he wants them to." He bit the meat off the fork and washed it down with a swig of buttermilk. "It's a damned hard row to hoe, being a judge in a county with a puppet for a sheriff."

And a cold-blooded killer too, Mercy thought. She couldn't forget the way the heartless man had smiled coolly after he'd gunned down poor Nelson Ross.

Victoria brushed a lock of dark hair out of her eyes. "Well, Reed is no more exactly like his father than I am exactly like you."

The judge studied her thoughtfully for a moment and sighed.

"You're a grown woman. If you want the stockyards in town, then you are entitled to that opinion. But don't think it's the only way to think just because some young upstart happens to agree with you. Use some of the brain God gave you and make your mind up for yourself."

Victoria finished her sweet tea and excused herself with a smile and a peck on the cheek for her father. These little conversations were nothing for those two, but they set Mercy's nerves on edge like fingernails on a writing slate.

Her husband took a strong stand on this stockyard business and whether he liked to admit it or not, there were a lot of people against him—a lot of cruel people like Sheriff Rance Whitehead. And now, to find out her own daughter was associating with his son . . . Mercy had worried that her husband might be facing trouble when she sent the telegram to Frank Morgan. Now she was certain. Her whole family was in danger.

8

“Mind if I ask you a question? It’s been eatin’ on me for sometime now.” Beaumont rode alongside Morgan, his short horse working almost at the double to keep up with Stormy’s ground-eating stride.

Morgan shrugged. He wasn’t used to having such a blabby companion on the trail, but when he was honest with himself, he realized he’d grown pretty fond of the stubby kid. “Fire away.”

“Who is this Mercy Monfore that she could get you on the road to recovery with a few words? I couldn’t get you on your feet for near two months of tryin’.”

Morgan glanced down at the stout little Ranger. “That’s a mighty fair question,” he said. He reached into his vest pocket, took out his gold timepiece, and clicked it open. He replaced the watch and stood in the stirrups to survey the dull green row of post oak ahead of them. “I’ll ask you a question and then we’ll see if you get an answer.”

“As you like to say, Frank. Fire away.”

“Why are you taggin’ along like this? I showed you I was fine back there at the contest. It’s not that I don’t enjoy the company, mind you, but you told me yourself you have plenty of things you could be up to if you didn’t have to fool with me.”

Beaumont leaned forward and patted his bay gelding on the neck, letting the reins dangle. "I don't know. Reckon I'm just doing what Rangers do. I'm rangin'. Besides, it's eatin' me up inside to know about this long-lost love of yours. I'm mean, that's who Mercy is. Isn't she?"

Frank cocked his head to one side and thought for a moment. "Unless I've missed my guess, that's Springtown up there. It's nearly two and I'm in a mind for a cup of coffee. If it's all the same to you, I'd like to chew on this for a bit so when I do spit it out, it'll be something you can understand."

Beaumont shrugged. He had a twinkle of youthful mischief in his eyes. "You up for a race with a short horse?"

"Son, I just got up from my deathbed a few weeks ago. I've got a feeling I'll be forced to prove myself soon enough. Suppose I'd better mosey for a little spell yet."

The Ranger kept his horse at a walk and shook his head. "I'm sorry, Frank. I shoulda known better. Now you got me feelin' bad."

Morgan grinned and took off his hat. "Oh, what the hell," he yelled as he put the spurs to Stormy and gave the horse his head, fanning the air with his hat.

"Wouldn't have been much of a race anyhow," Morgan said as he dismounted in front of Neff's Café in downtown Springtown. "With that little pony you got, I should have given you a half-a-mile head start."

Frank looped the Appaloosa's reins around a long

cedar rail. The ride hadn't been such a good idea, but he was never one to back away from a challenge. His ribs felt like they were on fire, but he wasn't bleeding; that was a blessing. He didn't know how fast a body manufactured the red stuff, but he was pretty certain he was still a little shy of a full dram.

Beaumont tied his stout quarter horse beside the Appaloosa. His hat was thrown back against his stampede string. "What was that all about? First you made me feel lower than an armadillo toe for not carin' about your health, then you leave me in the dust."

Frank slapped the Ranger on the back and pointed him toward the door of the café. "Remember what I said about not holding on to life too tight."

It had been so long since he'd been back to north Texas that Frank felt like a stranger in places he'd once called home. He brushed the front of his britches off and stomped his feet on the wooden sidewalk to get rid of any stray manure on his boots before he went into the glass-fronted establishment.

Mrs. Neff was older than he remembered. She'd once been a handsome woman with long blond hair she kept in a tight bun. He and Luke had often stopped by the café when they were out that direction just to lay their eyes on the pretty older woman. She'd likely been all of twenty-five at the time, but he and Luke had started pushing cattle at twelve and rounding up mavericks on their own when they were thirteen. To the two love-struck boys, Elizabeth Neff was a goddess of pure beauty. A creature so lovely, she was worth a day's ride and camping with the snakes two nights in a row, just to gaze at her angelic face while they ate a piece of her pie.

"And she was a damn fine cook too," Frank whispered under his breath, reminiscing.

She'd kept the bun, but it was gunmetal gray now. A little too much of her own good cooking had settled around her middle and hips. Her face, though aged, still held that timeless beauty that made it easy for Frank to see why he and Luke had taken such a fancy to the woman.

Morgan picked a table in the back where he could see the door and watch Mrs. Neff at the same time. It gave him a good view of the door, but it also happened to be the same table he and Luke Perkins had sat at all those years ago to do their awestruck gazing. He laid both hands palms down on the table—as if he could get a feel of the past from the polished wood.

"You all right, Morgan?" Beaumont flopped down in a chair with his back to the counter. He cocked his head over his shoulder. "You act like you know her."

Frank smiled and took a deep breath. "You might say so. I used to spend a considerable amount of time here as a boy."

Mrs. Neff came to the table to take their order. Her sky-blue eyes still held the same sly smile and mischievous twinkle. Frank remembered why he and his friend had been so smitten.

"A peace of pecan pie with that little dab of chocolate in it and a big cup of coffee," Morgan said, removing his hat.

Elizabeth gave him a querysome look and tapped

her pencil stub on her little pad of paper. "You just asked for my speci-ali-ty without me even tellin' you about it. I don't recognize you and I doubt my pie is all that famous."

"I grew up over near Weatherford, ma'am." Frank met her eyes like he'd never been able to bring himself to do as a boy. "When I was a boy, my friend and I used to ride out this way every chance we got."

Her lips pulled back into a shining grin. A sudden look of recognition flashed across the woman's face.

"I declare! You're one of the Moon Boys!"

"I beg pardon?" Frank looked at Beaumont and shrugged. "I think you may have me . . ."

Mrs. Neff wagged her finger and grinned from ear to ear. Her brightened eyes sparkled just as they had long ago. She put a hand to her chest and blushed. "No, I know it's you—Frankie, isn't it?"

"That's my name, but not Moon."

She patted him on the shoulder and winked at Beaumont. "Of course it's not Moon. Frankie here used to come in with his friend Lucas and ogle at me with their sad moon eyes so much, my husband told me that once they turned sixteen he was going to have to shoot them both. Mr. Neff started calling them the Moon Boys whenever they'd come around." She shook her head, doing some remembering of her own. "I don't mind tellin' you, Frankie, those were tough times for a young gal, what with all the Comanches raidin' every time there was a dark night. Hooligans coming around at all hours. It was a strain on the nerves to be sure. You two youngsters did a lot for me back in those days. Kept me from getting old before my time." She primped her hair.

Frank actually felt himself blush a little. "I hope your husband's not still the jealous type."

"No, I'm afraid poor Mr. Neff passed away a few years back. My lads, it's a good thing to see you again, Frankie. Puts me in such a mind of old times." She patted his shoulder again. "You just sit right there and I'll go get your pie and coffee."

When she'd disappeared through a back door, Beaumont gave Morgan a sly look. "What else am I goin' to learn about you—"

Morgan raised his hand. "Hold it right there. If you were about to call me Moon Boy—or anything close to it—I should remind you of who I am and the parts of your body I might be inclined to shoot off when you're not looking."

The Ranger slumped against the table, leaning on his hands. "All right. I get the message. Now, I'm ready to hear about you and Mercy. I think you ought to let me in on this little secret of yours before we ride into the middle of it and I look like a fool."

"She's an old friend of mine." Frank stared out the window into the sunny street. "From back before the war. We were awful young."

"She seems to think you are a man who could help her out of a predicament."

"We kept in touch some after the war, but she never wanted me to come back. She married shortly after I left. Had a child." He paused for a long while. "A daughter."

"How old's the daughter?" Beaumont crossed his

arms on the table and rested his chin on top of them, listening.

"In her late twenties, I suppose—about your age."

Beaumont pondered that for a moment, his eyebrows alternately working up and down as he ruminated on the information and did the math in his head. "The telegram said she has your temper—do you reckon she's . . ."

Morgan was saved by the tinkling bell at the front door. A young man in blue canvas britches and a pressed white shirt eyed the two men when he went to the counter. He wore a black, Mexican-style holster and a nickel-plated Schofield revolver. His flat-crowned black hat looked fresh off the rack.

Beaumont's Ranger badge wasn't visible, so the man likely dismissed the two as a pair of worn-out drifters—which in Frank's case wasn't far off the mark.

The newcomer pounded his fist on the counter. He acted like someone used to getting his way. He was so forward, at first Morgan thought he might be related to the Neffs.

Mrs. Neff had her hands full with a tray of pie and coffee, and she bumped the kitchen door open with her hip. She was smiling until she saw the new arrival.

"I'll be with you in a minute, Paddy." Her almost giddy voice slumped to a low drone.

The boy sneered. Frank decided this one wasn't old enough to be thought of as a man. "Drop off their order and get to it. I haven't got all day." The snide voice carried across the bright room on a thick Irish brogue not long from the old country.

Mrs. Neff set the tray on the next table and put

Frank's coffee in front of him. Her hands shook enough to rattle the dishes.

The gunfighter shot a quick look toward the kid at the counter, then back up at her. "Mrs. Neff, are you all right?"

She cast her eyes at the ground while she got the pie. She fumbled with the saucer and dropped it on the ground, narrowly missing Frank's lap.

Frank caught her eyes again. They were welling up with tears.

Paddy snickered. "Move your fat arse, lady. You knew I'd be comin' by on my rounds today."

Frank shook his head slightly to keep Beaumont in his seat. This was something he wanted to handle personally. He bent to help Mrs. Neff gather up the mess of pie and broken dish on the floor.

"Leave it and tend to me so I can be gone," Paddy clucked like a rooster. "I got other visits I'll be needin' to make."

Frank wiped his hands on his pants and stood up straight, gently pushing Mrs. Neff behind him as he did.

"Don't, Frankie," she murmured in a tremulous voice. "He'll kill you."

Paddy leaned back against the counter on both elbows, cocksure in his defiance. He acted as if he had a whole gang there with him.

"Why don't you run along, youngster." Frank glared. "It's likely time for your noon feedin'."

The boy swayed up and took a deep breath. "I ain't hungry. But if I was, I'd eat your liver."

"You know," Morgan said, "I've heard nothing but guff comin' from that mouth of yours since you walked in that door. I don't know what you think you got goin' here, but let me clear somthin' up for you. This nice woman is a friend of mine. Unless you have a strong desire to feel my boot in your ass, you'll be givin' her an apology." Frank mimicked Paddy's Irish accent.

"You're awful frail to be tellin' me 'bout my own fair business."

"Fair or not," Morgan whispered, "there are ways of talkin' to a lady and you don't seem to know them. I suggest you move your own arse on out of here before I move it for you."

Paddy's eyes fluttered. Everyone had a telltale, a twitch or tick that preceded their move. For the young Irishman, it was his eyes. Before he drew, his eyelids fluttered as if they might roll back in his head like a rank horse.

Mrs. Neff screamed as Morgan's Peacemaker roared and belched fire in the tiny café. Glass shattered in the counter behind the astonished Paddy as he dropped his pistol and slid to his knees. At the close range the bullet had pierced his chest and crashed into the display counter behind him.

"Who . . . who are you?"

"Frank Morgan." Morgan holstered his gun.

The boy licked blood off his bottom lip. "Morgan . . . ?" He shook his head, trying to clear it. "I heard of you. Thought . . . you were out west."

"Was," Frank said. "Thought I might try to come home for some peace and quiet."

Paddy's eyes fluttered again. He got one last look at his bloodstained shirt before they closed for the last time.

Morgan turned to Mrs. Neff. He could hear her sobbing behind him and wanted to calm her down.

"I'm sorry about this, ma'am. He left me no choice. I'll be glad to cover the damage to your glass here."

Her eyes were locked onto the Irish gunman. She spoke in jerking spasms between desperate sobs. "He's been coming in here getting money for his boss ever since my husband died." There was a flint-hard edge to the woman's voice. "Called it taxes. Extortion is what it was."

Morgan took her hand and stroked the back of it in an effort to calm her.

Beaumont stooped to check on Paddy, holding an open hand over the boy's gaping mouth. He looked up and shook his head. "He's dead."

"Oh, Frankie, I'm sorry you got yourself in the middle of this." Elizabeth Neff wrung her hands in her apron. Her eyes were wide with fear. "I know you were only trying to help me, but now you've . . ."

Morgan gave a tired sigh. "I'm sorry for you, ma'am. I reckon we need to report this. Who's the sheriff now?"

Mrs. Neff stopped her crying and looked sadly at Frank. "The sheriff's name is Rance Whitehead—and you just killed one of his deputies."

9

Chas Ferguson watched from the safety of a thick stand of cedars at the edge of town as Frank Morgan and his Texas Ranger friend swung onto their horses and trotted away to the south.

He'd had Morgan figured completely wrong, assuming the dried-up gunfighter was a tired old man, until he'd watched him shoot back in Amarillo. Now, the way he swung effortlessly up on the back of his broad Appaloosa said the man wasn't anything close to being frail.

Ferguson had seen the fight at Neff's through the large plate-glass window in front. He'd watched the speed and dispassionate manner the gunfighter had used to dispatch his adversary—and then snuck off to hide under the shadowed cedar fronds before anyone saw him.

The young dandy clutched his hat in one hand and used the other to steady himself on his saddle horn. An incredible dizziness had overwhelmed him when he witnessed the fight, and he'd had a difficult time staying on his feet. He knew Morgan was fast against another gunman, but up until that moment he'd just heard stories. Seeing the Drifter in action had had a much more sobering effect.

Ferguson had been working up the courage to challenge Morgan since following him out of Amarillo. The young dandy knew he was faster than Morgan. There was no doubt in his mind about that. But there was so much more to a gunfight than mere speed. His uncle had taught him that. You had to get your mind right. Let things flow. That was the hard part. So many things could go wrong that you had to stop caring just a little.

Ferguson's head reeled. His face felt flush. He untied the canteen from his saddle strings and took a long swallow. His stomach rebelled at the cool water and he vomited it back up. It had been this way for days now—ever since Amarillo. Whenever he got within a hundred yards of Frank Morgan, his insides turned to mush. If the gunfighter's voice drifted back on the wind, Ferguson would be seized with the sudden urge to turn tail and run away.

He'd never in his life been afraid of another human being, and it galled him that Morgan drew out the weakness in him like an illness. Morgan was a sickness, that's what he was. A putrefying illness that festered inside the aspiring gunman and gnawed at him until he was less than half a man. There was no cure for a sickness like that—it had to be located and cut out before it had a chance to take over.

There was only one way for Chas Ferguson to be whole again. Frank Morgan had to die and he had to kill him.

10

"I don't think I quite understand you, Purnell," Judge Isaiah Monfore said over the steepled fingers on his broad hands. He was seated in an overstuffed leather chair behind an expansive oak desk that would have dwarfed a smaller man. Well-worn law books lined the built-in cases that flanked the walls behind him.

"Oh, but I believe you will understand perfectly well if you would only think about it, Your Honor," Purnell said, tugging at his collar. Judge Monfore kept the window behind him open, and the smell of blooming irises and horse manure drifted in on the cool breeze. The lawyer's face was red as a beet even in the cool air, and beads of sweat dotted his steep forehead. "You have to listen to what I'm saying."

Monfore had never had much use for Purnell, considering him a mealymouthed attorney who could wind on for hours without ever getting to the point—which is exactly what he was doing at the moment.

The judge dropped his hands flat on the desk with a loud slap and leaned across it. "I've been listening to every word you've said and I don't understand one damn syllable. All you do is talk in circles. I can only assume all this has something to do with that Crowder boy."

Purnell gulped and nodded, staring at his lap. "It does, Judge Monfore." He suddenly looked up. "I have to represent him as best as I can, but I don't have much of a case. I have to tell you, his family gives me a few concerns, as well they should you—concern you, I mean."

The judge waved off the idea. "Hogwash, Purnell. Pure unadulterated hogwash. If I let every outlaw's family give me the vapors, I'd be as useless as you are."

The lawyer flinched at the insult but plowed ahead. If he'd have fought back, Monfore might have respected him more. He wouldn't have put up with such a thing, but he would have respected it.

"Your Honor." Purnell cleared his throat to cover a stammer. "The boy's father told me to warn you. He says if you allow his son to hang, you would surely see the same end."

"Excellent! That's just what I needed," Monfore said, pounding his huge fist on the table as if it were a gavel. The lawyer flinched at the noise. "I'll get Sheriff Whitehead to swear out a warrant for the old man—threatening a judge—we can't have that sort of thing, now can we?"

"I suppose we can't." Purnell looked deflated. "But the Crowders are pro-stockyard and the Smoot girl's parents are antis. It could look like they were using this as a platform to air their arguments with the Crowders' proposal. Maybe she led him on."

Monfore poured himself a drink of whiskey from the lead glass decanter on his desk. "You really think that Ellie Smoot got herself molested by young Crowder so she could help her parents slander the family? More to the point, do you expect a jury would believe such nonsense?"

Purnell shrugged. "I've seen worse."

"The boy stole a horse to get away from her irate father." Monfore took a drink and slammed the glass down so hard, half its contents spilled on the morning newspaper. "Purnell, when a man hurts a girl so badly she very nearly bleeds to death, I doubt she was doing any leading. If a jury finds him guilty, the boy will hang. Tell his mother I'm truly sorry for her if it comes to that." He leaned across the desk and narrowed his eyes, staring right through the squirming attorney. "And you understand me on this. I know what Crowder's position is on this stockyard issue, and I don't give a hoot in hell about it. What's more, I know that Whitehead happens to agree with him. But this has nothing to do with the yards or the railroad. This is about justice."

Monfore cleaned up the spilled liquor after Purnell slinked out of his chambers. The newspaper was ruined, but it didn't matter. There was never anything in it anymore but babble about the stockyard debate. Monfore already had a gutful of that.

The judge leaned back in his chair and swiveled it around to look out his second-floor window at the wagons on the square below. Across Main Street, Sheriff Whitehead's office door stood open, but the slimy lawman was nowhere in sight. Monfore had no doubt about how Silas Crowder felt about him, no doubt about the danger the wealthy patriarch posed if his family or fortune were threatened. As county sheriff, it was Whitehead's job to protect the judge from that kind of danger.

But Whitehead was Crowder's man. It was only a matter of time before he would be forced to show his true colors. That time was more than likely to come just when the judge needed him the most.

Monfore sighed and closed his eyes. This whole damned county was about to be torn apart and there was very little he could do except watch it happen.

11

Dog trotted out on point ahead of the two riders, nosing the air for signs of trouble, food, or fun. Any cottontail or red squirrel that happened to cross the scruffy cur's path didn't stand a chance.

Thick stands of scrub oak and mesquite lined the dusty road, and a pink carpet of primroses covered the ground on either side. Their petals were pinched closed until the sun set in the evening, which was still another hour away. Here and there a prickly-pear cactus sprang up from the rocky ground in a jumbled pile of flat green ovals.

"So, what do you aim to do?" Beaumont said a little south of Springtown. "Just ride up and say, 'Hello there miss. I do believe I might be your pa.'"

Frank turned and looked at the Ranger across his saddle. "I don't know that I plan to tell her anything at all. I expect I just need to see her—talk to her mama a bit. Mercy did say she needed my help."

Morgan gestured off to the east with the tail of his leather reins. "The Double Diamond spread is just over those limestone hills there. Before I do anything else, I plan to ride over and find out from Luke what's really going on around here. Sniff things out before I ride into the middle of something I don't understand. You're welcome to come if you like. Luke always was a man for havin' company under foot."

Beaumont gazed off to the south. "No, thanks. I believe I'd better go on in and do a little sniffin' of my own. There's a Ranger stationed over in Palo Pinto County. I'll send him a wire and see what he knows."

"Watch your bones then." Morgan smiled. "And don't get lost."

"I'll hook up with you tomorrow," Beaumont said. "When I get to town, I'll stop by and tell the sheriff you're on your way in to talk to him about the business with one of his deputies. I can say I witnessed the whole thing. That should help smooth matters out some. I'll leave word of where I'm staying with him in case you need to get in touch with me tonight." Beaumont put the spurs to his bay and the little horse leaped into a smooth rocking-horse lope.

Morgan trotted Stormy onto Double Diamond land just before sunset. The sun was behind him and he cast a long shadow across the dusty wagon road. Before the Perkins' ranch house was even visible, Dog perked up his ears and whined up at his master.

"Yeah, Luke's got dogs of his own, I reckon," Morgan said. "See if you can behave yourself around here. I haven't got too many friends left in this world."

The Double Diamond covered most of four sections of prime grazing land, with the house and ranch headquarters set well back from the perimeter.

The crickets were singing and it was well into dusk by the time Morgan trotted up in front of the main house. Two black and white cattle dogs scampered off the front porch and trotted out to sniff Dog. There was some low growling and a fair amount of polite whining before the whole mess of them ran off to get acquainted.

The Perkins house was a sprawling, two-story affair, large enough to take in plenty of the hard-luck strays Luke liked to adopt and fancy enough to reflect the size and worth of the ranch. It had whitewashed wood-lap siding and a cedar-shake roof. Fresh green paint trimmed the windows and covered the posts that supported a long wraparound porch.

The solid front door yawned open a crack, and light spilled out as Frank dismounted and tied Stormy to a little stone jockey holding an iron ring.

Luke Perkins stepped out the door in his stockinged feet. His bald head reflected the golden lamplight that surrounded him.

"I swan. It's Frank Morgan," the cowboy said, resting a big hand on top of his head in surprise. "You didn't die after all."

"Well, no, I didn't, Luke. What are you doing without your boots at this time of day? It's not like you to go to bed just because the sun does." Morgan stepped up onto the wooden porch and shook his friend's hand.

Perkins ducked his head and looked up with sheepish eyes. "Carolyn likes us to take our boots off when we come in the house. Says all the horse poop is hard on the new rugs."

"She's civilized you, eh? Do I have to leave my gun outside too?"

"No, and the way things are going around here, I'd advised you to keep it handy all the time." Luke scanned the dim line of trees behind Frank and motioned him through the door. "Come on inside and I'll fill you in. But you have to leave your boots there on that jockey or Carolyn will raise holy hell." He opened the door wider. "It sure is good to see you, partner."

"I seem to remember you were quite the coffee drinker," Carolyn Perkins said, putting a heavy mug on the table in front of Morgan next to a plate piled high with oatmeal cookies.

She was the picture of health, glowing with happiness in her new home and a baby in her belly that wasn't far from making an appearance—a far cry from the last time he'd seen her.

Carolyn rested her hand on Luke's shoulder and sidled up next to him. "I was awfully sorry to hear about Dixie. She was such a good woman. Saw us through some awful times, she did." Her face was drawn as she spoke, but she didn't cry. Frank supposed the poor woman had shed enough tears for a dozen lifetimes.

He'd been fearing the moment he'd have to talk to someone about his dead wife. The scars from losing her seemed more hurtful than the wounds on his own body. He swallowed hard, started to say something, but found there was nothing to say that didn't make the event sound small. Instead, he changed the subject.

"I swear, Luke." Morgan looked down at his feet. "I haven't had to take my boots off in front of civilized folks for some time now. My old socks have seen better days, that's for certain." His big toe stuck out the end of a hole in his right sock. He wiggled it to break the awkward situation.

Carolyn laughed. "I'll fetch you a pair of Luke's to wear while I wash and darn those. Shuck them off and give 'em to me. If you've got any other mending that needs doing, let me have it tonight. I'll have it done by tomorrow."

Morgan peeled off his socks. "We ought to just burn them," he said. "A few weeks on the trail can ruin a garment."

Carolyn snatched them away from him and started for the stairs. "Nonsense. No use throwing away what a little thread and time can fix." She turned. "It is good to see you, Mr. Morgan. I hope you know you're welcome here as long as you want to stay."

Perkins watched his wife disappear up the stairs. There was a light in the cowboy's eyes when she was near him. Even his drooping mustache seemed to perk up at her presence.

"Seems like she's treating you well," Morgan said, airing out his toes.

"Better than well." Luke's gaze lingered on the stairs for a moment after his wife disappeared before he turned his attention back to his friend. "She's due to drop that young'un in less than a month, but she won't hear of having someone come in and help with the chores. Next week I aim to hire a girl no matter what she says. Berta and Bea Fossman help out a bunch, but they're busy with their schoolin' and all." Luke reached out and picked up an oatmeal cookie, thinking.

Morgan took a long drink of Carolyn's coffee and saluted with the cup. "It's good to set foot on home soil, I'll say that much."

"You're likely wondering about Mercy." Luke kept both eyes locked on his old partner.

"She did send for me." Frank shrugged. "I reckon I coulda treated her some better . . . back then."

"You know she married?"

Morgan stared into his cup. "Yeah, I know. You told me that a long time ago. But you never told me she had a daughter."

"Didn't figure it was any of my business."

"How old is she, this daughter?"

"Mercy married Isaiah Monfore only a few weeks after you left town. He was just a young attorney then, new in town and without many prospects. The baby came sometime later—close enough it could go either way if that's what you're wonderin'."

Frank didn't speak for a time. This was a lot of information to try and digest. He'd heard from Mercy Monfore a grand total of three times in the last two-plus decades. If the girl was his, why hadn't she mentioned it?

"She's older than you'll remember her," Luke said interrupting his thoughts.

"I'm getting a little long in the tooth myself." Frank grinned.

"Do you remember that soft way Mercy used to talk with that Southern belle drawl—like she was fresh off a plantation in Alabama?"

"I do."

"Well, it's as soft a drawl as ever and I believe her

daughter has inherited it. If you can pass on such a thing as an accent."

Morgan felt uncomfortable talking anymore about Mercy and such things, especially on the heels of so many fresh thoughts of Dixie. He needed to change the subject.

"What did you mean about how things are around here? Ever since I got the telegram from Mercy, all I hear is how something sinister is going on in Parker County."

Luke leaned on the table and wrapped both hands around his own coffee cup. "Remember when we was kids and all there was to worry about was getting scalped by Comanche or drownin' in the Brazos River?"

"Don't forget the whiskey peddlers from Arkansas."

Luke took a drink of coffee to wash down the last of his oatmeal cookie. "The thing is, a man used to know who his enemies were. Nowadays it could be anybody—even someone you've known for years who puts the spurs to you.

"The railroad wants to put a spur through the county seat so they can situate a stockyard. They're tryin' to decide between here and Ft. Worth. There are those who would kill to have it and others who are just as fiercely against it. The two sides have done everything short of declaring open warfare on each other."

Frank put down the coffee and rubbed a hand across a week's worth of new beard. "I guess you'd be one of the ones all for it then. Stockyards in Parker County would sure make it easier for you to get your cattle to market."

"You'd think so, wouldn't you?" Luke produced a

corncob pipe with a short stem from his vest pocket. He tamped the bowl full of fresh tobacco, then used a burning splinter from the woodstove to puff it to life. Sweet smoke, the flavor of cherry wood, filled the dining room. He pointed at Frank with the pipe stem while he spoke.

"A stockyard and a railroad would make things a hell of a lot easier, but I'm against it. Ft. Worth is plenty close for me. Cow towns just aren't the kind of places to raise a family in my way of thinking. They bring in all sorts of riffraff." He winked at Frank and put the pipe back in his mouth so he had to speak around it. "Too many of those damned cowboys and drifters. Besides that, you know how I like the trail. A week or so just seems like a vacation."

"I see what you mean." Morgan drained the last of his coffee. It was good to get some of the real homemade stuff. "There are two sides to this, but none of it should be enough to get people's blood boiling."

"It's always about money," Luke said. "The land the railroad is considering is smack on a chunk of otherwise worthless rock and snake pasture owned by an old patriarch named Silas Crowder."

"Never heard of him," Frank said.

"You wouldn't have. He moved in with his family about ten years after you took to the trail. A real rank man, that one—meaner than a rabid badger. He runs his sons, and everybody else for that matter, like he's the Almighty himself. If the railroad chooses Parker County, he stands to double his net worth overnight—and he's already worth quite a bit. For some folks it's just a debate. For Crowder, it's enough to kill over."

"So what's all the fuss about if the railroad hasn't even chosen where they wanta put it yet?"

"Parker County has decided to vote on the issue to see if we will even allow the railroad to consider us. You'd think we were talkin' secession again the way everybody's worked into a lather over this."

"Anybody on the opposing side as vocal or stand to lose as much as this Crowder?"

Luke shrugged. "There's all kind of good folks besides me against the sudden boom the stockyards would bring. The Baptist church has spoken out strongly in favor of keeping Parker County stockyard- and sin-free. Course they're against near everything—dancin', gamblin', and even liquor by the drink. So far no one of them have gone anywhere past a little fisticuffs. Mercy's husband, Judge Monfore, is the most outspoken of what everybody's callin' the anti crowd. Crowder's youngest boy, Tom, has got himself in a speck of trouble misusing one of our local girls. He ended up in jail and Crowder's makin' it seem like it's all about the stockyards."

"How about the sheriff?" Frank filled Luke in on the incident with Mrs. Neff in Springtown.

When he was finished, Luke whistled low, under his breath. "That's not good, Frankie. Whitehead's a bad one. Crowder backed his campaign and helped him get into office. He's in the old man's back pocket, that's for certain. If I was you, I'd make sure that Ranger friend of mine was with me when I went in to explain everything. Whitehead's the type to shoot you, then figure out a reason later." Luke's eyes narrowed and he began to nibble at the corner of his thick mustache. "He's smart, Frankie. He's smart and he's got a lot to lose. Besides that, he's meaner than you by a long shot."

"Meaner than me?" Morgan wiggled his toes again and grinned. "That ain't likely—but even if it is, first he has to beat me to the draw."

12

Ronald Purnell tugged at his high collar and wrung his hands together in his lap. He tried to keep them quiet, but found it hard to sit still. From the time he was a fidgety little boy, Purnell had been uncomfortable around people with money. His own family hadn't had much, and he'd always felt like the rest of the world looked down on him because of it.

He knew the Crowders were well-to-do ranchers with enough money to buy him ten times over. Money wasn't the only thing about the family that set the lawyer's nerves on edge. Old Silas Crowder had a reputation for staring people to death with his one good eye. The story was that a black crow had swooped down out of a crepe-myrtle bush and pecked out the old man's eye. The way Purnell heard it, Silas Crowder caught the bird and strangled it to death with his bare hands to try and get his eye back. Local legend had it that Crowder cooked up the offending bird and ate it for supper. He was a hard man—and hard men with money were the worst.

Crowder land stretched nearly to Tarrant County. Except for the poor parcel that the railroad wanted to buy, the whole place was covered with fat cattle grazing on the grassy hills.

Native grasses sprang up in a vast blue-green carpet, with bright patches of bluebonnets scattered between groves of post oak and cedar. The land looked bright and alive.

The ranch house was a different story. From the outside, it looked all but abandoned. Paint peeled and split on the wood siding. Several weathered boards on the front porch had creaked badly when Purnell arrived, and he'd been afraid he might fall through. A large piece of oilcloth replaced a broken windowpane in one of the upper dormers. Faded shutters hung on by only one hinge. Except for the thin curdle of smoke coming out of the crumbling stone chimney and the telltale glow of lamplight through the dusty windows, the dilapidated house looked like it was about to fall down on its own foundation.

The lawyer supposed it was because the place was kept up by the old man and his boys without the benefit of a feminine touch.

In the parlor, Purnell found himself surrounded by the tintype photographs of a half-dozen dour members of the Crowder family. The women, dressed in high collars and severe hairstyles, looked as stone-faced and dangerous as the bearded men in Confederate gray. A layer of dust did nothing to dull the harsh stares coming from each of the stern portraits.

Cobwebs hung unnoticed by the all-male household in every corner of the high-ceilinged room. The hardwood floor in the parlor was cloudy and streaked from a lack of waxing. It was uncluttered, if not swept, but a silver spoon, encrusted with particles of some food Purnell couldn't identify, hid just under the edge of a well-worn leather couch. No female would have abided such a thing.

Mrs. Crowder had once been a beautiful woman from what Purnell understood—shy and withdrawn around others, she'd always kept a tidy house.

Now he could hear her quiet babbling through the peeling white door that connected the parlor to the kitchen. The incomprehensible noises sounded like a gurgling infant.

Purnell jumped like a guilty child when the door suddenly swung open.

Pete, the oldest Crowder boy, stood there staring and let the door swing shut behind him. He had hard brown eyes and a thick brow that ran together into one fuzzy line above his pug nose. He was ham-fisted and clumsy, with a lumbering walk that shook the house to the timbers with each plodding step.

"Pa says you should come in the kitchen and talk to him in there."

Purnell swallowed hard. He had hoped to avoid this. Mrs. Crowder was known for throwing tantrums now and again. When she did, it embarrassed the old man. When Silas Crowder was embarrassed, there was no telling what he might do.

Pete stomped impatiently, driving up a small puff of dust from the threadbare rug at his feet. "My pa wants to see you in the kitchen so you best get yourself movin'," he said. "He don't like to be kept waitin'."

Purnell gathered up his hat and coat and followed

Pete into the kitchen. He tried to keep his eyes off the swaying, gurgling Mrs. Crowder, and focused instead on the old man who sat at a long oak table feeding—or attempting to feed—his wife some sort of cornmeal mush.

Silas Crowder was dressed in tan canvas britches and a white shirt with the sleeves rolled up to reveal a thick rug of hair on his massive forearms. The hair on his head and face had gone white as ash, and was swept back as if he'd been riding into a hard wind without a hat. A black leather patch covered his left eye. A bit of jagged pink scar was still visible underneath. His right eye remained free to burn a hole straight though Purnell's chest if that was what he decided to do. Luckily for the lawyer, the old man was in a talkative mood.

"Having trouble getting her to eat this evening," Crowder said without looking up. He used a small wooden spoon to push the mush into Mrs. Crowder's mouth. Purnell could hear it thumping against her clenched teeth.

The poor woman sat mute in her straight-backed wooden chair. Cold, gray eyes stared blankly into space, but her mouth was clenched shut in a tight line. Her lifeless yellow hair hung damp from a fresh washing around frail shoulders. Purnell noticed a large galvanized tub beside the woodstove where Crowder must have bathed her. Bits of the mush dribbled down her chin and fell on the ragged red woolen shawl draped across her lap. He thought how much smarter it would have been to attempt to feed the poor woman before trying to bathe her—but kept the idea to himself.

There were worn spots around the uprights on

the chair back, as if someone had been tied there with a rope. Purnell looked away and willed himself not to think about such a thing. He was certain things went on inside this house he did not want to know about.

"What did *His Honor* have to say?" Crowder spit the words the way his wife spit out her mush. He set the spoon on the table and used a cloth napkin to wipe away the mush on his wife's chin. Some of it had fallen down onto her bosom, and Crowder blocked the lawyer's view with his broad shoulders while he cleaned her there.

Purnell coughed and scuffed at the hardwood floor with the toe of his shoe. "Mr. Crowder," he said, turning his head slightly like a dog that expected to be hit. "The judge will not give an inch. He's firmly entrenched with his own views."

Crowder drummed strong fingers on the table and ran a rough hand through his thick beard. It was flecked with the grainy remnants of yellow mush Mrs. Crowder must have spit in his face.

"Entrenched, you say? That figures. I can't say as I expected anything different from the pompous old son of a bitch."

Purnell found himself staring at the pitiful woman, and quickly cut his eyes back to the old man before he was caught. Staring was enough to get a man killed. "I can promise you, I'll give your boy the best defense possible."

Crowder waved that off with his dirty towel. "Tommy would still hang." The old man looked up suddenly, his good eye focused sharply on Purnell. "You know that, don't you? He'd hang because he's a damned idiot. Sometimes, I think it's a blessing that my Rebecca is unaware of how truly ignorant her boys are."

As if she'd recognized her name, Mrs. Crowder began to buzz, pursing her lips together and spewing mush in a sort of forced hum. She rocked back and forth slowly in her seat. Her dull eyes stared at nothing.

"I tell you what I'd like to do," Crowder went on, seemingly oblivious to his wife's antics. "I'd like to whip him bloody for that fool behavior—especially right now with so much at stake. But I can't let him hang. That would break his poor mother's heart for sure whenever she does come around."

Pete took a step forward. He was braver than Purnell when it came to his father—but just barely. "You want that me and Pony should go and bust Tommy outta jail?"

The old man shook his head. "Any other time and that would be fine. But not now. We need to be quieter about it all. We gotta convince the judge it would be in his best interests to let the boy go. This family has too much riding on the stockyard vote to stir the whole town up with a jailbreak."

Mrs. Crowder began to smack her mouth like she was ready for some more mush. At first Purnell thought she might be smiling. If she had anything to smile about, he couldn't see what it was.

The old man took up his wooden spoon again and stabbed it into the bowl of congealed cornmeal mush. "Judge Monfore, he's got hisself a daughter, don't he?"

Purnell nodded. "He does." Deep down he'd known it would come to this. He carried so many terrible secrets as a lawyer, sometimes he thought he might burst at the seams. "But Mr. Crowder, I . . ."

Crowder looked up at his oldest son. "You know where this high-and-mighty judge lives?"

Pete shrugged. "I can find it."

"Purnell will point it out to you. Now listen to me, Pete. Try not to hurt the girl if you can help it. Once you have her, you and Pony carry her out to the line cabin along Little Cottonwood Creek."

Purnell took a deep breath. He attempted to choose his words carefully to keep from getting shot. "Mr. Crowder, I don't see how I can be a party to a kidnapping. If I'm in jail, I won't be able to help with Tom's trial."

Crowder laughed out loud. His wife laughed too, a forced, mechanical giggle, as if she were trying to copy the old man.

"When we have the Monfore girl, there won't be any need of a trial." He turned his attention back to his cackling wife. "Now get moving. Both of you."

Purnell opened his mouth to continue his protest, but Pete glared at him from under a bushy forehead.

For whatever reason, Mrs. Crowder chose that moment to begin a song. She clapped her hands on the table in front of her. Her eyes stared blankly into space, but she crowed the words in a raucous monotone chant.

"Oh, do you remember? Do you remember? How you used to love me true?" She'd been holding some mush in her mouth, and it dribbled down the front of her face. *"Do you remember? Oh, do you remember? I do. I do. . . ."*

Old Man Crowder sat slumped in his chair,

wooden spoon in hand, staring forlornly at the pathetic figure of his damaged wife.

Purnell stood dumbfounded, not knowing what to say or do. He felt a pang of pity for the old man. No one deserved this, even someone as hard and cruel as Silas Crowder.

"We need to leave them alone. Let's go," Pete whispered. His voice was tight with urgency. He kept his eyes toward the floor. "Now!"

Old Man Crowder put his face in his hands and began to sob. His shoulders shook with grief while his wife kept up her song. Purnell tore his gaze away, turned on his heels, and fled through the door to the parlor behind Pete.

"Pa don't like it when anyone sees him get all down like that." Pete shot an accusing glare at Purnell, as if the whole incident was his fault. "He don't like it one bit. Now move your ass. We got us a girl to steal."

Purnell followed slowly, shuffling along without any will of his own, like people he'd seen in an opium daze. He was clinging fast to a runaway train that was moving much too fast for him to jump off—at least not without breaking his neck. This was all wrong.

Watching Mrs. Crowder's fits had turned the lawyer's insides into jelly, and he felt a pressing need to visit the outhouse.

13

Judge Isaiah Monfore made it his habit to work late on Wednesdays because his wife attended her weekly women's auxiliary meeting on that particular evening.

Although Victoria got along well enough with her mother and enjoyed lively debates with her father, she guarded her time home alone on those evenings like a precious treasure. For as long as she could remember, she had preferred her own company to that of anyone else. She'd yet to find a man who interested her remotely enough to make the prospect of marriage seem at all appetizing.

Often, when she was out for a ride by herself, she had to fight the urge to just keep riding—if only to see what was over the next rise. It wasn't the dangers that kept her from leaving, or any sort of fear of the unknown. If anything, these were the things that beckoned to her the loudest. The only thing Victoria Monfore feared was hurting her parents. They'd be heartbroken if she just wandered away the way she dreamt of doing.

Though she hardly ever spoke of it, Victoria knew her mother had been hurt before—desperately hurt—by someone who had wandered away, someone she'd loved more than anything in the world.

So, instead of following her dreams of travel, Victoria read books—any books she could get her hands on—books about sailing the seven seas, books about gunfighters in the Wild West, books about Europe. She didn't care as long as they took her somewhere else and allowed her to wander, allowed her to drift.

The day had been a warm one for April, but at sunset a cool wind had freshened out to the north. Victoria planned to have a long soaking bath with her new Charles Dickens novel. It was supposed to be about the French Revolution—full of intrigue and such. Peggy Langford said it had made her cry. Just the sort of book for a long soaking bath.

Dressed in a thick cotton robe, Victoria padded barefoot through the house, closing all the windows and drawing the drapes. That done, she stoked up the fire in the kitchen stove and checked to make certain the copper hot-water box attached to the side was full. Tiny bubbles formed along the side next to the stove signifying the water was just about the perfect temperature for the kind of skin-pinking bath she enjoyed while she relaxed with her book.

Gallows, her father's red bird dog, lay curled up on his blanket next to the box of kindling, warming his old bones. Flecks of white had crept into the hair around the faithful dog's muzzle. Victoria stooped to rub his ears, and he raised his head to give her a good-natured whine.

"So what do you think, boy? Would a railhead

and stockyards be a blessing or a curse to Parker County? How do you plan to vote?"

The dog groaned and stretched to meet her scratching.

"Come on and tell me what you think, boy," Victoria said. "I trust your opinion as much as Reed Whit . . ."

The dog suddenly came to his feet; his eyes glowed and locked on the kitchen window. A rumbling growl rattled his chest. His lips pulled back in a toothy snarl.

Victoria shot a quick glance over her shoulder at the window, then looked back at the dog. His growling grew more intense.

The back doorknob rattled. Victoria caught her breath and tightened the sash on her robe. If she was going to have to confront an intruder, she wished she'd worn something a little more practical.

Her father wasn't due back for another hour. Even then, he knew she would be in the kitchen having a bath, so he would never have come in that way if he decided to come home early.

Victoria glanced quickly around the room sizing up her situation. If she was going to have to fight half-naked, she would need a weapon. She reached behind the kindling box and grabbed the three-foot wrought-iron fire poker just as Gallows broke into a violent frenzy of barks and snarls.

The rattling at the door changed to a heavy knock.

Victoria stood beside the kitchen stove clutching the iron poker. "Who is it?"

She heard deep voices, muffled and tense.

"Who's there?" she asked again, struggling to keep her voice steady.

The knocking resumed. "Need to leave some papers for the judge," a muffled voice said.

"You'll find him still at his chambers." Victoria cringed and cursed her stupidity as the words escaped her lips. She might as well have told them she was home all alone.

The doorknob jiggled again, and Victoria thanked her lucky stars she'd been about to have a bath—otherwise the door would not have been locked. There had never before been a need.

She heard glass shatter as a window broke in the side parlor. Gallows bristled and growled again before tearing through the swinging door out of the kitchen toward the noise. The back door bowed on its hinges as someone outside put a shoulder to it.

Victoria considered screaming, but dismissed the idea. She really wasn't the screaming type. Beyond that, the women in the surrounding houses were all at the same auxiliary meeting as her mother. Their husbands likely used that as an excuse to leave the house and go down to one of the local saloons to do their weekly carousing. She could yell at the top of her lungs, even fire a twenty-one-gun salute, and no one would be likely to hear her.

Instead, she doused the gas lamp and moved up closer to the door to meet the intruder head-on. It was dark, but she had the advantage of knowing where everything was. As she passed the kitchen counter, she transferred the poker to her left hand and snatched a large meat cleaver off the cutting board for good measure.

She tensed as the door bowed in again. Wood

flew out in splinters. A booted foot crashed through a jagged hole under the knob. She took a swipe with the cleaver, but whoever belonged to the boot drew it back quickly and she missed.

She caught her breath and stood by, waiting. Her heart pounded in her ears. Gallows snarled in the other room, barking and howling as if he had something treed.

Slowly, a hand felt its way through the new opening in the door. Stubby fingers reached up, searching for the lock.

Victoria grasped the cleaver firmly and swung with all her might. This time, she didn't miss.

The hand, minus the ends of two fingers, jerked back through the hole. There was a loud yowl from the other side followed by a stream of molten cursing. Rather than dissuade the intruder, the injury seemed to infuriate him and he redoubled his efforts to get through the door.

Two hard shoves and he had it. The entire door flew off its hinges and crashed into the butcher block. A crouching figure followed it in. The figure stood up straight to get his bearings just in time to get a snoot full of twisted fire poker.

Victoria had dropped the cleaver, figuring the heavy iron bar a better weapon for close fighting. She swung with both hands, putting her hips into it. The figure slumped to his knees with a groan. She hit him again across the back, and was about to follow up with another to his swaying head when a shot rang out in the next room.

"It's a damned dog, dumb ass." The voice was a loud whisper. "Pa said not to hurt the girl. I don't think he'd mind it if we shoot a dog."

"Why don't you just shut up and get on with this." The other voice was strained and tense, like the man didn't really want to be there. Victoria thought she recognized it, but couldn't quite put a finger on who it belonged to.

She let her eyes play around the dark kitchen, trying to decide what to do next. She couldn't stay where she was.

The man at her feet muttered incoherently under his breath and tried to push himself to his feet. He wore a black hood over his head with two large holes cut out so he could see. It looked like the same kind of hood they put on people who were about to hang.

More voices came from the side parlor. Gallows was silent.

Victoria looked at the demolished back door, but decided against trying to escape that way in case there were more men outside watching the horses. In the books she'd read, they always left someone to guard the horses.

The door past the stove lead to her parents' bedroom. Beyond that was her father's study. He kept his guns in there. Victoria gave the man at her feet another whack on the noggin just to be sure he wouldn't follow, and ran for the door.

She'd never fired any of her father's pistols, but he'd taught her to use his shotgun when she was twelve. Up until he'd reinjured his leg, they'd gone to shoot doves in the maize field at the edge of town every fall. He'd been surprised at her skill.

Now, she tore at the coats in the closet of his study, pulling out the long double-barrel from its hiding place in the back. A bag of paper shells hung on a peg beside the gun and she had it loaded in no time. She could hear voices drifting in from the kitchen. Dogs barked up and down the street. She wondered if anyone had heard the earlier shot.

Backing up to the far wall, Victoria hid behind the corner of her father's heavy oak desk. She aimed the loaded shotgun at the door and used the heel of her hand to pull back both hammers. The first person into the room would meet a face full of bird shot. At this range—less than fifteen feet—that meant he wouldn't have much of a face left, or a head for that matter. She held her breath and waited, almost wishing for someone to come through the door.

Getting shot was an occupational hazard when you broke into other people's houses. Breaking in on a poor defenseless woman like this—if someone got their head blown off, it would serve them right.

14

Pony Crowder crouched low and played his pistol around the dark kitchen. Ronald Purnell turned up the gaslight on the wall.

"Good Lord above, look what she done to Pete." Pony's voice was thick, like he had rocks in his mouth. Blood trickled from Pete's ear and pooled around his mouth where it pressed up against a plush, handwoven rug. They pulled off their masks and looked around the room. "Don't worry, Pete. I'll kill her for you," Pony said, kneeling beside his addled brother.

Purnell shook his head hard enough to make his headache seem like it might explode. "Pony," he hissed. "Your father told us not to hurt her. Remember that?"

A cruel grin etched Pony's crooked face. His bottom jaw stuck out a good half inch further than his top, and he always seemed to have a string of drool dripping from the corner of his mouth. He sucked the spit back each time he spoke.

"That was before she beat the hell outta poor Pete. I'm pretty sure he'd want me to kill her now."

Purnell felt like his whole world was crashing down around his shoulders. He couldn't remember how he got mixed up in all this. If the pompous old judge would just listen to reason . . .

"Listen to me, Pony," the lawyer said. "We have to remember what we came for. Your pa doesn't want anything to mess up the vote, right?"

Pony nodded, blinking. "I reckon that's so."

"Well that's what he wants, take my word for it."

Pete groaned, pushing himself into a kneeling position. He held his head with his good hand. "Damn that little bitch." Pete staggered to unsteady feet, pulled off his mask, and stuck the nubs of his injured fingers behind his gun belt to stem the bleeding. He gave his brother a sullen gaze and looked like he might throw up. "I've a mind to kill her too, Pony. Maybe we'll get the chance later, but Pa would do worse to me than she did if we don't carry on just like he told us."

"She must've run in there." Purnell nodded toward the door that lead to the master bedroom. "We'd best hurry before she goes out a window. . . ." His voice trailed off.

The front door creaked open, then shut again. At first the lawyer thought it was the Monfore girl slipping out. He half-hoped it was, even though there would be hell to pay with Old Man Crowder if they came back empty-handed. At least then he might not hang for kidnapping.

He had no such luck. Footsteps approached the kitchen.

"What the deuce . . . ?" a stern voice said. A strange thudding tap accompanied the footsteps. A cane.

Judge Monfore had come home early.

Pete Crowder happened to be the closest to the

kitchen door when the judge came in, and the hapless outlaw caught the brass knob of his cane square in his prominent forehead, splitting his thick eyebrow down to his nose.

Pete was already too dazed to cry out, and slumped to the ground with a deflated whump. Blood poured from his head wound. His eyes rolled back in their sockets, and he blinked like a madman trying to clear his vision before he passed out.

The judge wheeled on his good leg, cane raised, seeking a new target. When he saw Purnell he paused, a puzzled look creasing his jowled face.

The lawyer cast his eyes toward the ground under the scrutiny of such a formidable man. Monfore had recognized him. He was as good as dead now.

"Judge Monfore," Purnell pleaded. "If you'd just listen . . ."

Monfore brandished the cane. His eyes went white and he bellowed like an angry bull. "What the deuce are you doing in my home, Purnell? Where is my daughter?"

"Your Honor, you must hear me out." The lawyer's head felt as if it were about to explode. His breath came in ragged gasps. The room began to spin and he found it difficult to see.

"Don't you *Your Honor* me." The judge raged. "What have you done with my daughter?"

Pony pointed his pistol directly at the back of the judge's head. His normally cross-eyed look cleared for an instant. His tongue flicked out to lick his lips, a sure sign he was about to do something.

Purnell prayed he wouldn't shoot.

Instead, he did the next worst thing. He clubbed Judge Monfore on the side of the head.

Monfore's cane hit the ground and gave one good rattling bounce as the judge followed it down with a crashing thud. He moaned once and lay still, a heavy arm trailing across Pete's ankle.

"You could have killed him, you idiot." Purnell stooped over the bodies and relaxed a notch when he saw they were both breathing. He heard the click of a revolver behind his ear.

"I'll be killing me somebody all right. Pa never said a word about not killin' you. Just as soon you call me an idiot again, I'm gonna splatter your brains from here to Sunday," Pony said. "I know I ain't none too smart, but I ain't no idiot." He prodded the lawyer's ear with the barrel of his pistol. *"Comprende?"*

Purnell swallowed and tried to calm himself. "I understand. We still have to find the girl." He hoped to appeal to what ever reason lurked deep inside Pony Crowder's thick skull.

Pony shrugged as if it was all so simple. "What do we need the girl for? We was supposed to get the daughter so we could make up the judge's mind. Now we got the judge, so we'll just make up his mind directly. *Comprende?*"

The lawyer gave an emphatic shake of his head. His brain was on fire. It was difficult to debate while staring down the maw of a Remington revolver. He struggled to keep his voice calm. "I don't think that's what your father had in mind."

Pony grinned and let his head loll side to side. "You're scared of my pa, ain't you? Fact is, I reckon you're scared of me and this judge and even that teensy little girl who whacked ol' Pete a good one. You're likely scared of your own shadow." Pony giggled and held up a thumb and forefinger half an inch apart. "Fact is, I bet you're this close to peein' down your own leg."

Purnell didn't say a word. He just looked at the gun barrel pointed at him and clenched his teeth, hoping the boy didn't see his knees shaking.

"You help Pete and I'll get the judge." Pony holstered his pistol and sneered. "Pete's lighter. I doubt you got the strength to lift a teacup, let along His Royal Highness here."

Safe from being killed for the time being, Purnell knelt and helped a groggy and bleeding Pete Crowder to his feet. The judge had seen Purnell's face, but it really didn't matter that he'd come along. The Crowders would likely decide to kill him anyway. If they were caught—and they surely would be caught—they would all hang.

Once they got outside, Purnell helped Pony heave the judge across the clumsy gelding they'd brought for Victoria Monfore. He was scared witless, but the lawyer was no weakling. Still, lifting more than two hundred pounds of deadweight across a tall horse left both men panting and covered in sweat. There was a chilly breeze blowing out of the north. Mounting his horse, Ronald Purnell felt as if the wind blew straight through his very soul.

Victoria sat listening to the creaks and snaps in the huge house that up until this point in her life had been her haven. The shotgun was heavy, and though she had more than her share of physical strength, the fight had taken a lot out of her. She rested the long Damascus barrel on the arm of her father's leather chair.

It was dark in the study and the smell of her father was everywhere. The heavy, sweet smell of pipe tobacco lingered in the red smoking jacket draped across the back of the chair. The rich fragrance of saddle soap and lanolin hung above the line of freshly polished boots along the wall behind her.

Years before, when she was still a little girl, she would often come and lie on the sheepskin rug at the foot of his desk and read while he worked on some case or another. He always asked her opinion, teaching her to defend her thoughts with viable arguments. This was the room in her home where Victoria had always felt the most grown up, the place she'd always felt safe.

Now she wondered if she might die here.

A door slammed shut in the kitchen. She jumped and took her eyes off the bedroom door long enough to check the mantle clock above her father's bookshelf. The scant light coming through the drawn curtain just allowed her to see it was still too early for her mother to be home.

Horses nickered outside the window. Grunts and hushed voices carried through the glass. Maybe the intruders were leaving and she would survive the night after all. Perhaps thievery had been their motive all along. Maybe they were just there to steal.

Victoria rushed to the window just in time to see four horses wheel and gallop away into the dark street. A limp body flopped up and down like heavy wings on the back of a stout sorrel.

The intruders had stolen something all right. She gripped the shotgun until her fingers turned white.

They'd stolen her father.

15

Morgan awoke to find his freshly darned and laundered socks folded in the hallway outside the door to his room. He poured water from a blue clay pitcher in a matching basin on top of the shoulder-high chest of drawers. His shirt off, suspenders hanging down around his sides, he surveyed the many scars across his upper body while he washed and rinsed the sleep out of his eyes.

A man with gaunt hollows for cheeks stared back at him from the small oval mirror beside the basin. Some of his scars—the deepest, most painful ones—weren't visible from the outside. He thought how glad he was that he didn't look quite as old as he felt, and slicked his wet hair back over his head.

The smell of frying bacon and fresh biscuits drifted up the stairs along with the flirtatious flurry of giggles.

Morgan smiled and listened to his stomach growl. He was suddenly hungrier than he had been in a long time. The Fossman girls were making breakfast for Luke's young cowhands, Chance and Jasper, no doubt. The four had been an inseparable crew the last time he saw them back in

Colorado . . . but he preferred not to dwell on that. It reminded him too much of Dixie.

Morgan grabbed his hat off the four-poster bed and strapped on his Peacemaker before heading down to the spacious kitchen. He'd gained enough weight back over the last few days that he found he could dispense with the holes in the gun belt he'd had to awl out back in Amarillo.

Both Fossman girls ducked their heads slightly when Morgan entered the warm kitchen. The sun was not yet up, and Morgan could just make out the cool mist hanging above the fields in the gray light of predawn. Chance and Jasper stood up from their spots at the long table. Jasper had a cloth napkin hanging from his top button. He motioned with an open hand to the empty chair next to him.

"Good to see you, sir," the young cowhand said. Despite his baby face, he had turned from boy to man in the short months since Frank had seen him last.

"Good to be seen." Morgan hung his hat on a peg along the wall by the back door and took the offered seat. Carolyn Perkins had her back to the stove, facing the table. She watched Morgan carefully, standing in that peculiar, hip-thrown-out way women who were heavy with child stood. She had a wooden spatula in one hand, tending to a pan of frying eggs. The heat from the woodstove had pinked her round face.

"You're looking poorer than I remember, if you don't mind me saying so, Mr. Morgan," Carolyn said before turning back to the huge pan of frying eggs.

Frank smiled and poured himself a cup of coffee from a speckled blue pot on the table. "I have to admit I'm thin as an old worn-out boot sole. But I swear, Mrs. Perkins, just the smell of these biscuits of yours could fatten a man up. I don't remember havin' such an appetite. I'm afraid I'm drooling like a hungry coyote."

"Good." She beamed a smile and brought over a steaming platter of fried eggs. "You dig right in and eat your fill then. We have plenty. Luke will be back in a minute. He had to go check on a first-calf heifer he's got penned behind the barn."

Perkins came in the door while his wife was speaking. "I'm back already," he said sniffing the air through his thick mustache. "I do love the smell of a good breakfast." He gave his wife a peck on the cheek and a gentle pat on the shoulder.

"Is that any way to say good morning to your wife?" Carolyn raised an eyebrow and put both hands on her hips. They'd obviously plowed this ground before.

Luke stammered and shot a squirming look at Frank for help. Frank shook his head to let the tough old trail boss know he was on his own.

"Well, darlin', I just thought I'd need to be treatin' you with a little lighter hand, what with you bein' in such a tender condition and all."

Carolyn kissed her husband properly, then shooed him toward his spot at the head of the table. "You're getting me mixed up with that first-calf heifer. I'm gonna have a baby. I'm not made out of glass."

"Mind passing me those biscuits, Frank?" Luke gave his friend a sheepish look. He lowered his voice while he took the plate. "Best not to argue with her when she gets a thought in her mind."

Carolyn served Luke three freshly cooked eggs she'd set aside on the stove especially for him.

"And you best not forget it," she said, planting another kiss on top of his bald head.

Frank couldn't help but wonder what it would be like to settle down and have a family like Luke's—surrounded by twittering kids, with a woman to kiss him on top of his head. He'd almost had the chance, back in Colorado. . . .

Outside, the dogs began to bark, and a knock at the front door interrupted Morgan's thoughts and his breakfast.

Luke and his wife exchanged worried glances. Both Jasper and Chance rose quickly and stepped away from the table. They both wore pistols.

"We don't get too many visitors out here early in the mornin'," Luke said with a wink. "The last one came out while I was diggin' a flowerbed out front for Carolyn. He went on and on spoutin' his views on the stockyard plan and makin' all sorts of veiled threats. He got his snout broke with the flat of my shovel."

"Tyler Beaumont, Texas Rangers," a husky voice called from the front porch. "I'm looking for Frank Morgan."

Frank nodded and settled back to one of Carolyn's cathead biscuits and some dark sorghum cane syrup. "You can put your shovels away, boys. Ranger Beaumont's a friend of mine."

The cowboys resumed their seats at the table beside Berta and Bea Fossman. Luke followed suit while his wife got the door.

Beaumont had his hat in both hands when he followed her into the kitchen. His brow was furrowed and a grim look crossed his normally serene face.

"Pull up a chair and have some breakfast, Ranger Beaumont." Perkins dipped his bald head toward an empty seat.

"I'd be much obliged, I would," Beaumont said. "But I really ought to get movin' and I need Frank to come with me."

Everyone at the table stopped at the tone of the lawman's voice. Carolyn shut the door to the firebox on her stove and turned to face him.

"What's happened?" she asked.

"The Monfores' house was attacked last night."

Morgan pushed his unfinished plate away from him and got to his feet. His appetite fled with the news. "The girl?"

The Ranger shook his head. "She's fine. She gave the bandits a sure-enough whippin'. Mrs. Monfore was not at home—but the judge walked in smack in the middle of all of it. And now he's gone missing."

"Judge Monfore, kidnapped?" Carolyn raised a hand to cover her mouth.

"Looks that way, ma'am."

Morgan was already putting on his hat. Carolyn gave him a hug and a peck on the cheek.

"Thank you for the hospitality, Mrs. Perkins." He smiled. "You too, Luke. I'll stop in again before I leave town so we can do some more catching up."

"Keep your powder dry, Frankie." Luke said. "I'll come if you need me to."

"With things shaping up as they are, you best stay here close to your wife." Morgan shook his friend's hand. "You might have to give someone else a snout full of shovel before all this is over."

* * *

Morgan had Stormy saddled in a few minutes and they mounted up to head at the trot for the county seat. It was early yet, and the morning mist swirled and eddied around the horses' hooves as they rode through the low draws and creek bottoms on the way into town.

Beaumont munched on a biscuit with some bacon Carolyn Perkins had given him for the road. The northerly breeze gave a chill to the morning air as it rustled the live oak leaves along the wagon road. Dog settled in to the rhythm quickly, and only occasionally darted off to chase after a jackrabbit or quail. His belly was full of biscuits too, and luckily for the rabbits his heart wasn't really in the hunt.

The cool wind filled the horses with boundless energy. Beaumont's little bay chewed nervously on the bits, and even Stormy pranced along with a kink in his tail. Morgan's bones were still too sore to sit a jigging horse, and he scolded the Appaloosa with a stern cluck and a tap of the reins to the animal's neck. The stout horse knew better and once reminded, calmed to a gentler gait.

"We'll stop in the sheriff's office first and straighten out this nonsense about the shooting in Springtown." Beaumont finished his biscuit and wiped his hand on the front of his shirt while he rode. "It's lucky you had another lawman there as a witness."

"It is at that." Morgan nodded. "If the sheriff will listen to reason. From what I hear about the man, that's still up for some discussion."

"He'll listen or go to jail his own self." Beaumont

spoke with the surety of a much older man. There was no false bravado in his whispery voice—just a statement of pure fact. It was difficult not to like such a man.

"Something's goin' on in Parker County," the Ranger continued. "I wired my captain and he said to go ahead and look into it. I haven't been able to talk to Sheriff Whitehead yet, but from what the captain says, he's a hell of a gunman. Shoots first and sorts out the mess afterward."

"That's what I hear," Morgan said.

He could see the tall clock tower on the limestone courthouse rising up from the center of town ahead as they came down the long hill from the north. It was still early and there were just a few wagons and horses out on the streets. Most people in the town were only now sitting down to their breakfast.

"Stay with me, Dog," Morgan said over his shoulder. "We may be in jail in a minute or two and you'll need the Ranger to post your bail."

Beaumont shook his head and sighed. "I told you I got it worked out, Frank. If the high sheriff of Parker County won't listen to reason, I got an ace up my sleeve he can't turn down."

16

The sheriff's office was located on the main street heading east out of town toward Ft. Worth, not far from a little fork in the Trinity River. It was a plain, stacked-lumber building with riveted flat-iron bars inside the shuttered windows. The heavy timber door was reinforced by the same riveted metal. It looked like a small fortress, because that's what it was.

Inside, his back to the door, a dumpy deputy sheriff stooped in front of a potbellied stove, poking at a smoking excuse for a fire. Half his freckled rear end rose above the sagging seat of his britches, which looked like they carried a load of freight. He banged his head against the door with a start when he heard Beaumont and Morgan come in behind him.

"Help you?" He rubbed the goose egg that was rapidly forming on the pink skin below his thinning hairline. The deputy wore a wide, brainless smile, though the bump on his forehead was already beginning to turn a deep shade of purple and looked like it gave him a powerful headache. His ponderous belly hung over his belt enough to hide the buckle, and he'd likely not seen his boots in years.

"Looking for Sheriff Whitehead," Morgan said.

The deputy glanced back and forth at the two men. He paid particular attention to Beaumont's *cinco-peso* Ranger star. "He ain't here just now. He's over at the Monfore place. I'm his town deputy, Bob Grant. Can I help you gents with somethin'?" He squirmed, but the painted-on smile remained.

Morgan grinned when he heard the man's name. Bobby Grant had been as awkward a boy as he was a man, but he was always a kind sort. Frank had always figured him more for a melon salesman, and was surprised to find he'd turned out to be a lawman.

"You don't remember me, do you, Bob?" Morgan held his hand out.

The deputy's smile tensed but didn't disappear. He took the offered hand. "I reckon I do too, Frank Morgan. I was just prayin' it wasn't you."

"Why's that?"

Deputy Grant turned toward the stove. "You fellers want some coffee? I got some right in this here pot."

"That's mighty kind of you, Bob," Frank said. The man was jumpy about something and wouldn't look him in the eye. "I'd not refuse a cup if it was offered."

Grant poured two black metal cups and handed them to the men. His hands shook a little, and the ever-present smile began to look more like a pained grimace. "Hope you like it black. I ain't had no time to go across the street to Carter's and get any sugar with the prisoner and all."

"Mind if I ask what's eatin' you, Deputy?" Beaumont spoke across the top of his cup. "Why would you be prayin' he wasn't Frank Morgan?"

The man gulped. "The sheriff warned me you'd likely be stoppin' by. He give me strict orders to arrest you when you came through the door."

Morgan took a drink of his coffee. It was passable, but not by much. "So what do you plan to do?"

The deputy gave a tight chuckle. "You remember my wife? She was Martha Alberry when you knew her."

"Sure I remember Martha, nice girl," Morgan said, though he really remembered her to have been an overbearing tyrant since before she was ten. It figured a man like Bob Grant would end up with a woman that could do most of his thinking for him.

"Well, sir. She brought me my breakfast this morning and I talked it all over with her." Grant looked up to make sure the other men were listening. "Martha would rather I talk most everything over with her. Anyhow, she said she remembers you well, Frank. From what she's read about you lately, she told me she's gonna go ahead and get out the suit she plans to bury me in if I try and do such a fool thing."

"That man doesn't need to be carryin' a gun," Beaumont said as he climbed aboard his little gelding.

"I don't know." Morgan grinned. "He had enough sense not to follow orders when it could get him killed."

"You wouldn't have shot poor old Bob the Boob, would you?"

"Nope," Morgan said. "But he don't need to know that."

"Makes a man not mind being single," Beaumont mused as they rode.

The wind died down by the time they reined up in front of the Monfore place. Frank whistled under his breath at the size of the gray mansion. A large covered porch wrapped around three sides of the two-story home. Lace curtains hung in each of four gables above the porch. The judge had been doing a good job of taking care of Mercy—at least when it came to a home. Even with all his money, Morgan had never sat still long enough to give a woman a place like this.

They tied their horses to the rail along the gravel coach drive that ran beside the house next to a small buggy barn. Morgan gave Dog a narrow look, and the cur flopped down next to the horses with a resigned sigh.

The front door was ajar. Morgan could just make out a raven-haired young woman sitting on a green velvet couch. She had high cheekbones, and even from across the room he could see her piercing blue eyes. They were red from crying, and he felt a knot in his gut from the thought of such a thing.

His boots clomped across the wooden porch and he walked in uninvited. Beaumont was right behind him.

Mercy sat in a high-backed chair across from her daughter. She was just like Frank remembered her: delicate as a new spring peach blossom. She had her hair pulled back in a single long braid. It was a fiercely shimmering blue-black, just as it was when he'd last seen her; though a startling shock of gun-metal gray swept back over her right temple.

A tall man with a coarse black mustache and matching eyebrows sat on a red velvet piano stool next to her. A grim look crossed his chiseled face.

Mercy's eyes were red as well, but she seemed to have gained control of herself—until she saw Frank. When she looked up, the floodgates opened again and she jumped to her feet. Much to the dismay of her daughter and everyone else in the room, including Morgan, she ran to him and buried her face against his chest.

"Oh, Frankie, I just knew you'd come. I fear that now you may have arrived too late." Her small body was racked with sobs. Luke had been right. She still had her honey-sweet drawl.

Morgan tried to console her, patting her softly on the back. She smelled different than he'd remembered, less like peppermint and more like lilac perfume. They'd both been so young back then.

"I'd have come sooner but I've been a bit under the weather."

"It doesn't matter now. You're here," she sobbed. Her voice was muffled against him.

Sheriff Whitehead got to his feet with a cold stare. "You're Frank Morgan?"

Mercy looked up when she heard the voice behind her. Her body stiffened in Morgan's arms. "Be careful, Frank," she whispered in his ear. She stepped out of his way and moved next to her daughter, wringing tense hands in front of her.

"You ought to be in jail." Whitehead took a step

forward. His hand wrapped around the grip of his pistol.

"That's what I hear," Morgan nodded. "Lucky for him and me, your deputy chose the better part of valor."

"If these poor women hadn't just lost a husband and father," the sheriff fumed, "I'd plant you here and now."

"You got a family, Sheriff?" Morgan squared off, keeping a close eye on the lawman.

"I do," Whitehead said. "Not that it's any business of yours."

Morgan's eyes narrowed. His voice became deadly serious. "Well, sir, you can go ahead and try to plant me here—if you're hell-bent on the notion. I gotta tell you, though, your own family will only end up without a husband and father."

"You son of a . . ."

"Here now, Sheriff." Beaumont put up his hands. "Tyler Beaumont, Company F, Texas Rangers. I was there in Springtown. Your man brought it on himself, bullyin' the lady like he did. He drew first and Frank had no choice."

Whitehead didn't move. His hand stayed at the butt of his pistol. "You can be a witness at the trial if he lives that long. You're under arrest, Morgan. It's up to you if you go to jail or to the undertaker."

Beaumont stepped in between the two men, his hands still in the air. "All right, he's your prisoner. Right, Frank?"

Morgan shot a surprised look at his friend. He hadn't counted on this.

"Get his gun then, if you're going to cooperate,"

Whitehead said. "Get his gun and tell him to stand down if you want to save his worthless life."

A tense silence followed while Morgan decided what to do. The ticking of the mantel clock and the hushed whisper of Mercy's breathing were the only sounds in the room. At length, he raised his hands and let the Ranger pluck the Peacemaker from his holster. Something he'd never given another living soul the leave to do. Instead of handing the pistol over to the sheriff, Beaumont tucked it in his own belt.

"He's all yours." The Ranger stepped away.

Mercy buried her face in her hands and began to sob again. "I'm so sorry, Frank. This is all my fault."

Her raven-haired daughter stared daggers at Beaumont with her beautiful blue eyes. She bit her full bottom lip to keep from crying.

Whitehead smiled smugly and let his gun hand relax. "Turn around, Morgan, and get out to your horse. Don't do anything foolish and you might live long enough to go to trial. One false move and I'll blow that fool head off your shoulders."

"Oh!" Beaumont smiled, stepping up again to hand the sheriff a folded sheet of paper. "It's a little thing really—almost slipped my mind. I got a writ here signed by Judge Kelly over in Palo Pinto County. It says you need to turn over one prisoner by the name of Frank Morgan safe and sound to the Texas Rangers." He pointed at his five-peso badge and whispered. "That means me."

"What the hell is this?" Whitehead unfolded the document and read it, moving his head from side to side as he took in the meaning. When he finished, he wadded it in a huge fist and threw it back to Beaumont.

"You got a choice to make, Sheriff," Beaumont said. Now he was the smug one. "You can defy this court order, in which case you can consider yourself under arrest. Your career would be done. Or, you can turn the prisoner over to me and go on with your job—which I assume includes seeing to the business of finding Judge Monfore."

Whitehead's deep chest heaved under his black leather vest with undisguised hatred. His eyes blazed when he shot a look at Morgan. "This isn't over."

"I never thought it was, Sheriff," Morgan said. "Never thought it was."

The sheriff slammed his hat down over his head and glared. "You better not so much as spit on a sidewalk or I'll have your sorry hide in jail. One false move, Morgan, and you're mine. Do you hear me?"

Frank gave a smiling nod. It was best to let the man fume a little.

"It would have turned out a damned sight different if you didn't have your sawed-off Ranger friend around to protect you." Whitehead didn't move.

Beaumont gave Morgan back his Peacemaker by the barrel. "You're right about that, Sheriff," the Ranger said simply. "If I wasn't here, you'd be dead by now."

17

Sheriff Whitehead slinked off and left Morgan and the Ranger alone with the grief-stricken womenfolk.

"My Lord, but you showed some spunk," Beaumont said, openly admiring Victoria after she filled them in on the events of the previous night.

Dark blood stained the thick green rugs in the living room. The sheriff had been is such a rush to leave, he'd forgotten the two fingers Victoria had liberated from one of her attackers, and they lay like two pieces of German sausage popping out of their casings in a bowl on the piano. Beaumont promised he'd take them away when he left.

Morgan sat beside Mercy on the couch. He was just as impressed as Beaumont with the girl's bravery and quick thinking under fire. Had the story come from a man, Morgan would have chalked most of it up to bravado and exaggeration, but Victoria told it with a calm indifference that said she really didn't care what anyone thought of her—she'd done what she'd done, and that was that.

He wondered where all that fortitude came from—certainly not from the girl's mother. Mercy had always been a quivering bird in the face of adversity. It was lucky for her she'd never had to fight her way through a Comanche raid like some of the women in Parker County. She was a fine woman, but bravery and a calm demeanor in battle had not been added to Mercy's makeup when the Good Lord was handing out personality traits.

"I'm certain the sheriff already asked this," Frank said. "But was there anyone in particular who might have a reason to kidnap the judge?"

Mercy sniffled in her hankie and shook her head. She worked to choke back more tears at the mention of her husband.

Victoria spoke up. Her voice was strong and matter-of-fact. "Mr. Morgan, my father is a district court judge for the state of Texas. During his time on the bench he has sent dozens of men to prison or the gallows. I'm sure there are an equal number of people who'd like to see him . . ." The girl looked at her mother and stopped herself. "See him gone."

"Anybody in particular lately?" Beaumont did not even try to talk to Mercy, but kept his eyes glued to Victoria's face.

"The whole county's embroiled in a wicked dispute over the railroad proposition. It's all coming to a vote a week from yesterday," Mercy said before blowing her nose. "My husband was . . ." She peered over the top of her hankie at Morgan. "Is very vocal in his opposition to the proposal."

"And Tommy Crowder is in jail for what he did to the Smoot girl," Victoria said. "The Crowders are the most vocal people on the other side of the stockyard issue."

"Miss Monfore," Tyler said. "I wonder if you would mind showing me where the outlaw kicked the door in. He might have left something behind that would help us track them."

"Certainly." The girl didn't appear to mind all the attention Beaumont threw her way. "We'll be right back, Mother. Will you be all right?"

Mercy nodded. She dabbed at her pink nose with the hankie.

Victoria rose and pinned Morgan to his chair with a look from her deep blue eyes. It was a look of accusation, gone in a flash, but it still made his insides crawl. Frank told himself it was just his imagination, but he knew better.

"It's this way, Ranger Beaumont," she said, with just a touch of her mother's accent.

When they were alone, Frank turned to Mercy and smiled wearily. She looked much as he remembered her, only thinner, with a few more lines around her eyes. He wondered if most of them came from laughing or crying. He found he could not pull out any words to fit the occasion.

It was Mercy who broke the awkward silence. "You're looking thin."

Frank looked down at the rug. Up until now, he'd forgotten why he'd been taken with Mercy so, all those years ago. She had a way of taking care of him, mothering him and seeing after his every need.

"I got in a little scrape with a bandit up in Colorado, then again with the same bandit out in the Panhandle."

Mercy's eyes were wide and her lip trembled the way it always had. Memories flooded Frank's mind.

"From what I hear," Mercy said, "bandits who

have a scrape with Frank Morgan don't usually have a chance to have another."

Morgan shrugged and toed at the thick Persian rug. "This one was a particularly nasty kind."

"I heard about it. I'm so awfully sorry about your poor wife." Mercy's drawl dripped with genuine concern.

Frank felt his neck burn. The bitter taste of boiling acid churned up from his stomach. He didn't like the way the conversation was going. Lately, all talk about him seemed to lead straight to Dixie. He needed to change the subject.

He looked around the well-furnished home. It was comfortable enough, but a little dark to suit his way of thinking. The deep mahogany furniture and pine-colored rugs gave the place the shadowed air of a cave.

"You seem to be doing well for yourself. You got a huge house and more nice paintings and furniture than I thought there was in all of Texas. The judge is taking good care of you and I'm glad."

"He does take care of me," Mercy said. She looked up at Frank, but when he tried to meet her gaze, her eyes darted back to the safety of her lap. "Isaiah provides a very comfortable life for Victoria and me." She toyed at the white lace corner of her handkerchief.

Morgan knew it would take some time for her to work up to whatever it was she intended to tell him. Mercy had never been one to let everything out all at once. He sat quietly beside her, close enough to feel her body move when she breathed. If rushed, she was the type who might bottle it up inside forever.

Mercy's warmth and the smell of her hair

brought back a thousand tender memories, memories of another life, before the war. Frank had never felt more awkward. He coughed to give himself time to think.

"Mercy," he said softly. "I need you to tell me a little more about the judge. That way we can get to work locating him and take care of the men who took him."

Victoria sat at the kitchen table and watched as Beaumont took a closer look at the damage done to the kitchen door. She could see the muscles of his powerful shoulders as they bunched and moved under his thin cotton shirt. Watching him made her mouth feel dry.

"How long have you known Mr. Morgan?" Victoria had always found it easier to relax when she was talking, as if the words helped bleed off some of her tension.

"Met him a few months back," the Ranger said, still looking at the door. "We were after the same bold killer and he took the time to save my worthless neck. Thought we were going to lose him for a spell there. He's a tough old bird, but don't let him fool you. He's got a soft spot in there somewhere. All those books about him are nothin' but a pile of horse sh—"

She laughed and Beaumont caught himself.

"Sorry," he said. "I about forgot my manners. In my line of work, I don't get to spend much time around too many upstanding women."

She let him off easy. "There are books about Mr. Morgan?"

"Ten or twenty, I reckon. None of 'em worth the paper they're printed on if you ask me."

"You're not like any Texas Ranger I ever met," Victoria said. She had to fight the unsteady feeling she was getting from being so near the handsome Ranger.

He seemed particularly interested in a bit of cloth stuck in the splinters of the door frame, and worked to free it with the point of his jackknife.

"You've met a lot of Rangers, have you?" He spoke without looking up.

Victoria shrugged. "My fair share, I suppose. My father is a judge after all."

"Hmm," Beaumont grunted. "I reckon that's so. What's so different? All those other Rangers over five feet tall?"

"You hush." Victoria chuckled despite herself. "You're well over five feet tall."

"Depends on what you mean by *well*. I'm not quite halfway to six."

"It doesn't seem to bother you."

He looked up and grinned. His eyes sparkled in the light that poured in from the open door in front of him. "I can't say that it does."

"Me either," she said. And she meant it.

18

"Keep those heels down, ye blasted no-ridin' sons of bitches," Sergeant Percy Cleary yelled at the top of his merciless lungs. A bright sun beat down on top of his bald head as he stood rooted to the middle of the open parade ground. There were twenty-three other men in his column, but Lieutenant Isaiah Monfore knew the tough Irish master of horse was speaking directly to him.

Monfore's head ached as though he'd been stepped on by a mule. At times like this, the young lieutenant cursed his father for making him join the military. He'd studied law and intended to pursue it as a career, but with a war between the states looming ever closer on the horizon, the elder Monfore was insistent. "Lawyering is all well and good," he would say. "But if a man were to want himself a judgeship someday, he would need to be a military veteran. Connections are what it's all about, my boy. . . ."

Isaiah couldn't understand what a connection to anyone like this Irish loudmouth could get him besides a sore back.

"Column of fours! Left face, at the walk! Hooo!" Sergeant Cleary's voice had only two volumes:

silent and full-bore, red-faced, purpled-veined screaming. "Monfore, fall out," the sergeant barked. "And don't ye quit ridin' just because I call ye over! Shoulders back, lad!"

Monfore kept his heels pressed down in the iron stirrups and his eyes forward as he drew up alongside the ranting teacher.

"Ye ride like ye got a broomstick stuck up your arse, Leftenant." Sergeant Cleary's voice was loud enough for the rest of the riders to hear. "What do you have to say for yourself?"

"No excuse, Sergeant." It was the only answer allowed, but it was never accepted.

In truth, Monfore rode just as well as or better than anyone else in his class; it just happened to be his day under the sword of Sergeant Cleary. The focus of wrath from the tough master of horse was something each student dreaded—even officers like Monfore. Cleary was on loan from a prestigious cavalry school in Europe, and thus not constrained by the structures of normal command. Rank indeed had no privilege when it came to his classes in equitation.

"It's a wonder your nag can still stand with all the bouncin' nonsense you're doin' on his poor back."

The insults stung, but experience had taught the junior officer that when Cleary called attention to you, he generally let you prove him wrong.

The students had been hard at work on what the sergeant called "correct seat" for two weeks solid. Each day they listened to the scolding rants and personal jibes as they walked, trotted, and cantered in circles and figure eights. Each night they fell asleep on weary backsides with cries of "Heels down!" "Quiet those blasted hands!" or some other barked curse or order ringing in their ears.

Cleary believed that no soldier deserved the privilege of a saddle until he earned it by completing a series of contests, the most difficult of which was a bareback jump over a four-rail fence.

"Column halt! Ho!" Sergeant Cleary bellowed lest the obedient class carry on all the way to the Okalahoma line without another order. "Lieutenant Donaldson, form the men up along Parade Ground B."

"Aye, Sergeant!" A lanky cavalryman at the rear of the column squeaked out the orders to return the men.

Cleary focused a blazing eye on Monfore. "I'm disinclined to give ye this opportunity, but I feel it's a waste of the government's resources to put you through any more drill. Let's let ye have a go at the fence so we can go ahead and send ye back to the line as a foot where ye belong."

To call a cavalryman a *foot* or infantryman was the worst insult of all.

"I'm ready, Sergeant."

"We'll see about that." Cleary glared. "We'll see about that."

In Sergeant Cleary's way of thinking, nothing was ever the horse's fault. If an animal stumbled, the rider was too heavy-handed. If it shied, the tentative soldier on board was to blame.

Monfore had no one to blame but himself when the tall black gelding refused the jump and sent him flying into the fence. His leg snapped like a piece of kindling, twisting backward at an absurd angle and ending his career in the military forever.

"Well, my boy." The sergeant looked down at him as he hung upside down between the rails of the fence. "Knew right off you'd never be a horseman. Now you won't even make a good foot. I'll get the paperwork started to make you a judge. . . . I have connections, you see. . . ." Cleary smiled.

That was all wrong. Sergeant Cleary never smiled. . . .

Judge Isaiah Monfore woke with the pain in his leg as fierce as the day he broke it. The bouncing horse ride, tied across the saddle like a sack of grain, had ground bone against bone in the old wound and his right knee was swollen to half again its normal size.

His head was on fire. For a moment he thought his neck might be broken. He dismissed the notion when he realized he'd not be able to feel such pain if that were the case.

He was lying on his side, his hands tied in front of him with stout pigging strings like cowboys used to tie up calves for branding. The bonds were tight and his hands had begun to turn a sickening purple. His boots were gone and though he couldn't see his feet, the fact that he couldn't feel them either told him they were bound the same way.

A shaft of sunlight cut through the single window on the south side of the stuffy log cabin. As far as Monfore could tell, he was alone. He'd heard men's voices earlier—the sounds of drinking and a riotous card game. The stench of old whiskey and human sweat filled the room.

The judge prayed that the men hadn't harmed Victoria. They'd been in his house, but he clung to the hope that she had somehow escaped by running out the back as they came in.

The thought of anything happening to her made him sick to his stomach. Without him there to protect them, his whole family might be in danger.

He struggled against the ropes, but they wouldn't budge. Falling back in exhaustion, he looked around the room. He was surprised they'd left him alone—and even more surprised when he saw a broken whiskey bottle on the floor five feet in front of his nose.

The judge strained his ears to listen for anyone approaching. When he heard nothing, he inched his way across the dirt floor like a worm, fighting the pain in his leg and neck as he went. His hands were all but completely numb, and five minutes later, when he'd cut through the ropes around his wrists, he found he'd shredded his own fingers in the process.

Wincing at the hot spasm that shot up his knee, he bent to cut his feet free. That done, he tried to stand, using the edge of a wooden table to aid him.

His head spun and he found his leg would not hold him. He fought back the urge to vomit, and collapsed writhing and clutching his injured knee with blood-soaked hands.

When he caught his breath, Monfore looked at the door to his right. Light shone through the many cracks in the rough slab wood. He half-crawled, half-dragged himself across the dank earthen floor. He hadn't gotten where he was in life by waiting for conditions that were easy.

He used a stick to push up on the latch above

him. It was unlocked. Luckily for Monfore, he'd been kidnapped by brainless imbeciles.

The door groaned open with painful slowness, and creaked loud enough to call in any nearby guards. The judge poked his head over the rough-hewn threshold and chanced a look outside. A dozen yellow butterflies danced on a warm breeze in the otherwise-vacant clearing between the cabin and a dense line of trees and vines that looked like it might be a creek bed.

It took him ten minutes to cross the twenty yards to the tree line. Every inch gained came at tremendous cost as he pulled himself forward on tufts of grass and clumps of rock and dirt. The journey left him panting and bilious. He collapsed in a tangle of grapevines and poke salad in the cool shadows.

He watched a brown dog tick shinny up a green stem in front of his nose, felt it drop down on his neck. He was too tired to care.

The land gave way rapidly to the creek fifteen feet below. Monfore had no idea where he was, and had only a vague plan of what he would do when he got to the water. He hoped the creek would be deep enough that he could float downstream and put as much distance between him and his captors as possible before they noticed he was missing.

After a short rest, he began the painful job of towing his injured body over the thorny briar vines and deadfall. An Osage orange tree had littered the sloping ground with fist-sized green fruit from the previous year. The rotting bumps each formed a hurdle he had to pull himself over or through.

By the time he dragged, tumbled, and rolled his way to the creek, his belly and legs were soaked with mud and stained purple-green from crushed vegetation and rancid, year-old mustang grapes. His back was soaked with sweat.

He collapsed on a damp sandbar just feet from the cloudy stream and fainted.

Monfore shivered himself awake. His teeth chattered and his head pounded as if it were locked in a vise. He couldn't tell how long he'd been unconscious, but the shadows had moved across the sandbar in front of him and he supposed it had been a while.

His whole body felt stiff and bent as a mesquite branch. There wasn't an inch of him that didn't hurt. He thought of his poor wife. She wouldn't be doing well alone. Mercy was one of the few people in the world who truly needed him. Of course, she might not be alone. Monfore knew his wife had sent for that old flame of hers—a desperate outlaw from what he'd heard. She said he'd be able to help, but a man had to wonder about such things. He closed his eyes and pushed such thoughts out of his mind. Years on the bench had made him cynical. If he trusted anyone it was Mercy—except for her handful of little secrets, she was truly a woman without guile. Tender Mercy, he often called her.

He wondered about Victoria. She'd be worried sick, but she would do fine on her own. Her blasted independence had always galled him and made him proud at the same time. She had very little in common with her mother besides her looks.

Monfore shivered again. He knew he had to move, to put as much distance between himself and the cabin as he could. He couldn't go fast, but he could move, and that was better than lying down and giving up. When he tried to push himself up, he felt a strange tickle along his right side, along his arm. He didn't have enough energy to flinch, but when he moved again to look, a rasping hiss hit his ears and made his blood run cold.

Slowly, he shifted his gaze, trying not to alarm the thing he already knew he would see.

On top of all his troubles, a fat water moccasin had slithered in to take advantage of the relative warmth of his body. As thick as his wrist, the deadly snake lay like a black sausage in a three-foot S curve from Monfore's swollen knee to his chest. The beast opened its cotton-white mouth and hissed again at the movement of his breathing. Like every other moccasin he'd ever seen, this one was in a bad mood.

In his present condition the judge knew he'd never be quick enough to roll away before the viper could strike. One bite from a cottonmouth wasn't always fatal—but two or more would spell disaster.

Monfore thought he might try to wait the snake out, hoping it would move away, but he was shivering badly and he feared the movement would soon aggravate the animal to the point where it would bite. His pitiful wet cotton clothing would offer no protection at all from the sharp fangs.

He pressed his face into the cool sand and racked his brain for a way out of this mess. He cursed Silas Crowder and Ronald Purnell—swore he would live to see them hang.

Without warning, a deafening boom rocked the narrow creek bed. Sand, mud, and bits of bloody snake flew through the air around Monfore's head, peppering the water in front of him.

Brown water seeped into the muddy crater where the snake had been. Half the moccasin's thick body lay three feet away bobbing in the edge of the creek.

"That was a big-un," Monfore heard a voice say.

The judge didn't have to look up to know it was Pony Crowder.

The drooling cowboy squatted down next to his face and prodded him with a rifle barrel. "Now what do you think you're doin' out here all by your lonesome? That big ol' booger woulda kilt you for sure if we hadn't come along to rescue you." Pony sucked spit in from his hanging lower lip. His gaze hardened and he stood, looking down. "You might as well get over the idea of tryin' to escape, Your High and Mightiness."

A brutal kick to his unprotected ribs drove the air from Monfore's lungs. Pain washed over his side and cascaded down his leg as he writhed and coughed in the mud.

Crowder spit at his face. "Now we have to carry your damn carcass back up that hill. This time I aim for you to stay put. *Comprende?*"

The outlaw drew back his boot and planted it squarely in the side of Monfore's face.

Brilliant colors exploded in the judge's head. He cried out in spite of himself, and then found he could close his jaw. He heard Crowder grunt from the effort of his beating. The kicks fell on him like rain. After the first half dozen he was beyond feeling.

The judge felt certain he was a dead man. He

couldn't hold on much longer. The human body could only take so much. He drew his arms up around his head, tried to cover as best he could, and began to picture Mercy's face, hear Victoria's voice. He needed to say his good-byes.

Pony's boot connected again, snapping Monfore's head sideways with the well-placed kick.

Orange and purple lights flashed like fireworks behind his eyes, then slowly faded to black.

19

The Whippoorwill Saloon, a squatted pile of rotten lumber and rusty nails, was in a wide spot on the dusty wagon road toward Poolville. Chas Ferguson slouched at a rickety table looking at the dots of light where the sun came in through dozens of bullet holes and wide cracks in the wood.

It was early afternoon and the place was nearly deserted except for a couple of card games at the far end of the open room. A heavy pall of tobacco and lamp smoke curled in a thick layer below the ceiling rafters like a fog bank along a river bottom. The smell of spilled beer and stale coffee hung in another unseen layer closer to nose level.

Ferguson was mad enough to boil an egg in his fancy hat. His life had been fine before he met Frank Morgan. He'd been handy with a gun for as long as he could remember. There'd never been a single town where the sweet young ladies didn't pull each others' hair out to spend time with him. Before he had the misfortune to cross paths with the infamous Drifter, Ferguson had been brimming with confidence in his stellar abilities.

Then he had to run up against the damned gunfighter. Something about Morgan turned his guts into jelly. It was as if the man looked right through him, as if he saw every weakness, read his every thought. Worse than that, just talking to the renowned gunfighter made Ferguson want to turn on his heels and run. The thought of such a thing made him furious. He had never run from anything in his life, and he wasn't about to start now.

He would have to face his fears sooner or later; he'd have to stand in the street with Frank Morgan and meet him head-on.

The dandy threw back a shot of whiskey, grimaced as the heat of it hit his belly, and refilled his glass. He'd need a few more drinks before the pain in his head would dull to a manageable level. He popped his neck from side to side.

He'd made this same decision a hundred times already. It was an easy thing to do when he was alone. Alone, he could lay his plans to step into a dusty street where he would face Frank Morgan and take his rightful place as the best gunman in the country. Alone, he could load his pistol, stand at twenty paces, and send six rounds through a hole the size of a silver dollar before most men could even get off three shots.

Then, he'd catch a glimpse of the cocksure Frank Morgan somewhere on the street—and all the bravado, all the sauce he'd built up in himself drained away. Then all he felt was a knot the size of his fist, low in his stomach as if he'd been gut-shot. During those times, he wasn't certain if he'd be able to hit a plow horse in the ribs from five paces.

"Damn you to infernal Hell, Frank Morgan, you sorry sack of horse shit." Ferguson saluted the air with his shot glass and killed another shot of whiskey. His voice had a catch in it and his eyes were glassy with tears of frustration. The men at the table closest to him looked up from their game and chuckled.

"Somethin' on your mind?" Ferguson slammed the glass down hard on the table and glared, wiping his forearm across his eyes.

All four men turned quickly back to their cards, whispering and grunting among themselves.

Ferguson calmed down a notch and flicked his hand toward the girl standing next to the bartender. She rolled her eyes and swayed up from the bar to ease in his direction. He fumed inside at her attitude, as if it was a damned nuisance to serve him. She wasn't much to look at herself with her heavy face paint and protruding squirrel teeth. It hadn't been all that long ago that a girl like this would have counted herself lucky to wait on Chas Ferguson's table.

"What can I do you for?" the girl said. She held back a few feet as if he had the pox.

Ferguson grunted and filled his shot glass again. He held up an empty beer mug. "I'm thirsty. I will require another beer to go along with my main course of this rotgut you folks call whiskey around here."

When she reached for the glass, he let it fall, then grabbed her wrist and drew her to him. "Besides the beer, I'll require a little of your company."

The girl squirmed and tried to pull away. She didn't cry out or panic. It was obvious she was used to a certain amount of man-handling, and it appeared she was more annoyed than frightened. If she'd at least feared him, that would have been something. Her attitude infuriated him. There had been a time when a focused look from Chas Ferguson could make a grown man go pale. Now he couldn't even intimidate a filthy saloon girl with an ugly overbite.

"Turn a-loose of me, you imbecile." She smacked him across the arm with her free fist. She had a way of clicking her prominent teeth when she talked that made it sound like she was spitting.

"Whatever you say." He let go of her arm suddenly and she tumbled over backward. When she scrambled to her feet, he kicked her in the rump with the toe of his boot. She fell headlong to the filthy barroom floor. "But scurry that little tail of yours back with my beer."

A stub of a man with hairy arms and broad shoulders pushed back his chair at the card game next to the far wall.

This was exactly what Ferguson had been hoping for.

"You got no call to treat the lady that way," the burly man said. He wore no hat and his wispy black hair was combed straight back over a round head. Even from across the smoky room, Ferguson could see the man's lips trembled as he spoke.

"Her?" Ferguson hooked his thumb toward the buck-toothed barmaid and sneered. "She ain't no lady. I guess I'll treat someone who's rude to me any way I please. Not that it's any of your business, Grandpa."

"Betty happens to be a friend of mine, so that makes it my business." The man wore a pistol, but Ferguson doubted he ever took it out of the holster. The line of spare cartridges on his belt showed green corrosion where they met the leather loops. He was obviously a stalwart citizen ready to look out for the weaker types—like Betty, the squirrel-faced barmaid. Full of good heart and lofty intentions, but his equipment showed he was no gunfighter. Most every man in town wore a gun, but few were truly gunmen.

"You should sit your ass back down and forget about this," Ferguson said. He knew as he spoke that there was no chance of that happening. No chance at all.

"I think you need to move on out, mister."

Ferguson ignored him and pounded his hands on the table. "How about that beer, Betty? A man could die of thirst around these parts before he got a little service."

"She ain't bringin' you no beer, so clear out."

"You got a name?" Ferguson pushed back his chair and stood. He turned to face his challenger. The other men at the table scattered, leaving the husky man alone.

"What's my name got to do with anything?"

Ferguson smiled and took a wider stance. "I got this little quirk where I like to know the name of a man who's bracin' me—before he makes me kill him."

"Name's Vince Lee." The man worked hard to keep from stammering. "Now, look here. You just had a little too much to drink, young fella. Clear out and nobody has to get hurt."

"Well, Vince. I don't aim to leave. I've made my decision. Now I guess it's up to you to make yours."

"For hell's sake," Betty said, bringing out another beer. "Here. Now both you foolish boys sit back down and stop all this he-man stuff and nonsense. I ain't hurt, Vince; nobody needs to get killed over me."

Ferguson swatted the beer out of Betty's hand when she got close enough. The barmaid recoiled and hurried out of the way. She was at least smart enough to see what was about to happen.

"Now, Vince. This is your show." Ferguson stood relaxed. This was all going better than he had hoped. "Where do you want to take it from here?"

Betty's would-be hero stood blinking. His round face twitched. There were too many folks watching who knew him for him to quit. Ferguson saw it coming. Vince Lee couldn't back down—not now. He looked smart enough to know he couldn't win. But he had to try.

Ferguson fired three times. Lee's gun clattered to the floor amid a cloud of smoke and the roar of gunfire. The dandy's first shot hit the other man in the head, above his right eye. The next two struck square in the chest. The last shots were just for show.

The dandy breathed in the smell of burning gunpowder and smiled. It felt good to be in control again.

Focused as he was on his therapeutic battle with poor Vince Lee, Ferguson failed to notice the burly sheriff stalking up behind him.

Whitehead had his pistol out, ready to shoot the rowdy upstart. Between the Crowder business and that meddling gunman Frank Morgan riding into town, he hardly had time to keep the peace. It was only by sheer happenstance that he had walked into the Whippoorwill Saloon looking for one of his deputies and seen the gunfight.

Vince Lee had been an outspoken adversary of the stockyard proposition, and people like that tended to make Whitehead's job all that much harder. Lee had even talked about running against him in the fall elections. The sheriff wasn't the least bit sorry to see him meet his maker, so he'd waited for Ferguson to get the job done.

Good riddance to a man like that.

Still, the sheriff couldn't very well have a mad gunman on the rampage, running roughshod over Parker County, no matter how many favors the man unintentionally did for him.

Whitehead cocked his pistol and pointed it at the young gunman's back, ready to shoot when he turned around.

"You're next, Mr. High-and-Mighty Frank Morgan," the dandy whispered, spitting into the spilled beer at his feet.

The sheriff froze, paused for a moment before quietly letting the hammer down on his pistol. He took a step closer and in one quick motion, brought the heavy barrel of the weapon down squarely on the back of the dandy's curly blond head.

20

Ferguson moaned and touched the tender knot behind his right ear. It burned as if it was on fire and was swollen to the point that he wasn't certain he'd be able to get his hat on over it. He was lying on his side with his legs drawn up to his belly. It was the only position where he didn't feel like he was about to throw up.

It took a moment for his mind to clear, and a little longer to settle his churning stomach. A high-pitched, maniacal laugh bounced off the thick, timber wall and landed at his feet. For a moment he thought he might be in Hell. He blinked to clear his vision.

He sure felt like hell anyway.

The filthy ducking tick was matted and torn. When Ferguson swung his feet to the floor and sat up, he could see the grimy outline where countless prisoners had rested their greasy bodies on the same mattress. The air inside was close and damp. It smelled of urine, sweat, and stale cigarettes.

"You're in as much trouble as I am now, Mr. Fancy Pants." A sallow-faced demon in a tan wool shirt and faded blue trousers clung to the riveted flat-iron bars in the cell next to him. He swung back and forth against the bars like a monkey Ferguson had once seen in a traveling circus.

The other prisoner cocked his head sideways, studying him, his big monkey eyes darting up and down the cell. "That man you killed, he had a lot of friends around these parts. Yessir, they gonna hang you for sure. I'm sorry for you, but I was beginnin' to get lonely in here by myself."

Ferguson looked around to try and get his bearings. "I'm in jail," he whispered to himself.

"No shit," the pale prisoner hanging on the bars cackled. He had big ears like a monkey too. "We're both in jail till we hang." He raised his voice as if he was talking to someone on the other side of the heavy oak door. "That is unless *somebody* would do their job and get me outta here like they're gettin' paid to do."

The outer door swung open and a tall man with a thick charcoal mustache and dark, brooding eyes strode into the cell block. He leaned against the heavy timbers on the wall and crossed his arms below his silver star in front of a chest that looked just as thick as an East Texas pine.

He nodded toward the barred window high above them in the back of the cell. "That's real good, Tom. Why don't you go on and announce to everybody in the county that I'm on your old man's payroll. I'll be able to do you a hell of a lot good then. Why don't you hoot out all the details of our arrangement; then the mob can come on in and lynch us both?"

Tom dropped from his perch on the bars and bowed his head. "I'm sorry, Sheriff." He shuffled off to lie on his bunk and sulk facing the wall. Ferguson couldn't be sure, but he thought the kid might actually be sucking his thumb.

The sheriff kept his position by the timbers, staring holes through Ferguson.

"You got something on your mind?" Ferguson said.

The sheriff nodded. "I'm Sheriff Whitehead. And you are?"

No harm in telling the man his name. "Chas Ferguson."

"Like the rifle?"

Chas nodded. These Texans knew their firearms.

"You're not from around here, are you?"

Ferguson shook his head. The small movement sent a current of pain rushing behind his ear. "South Dakota."

The sheriff smiled under his dark mustache. "Well, sir, Mr. Ferguson, you're a long way from home. What brings you to our little Texas burg?" The smile still lingered, but the eyes went stone cold. "And I'm gonna warn you now to be completely truthful with me or this is the last conversation we'll ever have."

Considering the fact that the sheriff appeared to be on the payroll of another prisoner's father, Ferguson could see no reason not to tell him the truth. He'd play it safe to be sure.

"I'm looking for someone."

"Who?" Whitehead wasn't about to let him off that easy.

"A no-account son-of-a-bitch gunfighter."

"What is it you got against this gunfighter? He kill your kin or somethin'?"

Ferguson scoffed. He'd learned not to shake his

head. "No. Nothing like that. I just can't stand livin' in the same world he does." He'd never said it out loud before, but that's what it boiled down to.

"Is he here in Parker County? This no-account gunfighter."

"Sure is."

"What's his name?"

Might as well let the sheriff have it all. "Frank Morgan. Hope he's not a friend of yours."

"Not hardly," Whitehead spit.

Tom rolled over in the other cell and faced them, still on his side. He whistled low, under his breath. "You bite 'em off big, that's for shore, Mr. South Dakota Fancy Pants."

Whitehead looked Ferguson up and down while he chewed on the end of his mustache. After a bit, he rubbed his chin and disappeared through the heavy oak door. Ferguson slumped on his filthy mattress until the sheriff came back in with a big ring of iron keys and unlocked the heavy cell door.

"Come with me," the lawman said, turning his back.

In the front office, Whitehead motioned to a chair covered in a brown and white cowhide. He picked up a well-used coffeepot from the stove and held it up in front of him.

"Can I offer you a cup?"

Ferguson nodded. His head pounded worse now that he'd stood up, and he hoped the coffee might help.

"I'm at a disadvantage here. What do we do next?" He took the battered tin cup. It had a bit of dried egg on the rim, so he turned it around.

The sheriff sat at his cluttered desk and rested his

feet up on an open drawer. "You said the magic words, son: Frank Morgan."

Ferguson didn't like where this was heading, but he had no choice but to listen. He sipped his coffee. It didn't help his head, but it tasted good enough for jailhouse coffee.

"You see, Mr. Ferguson, I gotta be honest with you. This gunfighter of yours is Parker County's own prodigal son. If I were to call him out, I'd make some people happy and others furious." He leaned back and stared up at the ceiling, strumming his fingers on his chest. "I'm ashamed to admit it, but a sheriff is no more than a politician who totes a gun. I have to pay attention to my constituents or I'll find myself out of a job—or worse."

"I'm not sure what your politics have to do with me," Ferguson said, even though he understood all too well.

"I'm just askin' you to keep hoein' the row you started. Finish what you came here for. That's all."

Ferguson studied his boots. "I see. And if I do your killing for you, I can be on my way?"

"It's mighty direct." The sheriff shrugged. "But I'd say you get the picture."

"What about Mr. Lee's friends? I understand he had a few who might not be so happy to have me walking around a free man."

"I can't help you there. But this is a civilized town for the most part. People are long on threats and short on action from what I've seen. I doubt anybody will throw you any trouble you can't handle."

"Can I take care of Morgan my way?"

"You're thinking you want to face him in the street?" Whitehead raised an eyebrow. "From what

I hear, he's as fast as they come. Those are long odds—facing someone like Frank Morgan."

"Eventually," Ferguson mused into his cup. "I'm sure it will come to that. Who's the toughest, meanest man around here?"

"You planning to sublet this job?"

"Maybe. I want to see Morgan shoot again one more time." Ferguson wondered if his emotions showed in his eyes. He wasn't ready to face Morgan yet. He needed more time to get his head straight. More time to focus. "It doesn't matter to you who does it, as long as the job gets done. Right?"

"I reckon not."

Ferguson got to his feet and handed the sheriff back the empty cup. "Could I get my gun back then?"

"Comin' right up." Whitehead let his feet fall to the floor and took a folded gun belt out of the drawer he'd been resting them on. "Here you go." His voice became low and piercing. "But don't forget who to use 'em on. You go and kill any more of Parker County's good citizens and I won't be able to help you."

"Understood," Ferguson said, strapping on the belt and reloading the pistol. "Now, you were about to tell me the name of the meanest hombre you got in this part of Texas."

Whitehead leaned back in his chair. "Son, that would be me, and don't you forget it. Next to me, well, I have a name or two for you to choose from."

21

Victoria heard Tyler Beaumont's quiet, breathy laugh coming through the front door of Bailey's general store minutes after she'd arrived. She'd yet to begin her shopping, and gave her order slip to Mrs. Peck at the register. She hurried outside before Beaumont could ride away, trying to look like she wasn't hurrying at all.

As it turned out, the handsome Texas Ranger was only just arriving. Frank Morgan rode beside him on a beautiful spotted horse. They were sharing some joke, and she felt out of place standing in front of the store clutching her handbag. Up on the raised walk she could look both men and their horses in the eyes.

Morgan noticed her first and cleared his throat, taking off his hat. Tyler did likewise. He brought his horse to a stop and swung a leg over his saddle to dismount with a flair.

It was the first time anyone had showed off for Victoria in a long while. To her surprise, it felt extremely satisfying.

The Ranger flipped the reins of his horse around the hitch rail and hopped up on the boardwalk beside her. The big rowels on his spurs jingled in time to his footfalls against the wood. "Would you care for an escort somewhere, ma'am?" He bowed.

"No, thank you. My mother's not feeling well so I was just picking up a few things at the store here."

Morgan smiled at both of them, then glanced up the street behind him. His smile faded.

Victoria couldn't help but notice the sudden look of pure exhaustion that crossed his already tired face.

Beaumont followed Morgan's gaze up the street and shook his head slowly. His broad shoulders slumped as if his plans had been dashed.

"What do you want to do, Frank?"

Morgan took a deep breath and crossed his arms over his saddle horn, slouching forward. "Not much I can do, but wait."

Victoria looked back and forth at the two men. "What's happening?" She could see a man on horseback ambling slowly down the street toward them. He wasn't doing anything out of the ordinary. "Who is that back there?"

"A very angry man," Beaumont said under his breath. "He's decided to take out some of his hate for the world on Frank. Miss Monfore, there's fixin' to be some blood shed. I think it's best you went on back inside the store."

"How can you be sure there'll be a fight?"

"This bandit's been planning a little run-in with Frank since we were in Amarillo. Name's Lefty Cummins—he's got a bad right hand."

"If he didn't do anything to cause a fight then, what makes you so sure he'll do anything now, here in Weatherford?"

"I just know," Frank said. "It's a feeling mostly.

You get so you can recognize it over the years. He'll make his play in the next few minutes. His eyes are locked on me and he's sitting his horse like his mind's made up."

This was all foolish man talk, full of bravado and the sheer stubbornness that made men the sort of querulous creatures that they were. "What if he's just made up his mind about what he plans to have for lunch?"

Morgan chuckled and sat up in the saddle, arching his back to stretch. "I wish you were right about that, Miss. Monfore—but unfortunately you are not." He reached in his pocket and took out a gold piece. "Fortunately, it is lunchtime. Tyler, I'm willin' to spring for a phosphate if you'd be so kind as to accompany the young lady off the street to safety." He leaned forward and handed the money to Beaumont.

The Ranger bit his lip and cocked his head slightly, looking back up the street. "I don't like to leave you now, Frank," Beaumont said through clenched teeth. "Feels wrong."

"Go on with the pretty young lady. I'll be fine."

"You got to play this close, you know." Beaumont stepped back beside Victoria. "Whitehead is just lookin' for a reason to arrest you. A gunfight is as good a reason as any to throw you in jail and take time to sort things out—or worse."

Morgan climbed down and tied Stormy beside the Ranger's little bay. He'd stopped paying attention to anyone but the man approaching on the street. "I'll be fine. Order me a phosphate too; I'll be there to join you in a bit."

Beaumont slumped, looked at Victoria, and held

out his arm. "Morgan the immovable has spoken. I guess we should get on down to the drugstore and order his phosphate."

She took the offered arm. "Doesn't anyone care what I think? I might not even like phosphates for all you tough-talking men know."

The Ranger stopped in his tracks. "We can go somewhere else."

"This is so exasperating. Phosphates are fine. That's not what I meant. I'm just not accustomed to being ordered around like this. Who does Frank Morgan think he is anyway?"

Beaumont held back a laugh. "Darlin', if you only knew the half of it." He glanced back up the street, then shooed her quickly to the drugstore three buildings down the street.

The door to Stidom's Drugstore was propped open to catch some of the cool noon breeze. Mrs. Stidom had quite the green thumb and a row of whiskey kegs lined the walk in front of the shop. Bluebonnets, sweet peas, paintbrushes, and Indian blankets filled each half barrel. Some type of vine Victoria couldn't identify overflowed the sides. The smell of all the flowers drifted through the door with the breeze, and helped cover the smell of camphor and other salts inside the apothecary.

Beaumont stood, his hat tilted back, and studied the slate board behind the counter. "Looks like they got strawberry and chocolate. Seein' as how no one's been asking your opinion in the last few minutes, I'll let you order for the both of us. I should warn you, though, Frank is partial to strawberry."

Victoria stood, glued to the large picture window at the front of the store, staring down the street at Morgan.

"I don't particularly care what kind of . . ." She stopped and softened her words. She didn't want to start a fight with Beaumont. "I'm not fussy about the flavor. I'll just have what you do."

It was impossible for her to think about what kind of phosphate to order when someone was about to die in the street. Weatherford was a quiet little town, full of respectable, churchgoing folks. This kind of thing just didn't happen here every day.

Through the window, she watched Morgan bend down and begin to pick up each of his big Appaloosa's feet in turn. He used a hoof pick he got from a little pouch on his saddle to clean them. He had hung his hat on the saddle horn while he worked, and his dark hair shone brilliantly in the harsh noon sunlight. Victoria couldn't tell for sure, but it looked like he'd put on a little weight in the short time he'd been in town. In any case, he seemed to swell into a force of nature as the other gunman approached and tied his own horse to a hitch rail across the street.

Victoria used the flat of her hand to shield her eyes from the glare, and tried to make out the man across the street. His right hand was drawn up in a pitiful claw and he carried it high and close to his chest, like a bird with an injured wing. He was close enough now that she could hear him through the open door.

"Morgan, it's time for you and me to have a little talk," Cummins yelled from beside his horse.

Frank kept on with his hoof business, apparently ignoring his challenger.

"You hear me, Drifter?"

"I hear you," Frank said, grunting a little under the strain of being bent over. "My horse picked up a stone a little ways back. It's wedged down deep by the frog here and I'm tryin' to dig it out before he goes lame on me." He waved the hoof pick in the air. "Hold on and I'll be with you in just a minute."

Cummins stopped in his tracks and scoffed, throwing his head like a horse fighting the bits. "I said I need to have a word with you. I don't give a damn about that spotted bag of bones you call a horse."

The man was yelling now, and a small crowd of passersby began to line the boards waiting to see what was about to happen.

"Cummins has made his play, hasn't he?" Victoria heard Beaumont's husky voice in her ear.

She nodded, realizing her jaw was clenched. She was gritting her teeth the same way she had when the men had broken into her house and taken her father. "Mr. Morgan is stooped over there by his horse. He hasn't looked my way as of yet." She could just make out her reflection and that of the Ranger beside her in the window glass. She liked what she saw.

"I wonder what Frank's up to," Beaumont mused, rubbing his chin. "He's sly as a fox and twice as quick."

She pulled her eyes away from the scene on the

street to look over at him. He was empty-handed. "You decided against the phosphates?"

He shrugged. "Knew you wouldn't drink it till after this is over. Truth is, I couldn't either. I didn't want them to go flat on us. Besides, Frank told me to look after you."

"I didn't hear him say that." Victoria peered at him through narrow eyes.

Beaumont gave a sheepish grin. "Okay, I told myself to look after you—but I know Frank would have wanted me to." His eyes danced when he looked at her.

Out on the street, Cummins was boiling over. "Morgan, you stand up and face me, you spineless bastard. I seen the way you looked at my bad hand back in Amarillo. You and that little Ranger friend of yours was laughin' at me all the way out of town. I'm thinkin' you owe me an apology."

"I'm sorry then," Morgan said, still working at Stormy's hoof with the pick. "I don't remember doing anything unneighborly to you, but if I did, I do apologize for it, you can count on that."

"You gonna stoop there and show me your ass and call that a proper apology? Mister, I'm gonna shoot you where you stand and take my apology out of your hide if you don't stand up and face me."

Just then, Anthony Pierce, one of Sheriff Whitehead's rawboned deputies, came out of the barbershop into the middle of the commotion. There were enough citizens along the street watching that he couldn't very well walk away.

"What's going on here?" the deputy shouted, his hand clutching the handle of his side arm.

Frank acted as if the lawman was interested in his

horse. "My fool horse stepped on a little stone up the trail a ways and it's wedged in between the sole and the frog." He grunted at the effort of stooping to work on the hoof.

Beaumont chuckled and gave Victoria a wry wink. "I see what he's up to. That fool deputy is in a pickle now, sure enough. I'm pretty certain Whitehead's given him strict orders to arrest Frank for any misdemeanor. Now he's forced to arrest the other fellow 'cause Frank ain't doin' a damn thing." He glanced over at Victoria. "Sorry about the cussin'."

She waved him off with a smile.

"This is none of your affair, lawdog." Cummins's chin quivered in anger. His eyes glowed yellow like a cornered animal. He wasn't about to give up and everyone on the street knew it, including the deputy. "My beef is with Morgan. He owes me a word to my face."

"Mr. Morgan is only trying to do little doctoring on his horse's foot and this yahoo comes and starts in callin' him out," Harry Roberts piped up from in front of the tobacco shop beside his butterball of a wife. "I thought Morgan woulda blasted him by now, but he hasn't. What are you gonna do, Pierce? Handle this yourself or go and get the sheriff?" Roberts was a county commissioner who didn't care much for the present sheriff. There was a snide air of accusation on his voice.

"Shut up, Harry," Deputy Pierce muttered. "Of course I'm gonna handle it myself. That's what you pay me for, ain't it?"

Beaumont giggled. "Yes, ma'am, he's got his self

in a sure enough pickle all right," he said under his breath.

"Mister," Pierce said to Cummins. "You keep your hand away from that pistol and come with me. We'll get this all sorted out and you can be movin' on out of this county."

Finally, Frank stood up. He dusted off the front of his britches before turning around. Victoria saw him throw a glance up the street at her and Beaumont. He wore a sly, cat-that-ate-the-canary grin.

Cummins let out a deep breath and played his eyes back and forth from Morgan to the deputy. He swallowed hard and let his good hand swing away from his gun before raising it above his head.

"This ain't over, Morgan," he spat as Deputy Pierce walked toward him.

"I know," Morgan sighed. "It never will be."

The ill-tempered sheriff's deputy took Cummins's raised hands as a sign of contrition, and put a hand on the crippled man's shoulder to turn him toward the jail. He had his own gun drawn, but didn't bother to take the gunman's pistol.

"Get moving," the deputy said—more to the crowd than the gunman. He gave his prisoner a slight shove to add to the show.

Cummins reacted with the speed of a viper. He shrugged the deputy off his shoulder and struck out with his withered hand to claw across the young lawman's face.

Instead of shooting, Pierce threw up a forearm to protect his eyes. Cummins drove a hard left hand into his gut, then sent another into the tottering man's nose, knocking the pistol out of his hand and sending him sprawling to the dusty street. The deputy cowered there, squinting up into the sun, his arm across his face.

Cummins drew his own pistol and pointed it at the stunned lawman. He thumbed back the hammer. "No snot kid of a lawdog is gonna take me in while I can still shoot, and he damned sure ain't gonna push me around. I'll plant you, then I'll kill . . ."

Morgan whistled to get the left-handed gunman's attention. "Hey, Cummins," he shouted.

The gunman wheeled, pointing his pistol as Frank drew and shot him in the chest.

"I apologize," Morgan said. He strode across the street to kick the gun out of the dying man's hand.

Cummins stumbled backward, blinking his eyes against the bright light. He fell back as the life drained out of him. "Morgan, you . . ." The wounded gunman slumped to one side, lying on his gun hand. "Hell, Morgan . . ." He moaned and lowered his head for the last time.

Frank rounded up Deputy Pierce's pistol and handed it back to him. "Thanks for comin' by when you did," the gunfighter said. "I didn't think he had the peach pits to follow through. Couldn't let my horse go lame on me, you know."

Even from across the street, Victoria could see Pierce stare holes into Morgan. He took the gun, but jerked away when Frank offered him a hand up.

"You go ahead and drink my phosphate, Tyler," Frank said a short time later when he walked inside the drugstore. "I feel more like a cup of coffee right now."

"We haven't even ordered yet," Victoria said, trying to understand how Morgan must have felt. She was glad he hadn't gloated over the way it had all come to pass.

"Good. Fact is I could use a little of my own company right now, as odd as that may sound."

That was one thing easy for Victoria to understand. She often felt that way.

"You say your mama's feelin' poorly?" Morgan matter-of-factly reloaded his Peacemaker while he spoke.

"I'm afraid the stress of my father's kidnapping has taken its toll on her." Victoria shot a glance at Beaumont. His eyes still danced.

"Maybe I'll ride on over there in a few minutes and make me and her a pot of strong coffee," Frank said. "What say you two youngsters go ahead and enjoy those phosphates? Tyler can help you bring your shopping home from the general store." He looked over at Beaumont with sad eyes. Eyes that must have seen dozens of such killings—too much bloodshed for one man.

"I'll meet you at the Monfore place." Morgan holstered his pistol and took out his timepiece. "Say an hour? We'll ride out and have a talk with the Crowders then—see what they know."

"Sounds good," Beaumont said. "I'll take good care of her." The Ranger winked at Victoria.

"I'd be willin' to bet on that," Morgan said. He looked at her and grinned. "He's a cocky little rooster but he generally knows how to handle himself." He turned to go. "An hour then."

* * *

Ten minutes later, two bearded men in dusty coveralls drove up in a buckboard wagon. They heaved Cummins's body in the back with an unceremonious thump. His bad hand hung limply over the back, waving in a final irony to the gathered crowd.

The object of interest gone, people began to disperse and go back to the mundane daily grind of life in Parker County.

A minute later only one man was left across the street from the drugstore. He stood frozen, intently watching the large picture window on the drugstore. He wore light tan trousers and a pressed white shirt with a silk tie. He had his suit coat over his arm, having removed it because of the afternoon heat. Now, something more than the beating sun sent a burning glow to his neck and face.

Reed Whitehead cursed under his breath as he watched Victoria Monfore, who was supposed to be his woman, sit and flirt across a tiny drugstore table with the sawed-off upstart of a Texas Ranger. She giggled and laughed, and put her hand to her face the way she never had when he told her jokes and funny stories.

The runt of a Ranger twirled his hand over his head, telling some ignorant tale, no doubt about his feats of daring and bravery. Victoria—Reed Whitehead's Victoria—sat entranced with rapt attention, her beautiful eyes fixed on the lawman.

Reed's father had warned him about the Monfore girl. "She'll never stick by you, son," the old man had said. "She's too damned fixated on herself and her own family to let a man in her life."

She was sure letting this man in.

Whitehead felt the steak he'd had for lunch roll in his belly. He spit into he street to get the bitter taste out of his mouth.

"Filthy little whore," he fumed. "I'll show you how a proper lady should behave."

Reed stepped down off the boardwalk and started across the street. The sorry little tramp would pay for this sort of behavior. Beaumont, busy with his story, stood at the table inside and twirled his hand around his head again. The huge pistol was plainly visible on his hip.

Reed stopped, then spun quickly on his heels before anyone could see him. Victoria Monfore would get her just desserts, but he could wait until the meddling Ranger wasn't around.

Oh, yes. Her time would come, and soon. He smiled to himself and began to form a plan in his head. His stomach was already feeling better when he rounded the corner leading back to his office.

22

Morgan found Mercy sitting alone in her parlor reading from a leather-bound book of poems. Seeing her there in her shining black skirt and spotless white blouse, he remembered how much she'd always liked to read.

She stood when he came in and gave him a weary smile, touching her hair to primp out of nervous habit.

She motioned him to a seat in the chaise lounge next to her high-backed wooden rocker. "You know what just upsets me to no end?" Her sweet Southern drawl rolled off her tongue like nectar.

"What's that?" Frank braced himself for whatever she might say. He felt sure he'd done a dozen things that Mercy deserved to be upset with him about. Any one of them was likely to hit as hard as a bullet.

"Well, look at us. Here you are thin and fit. Oh, you may have a little touch of distinguished gray around your temples and a laugh line here or there, but other than that, you are the picture of health and vigor." She sighed. Even the soft sound of her breathing carried a hint of the Deep South. "I, on the other hand, look and feel old as one of those drooping live oak trees out front of the house."

"Well that's about as foolish a thing as I've ever heard a woman say. You're as pretty as . . ."

She cut him off. "As the day you left?" Though her name was Mercy, when she attacked, she aimed straight for the throat.

Frank leaned forward in his seat and stared at the back of his hands. He tried to decide what to say, wishing he could do something to make amends for the sins and weakness of his youth. When he finally did look up, Mercy was leaning back in her rocking chair, staring up at the ceiling. Tears streamed down her cheeks.

"Mercy, I . . ."

She sniffed and held up a hand to stop him with uncharacteristic firmness. "Don't. I don't want you to have to lie to me. What's done is done. Things have turned out for the good or bad in spite of anything you or I may have done."

"I know it's a poor substitute for good behavior." Morgan looked her square in the eye. "But I want you to know I am truly sorry for any hurt I caused you." Mercy would never have any idea, but he could count all the people he'd ever apologized to on one hand. Not that he thought he was perfect, that wasn't it at all. Apologizing admitted a particular weakness—and in his line of business, admitting weakness was like the scent of blood to a pack of wolves. It could get a man killed.

Mercy looked away, her eyes cast up at the ceiling again. She began to speak, but her chest quivered with sobs. Frank looked at the pale skin of her throat and the soft lines of her collarbones where they disappeared below the white fabric of her blouse. He didn't think he'd ever seen anything quite so white. She was right in that she'd aged, but with her blue-black hair, high cheekbones, and slender neck, Mercy Monfore was yet among the most handsome women he'd ever seen.

He felt his face flush when she finally met his gaze and caught him looking at her. He closed his eyes and tried not to think about their times together all those years ago.

"We were little more than children," she said, using a flippant tone he could tell she didn't really mean. She'd never been able to hold a hard demeanor with him—or anyone he'd ever known for that matter. "Old enough," she continued, "to do the things older folks did, but too young to understand the consequences of our own actions."

She brought the hankie to her face and sobbed into it with both hands. She was the only woman Morgan had ever known who could blow her nose and keep her ladylike demeanor.

"Mercy," Frank said, his voice a hoarse whisper. He'd been working up to this for some time. It was something he had to say.

She looked up from her crying and sniffed. Her nose was red and swollen. Her eyes still brimmed with tears, but they sparkled with happiness that he would still want to talk. Happy to hear him say her name. "What is it, Frankie?"

"I'm nothing but a tramp, Mercy. I could have never given you something like this." Morgan tugged at his hat so hard he thought he might tear it in half. "After the war, I just couldn't see myself rooted to one spot. Especially not here in Parker County."

He'd never felt more awkward in his life. "I've done a heck of a lot I'm sorry for; most of it I couldn't make right if I had a hundred lifetimes. All I can do is push ahead on the road I'm already on. I'll never be able to make it up to you for leaving the way I did. There's a bushel full of things in my life I'm not very proud of, and I sure do carry the blame on this one, for a fact."

"Not all of it, Frank. None of us are blameless." She moved to the chaise lounge beside him and took his hand, holding it in her lap. "I'm certainly not without guilt." She paused, meeting his eyes. "But I am repentant, and that ought to count for something."

"If I'd known about the girl," he said, "I never would have gone. You know that, don't you?"

"What difference would that have made?"

"You know what I mean," he said. "I wish you would have told me."

"What makes you so sure she's yours?"

"Isn't she?" He watched her face, looking for a sign he was right. Morgan was better than most at judging human character, but Mercy didn't give him a single clue.

Instead, she smiled slyly and looked at him through narrow, swollen eyes.

"Victoria looks like you. That's an undeniable fact. But you know, people always said you and I favor one another." She sniffed. "And sometimes, she acts so much like Isaiah it frightens me. Some folks on his side of the family say she's the spittin' image of his younger brother, Theo."

"This is just like you." Morgan threw back his head. "You always did love to toy around with me."

She took his hand again and traced a vein on the back of it with the tip of her finger while she spoke. She didn't look at him, but kept her eyes on her own lap while she spoke.

"I was devastated when you left. I wanted to tell myself you felt some foolish duty to go fight in that foolish war. . . ."

"I . . ." Morgan interjected.

Mercy squeezed his hand to stop him. "I knew it could not have been something as simple as that. If it had been, then you would have at least said good-bye to me. I finally had no choice but to assume you were not running to the war, but from me." She took a deep breath. "Then Isaiah came into town, a handsome young lawyer with the promise of a good future. He showed a bit of interest in the poor broken creature that I was . . . am, and we married a few weeks later."

She looked up at him for the first time since she took his hand. Her eyes were wide now and painfully honest. "You see, Frank, you broke my heart, but Isaiah put it back together, without any questions. I grew to love him almost as much as I need him."

"I don't know what to say," Frank whispered.

"Only two people in this world are certain who Victoria's father is, and you aren't one of those two. You would be doing me a great favor if you didn't ask me about it again."

Morgan hung his head. "I won't."

She traced a knife scar up the palm of his hand to his wrist. "Think of it this way, Frankie. Victoria already has a father. I am trusting in you to find him and bring him home to us safely. But she could always use another friend."

Horse hooves crunched on the gravel drive and footfalls sounded on the porch. Morgan drew his pistol and stood, motioning for Mercy to stay put in the chair. He didn't need her hanging on him if the visitor happened to be Sheriff Whitehead.

"Hello the house." It was Beaumont.

Frank opened the door to find the Ranger standing with a grinning Victoria scooped up in his arms. She wore his jacket and both wore the smiles of recent laughter on bright faces.

Mercy rose quickly. "What's happened? Are you all right?"

"It's nothing, Mother. I stumbled coming off the boardwalk in front of Stidom's and twisted my ankle, but I'm fine, really. I told Tyler I was all right and could walk, but he refused to let me try."

"I'm not very tall," Beaumont joked. "If I drop you, you won't have far to fall."

Beaumont put the girl down and she limped over to her mother. "You've been crying again," she said.

"I'm fine, dear," Mercy said. "Really. You look a fright, though. Are you sure about your ankle?"

Morgan motioned toward the door with his hat. "We'd best get on the move. We'll not accomplish much sitting around here talking." His voice sounded hollow and as faraway as his thoughts. In a way, he wished he'd had a few more minutes alone with Mercy, but he was just as happy Beaumont had come along and rescued him from the conversation.

"You be careful, Ranger Beaumont," Victoria said. The smile had never completely left her face.

Tyler tipped his hat. "You ladies watch yourselves now. Don't let anyone in unless you know and trust them."

There seemed to be a sudden lack of air in the house, and Morgan felt a desperate need to be on his way. "See if you can get some rest, Mercy. We'll go have a talk with Old Man Crowder—find out what he knows about all this."

"Thank you for checking in on me," Mercy said as they went out the door. "I'm thankful for the chance to talk with you some."

Morgan settled his hat over his head and looked over his shoulder as he went out the door. "Me too, Mercy," he said, and he meant it.

"What do you think of Ranger Beaumont?" Victoria asked after the men had gone. Mercy sat on the edge of her bed and watched her change into fresh clothes after her tumble into the street. "He was a perfect gentleman. I only stumbled and he treated me like I'd broken my leg. Wouldn't hear of letting me walk on my own."

Mercy smiled. She'd never seen her daughter bubble over so. It was strange how happy she sounded considering the circumstances and all they were going through.

"He seems the decent sort of fellow," Mercy said. She handed Victoria a clean camisole.

"He is, isn't he? He told me he intends to stay here in Parker County for a while and base his

Rangering from around here. What do you think he means by that?"

"I'd say you know what he means by that."

Victoria finished buttoning up her blouse and sat down by her mother. She ran a brush through her long ebony hair. "Daddy's going to be all right, you know. With two men like Ranger Beaumont and Frank Morgan going after him, he'll be just fine."

"I know." Mercy bit her bottom lip. She felt tears welling up inside her again.

Victoria, caught up in her own emotions, didn't seem to notice. "That Frank Morgan is a great man. You're lucky to have known him when you were both young."

Mercy could do nothing but offer a closed-mouth nod.

"Tyler practically worships him. It's always Frank this or Morgan that—Tyler thinks he hung the moon. Did you know people have written books about him and his bravery and skill? If Tyler believes so strongly in him, he must be quite a man."

Mercy swallowed back a sob and touched her daughter gently on the shoulder.

Victoria stared into space, thinking. "There's just something about him. . . ."

I know, Mercy thought, but she didn't say a word. She didn't need to.

23

The Crowders' Ranch actually started a half mile out of town—the part of the land the railroad was interested in for stockyards—but the main house was nearly three miles out over cactus and white caliche and rock-covered hills. The land nearest town was too poor for ranching, and would take a good fifty acres just to support one cow-calf pair.

"It's no wonder Crowder wants to get shed of this hunk of ground," Ranger Beaumont said, twirling the end of his reins as he skirted his horse around a particularly nasty patch of prickly-pear cactus.

"It is slim pickin's, that's for certain." Morgan scanned the countryside around them. There were more gnarled mesquites springing up than Morgan remembered as a child. The thorny trees seemed to be traveling further and further north each year with the passing herds of Mexican cattle that ate their beans and deposited them elsewhere in their manure as they traveled. Here and there, a patch of bronze-and-rust Indian blankets made a go of it on a bit of shallow gray dirt, but the biggest crop going by far seemed to be yucca plants and red-ant hills.

"It gets better on up a ways." Morgan nodded ahead.

"Can't get much worse." Beaumont grinned, then reined up sharply and looked at Frank.

The flat crack of a rifle report echoed across the rolling hills in front of them.

"Any other time I'd chalk that up to somebody takin' a potshot at a coyote." Morgan craned his head toward the sound of the shot. "But the way things are goin', I'd say we ease on up, real carefullike, and reconnoiter."

In the rolling country it was impossible to tell exactly where the shot came from, but it sounded close, maybe even over the next rise. To be on the safe side, both men dismounted and led their horses so as not to be such large targets coming over the hill.

They left their mounts a few feet below the crest and inched up on their bellies, skirting cactus and anthills as they went. Morgan carried his .44/40 Winchester.

On the road below them, about two hundred yards away, four cowboys sat astraddle their horses surrounding a single buckboard. A black man held the reins, and a little girl of about four or five sat beside him on the seat.

The cowboys milled around the wagon, shouting and taunting the driver. One of them had a rifle in his hands and fired it into the air, waving the weapon and shouting to make some point. None of the ne'er-do-wells looked to be over twenty.

"We best hurry on down," Morgan said, backing quickly down the hill. He slid the rifle back in his saddle boot and swung aboard Stormy gathering the reins.

Beaumont climbed on his bay. "Four against one

and a little young'un—it's mighty lucky we happened along when we did."

Morgan urged his stout Appy into a trot. He spoke over his shoulder. "Yes, it is at that. I happen to know the man driving the wagon. If we don't hurry, there'll be four dead cowboys down there very shortly."

Morgan and Beaumont covered the ground in no time, and trotted up to the little group like they owned the world. All four cowboys bunched up on one side of the wagon to meet them. They stood stirrup to stirrup and ignored the black man they'd been teasing only seconds before. It appeared they needed each other for moral support.

Morgan pointed his horse straight for the kid with the rifle in hand. Beaumont veered off toward a cowboy at the end of the group on a small mouse-colored mare.

Stormy was a stout animal with powerful hindquarters. He didn't know the word quit. Though the armed cowboy's pony stood its ground, the big Appaloosa plowed on through knocking the smaller quarter horse back and peeling the rider to one side. Morgan took advantage of the boy's surprise and slapped the rifle to the ground before grabbing the scrawny kid by the scruff of the collar and dragging him across to his own saddle. He felt surprisingly light, and Frank couldn't help but smile to himself that his old strength was coming back.

The kid attempted a struggle, but Morgan hammered him on the noggin with the side of his fist before letting him slide to the ground. Beaumont gave the mouse-colored mare a sharp slap on the ears with his quirt. She squealed, then bolted, dumping her hapless rider on his rump into a wide patch of prickly-pear cactus.

Out of the corner of his eye Frank saw the others glance down at his side arm. He drew and thumbed the hammer back on his Peacemaker before either of the two remaining cowboys could lay a hand on their own weapons.

"If you boys would settle down a little," Frank said as he tipped his hat at the wagon driver with his free hand. "We're trying to save your miserable lives here."

The cowboy who'd landed in the cactus cussed a blue streak that made the little girl cover her mouth and go wide-eyed. She giggled when he clucked and waddled around trying to catch his horse. He had enough sense not to make a play for his gun. The one Frank had walloped lay groaning on the ground. Dog stared him in the face and growled. The two who remained mounted sat dumbfounded at their new predicament.

"How you been, Bose?" Morgan smiled at the man in the wagon.

The black man dipped his head. "Just fine, Frank. I was on the way to town with . . ."

"You know this here nigger, mister?" the mounted cowboy nearest Morgan sneered. His hat was thrown back in the manner of so many of the cocky youth Frank had met in his travels. It seemed like young people just couldn't figure out the proper way to wear a hat.

"I do," Morgan said patiently, directing his pistol

at the loudmouthed cowboy's belly. "But it's apparent you do not. All I can figure is that you're not from around here. Gather near, boys, and let me introduce you to an old friend of mine. If you listen close, you might even learn some history."

The wagon driver shook his head and looked a bit embarrassed by the show Frank was putting on.

"The gentleman you chose to harass today is my friend Bose Ikard, trail companion of Charles Goodnight and Oliver Loving of Goodnight-Loving Trail fame. Mr. Ikard was killing Comanche and dodging outlaw bullets while you boys were still trying to figure out how to button your own britches. Like Mr. Goodnight, I'd trust him with my money and my life." Morgan stopped suddenly and motioned with the Peacemaker back toward the wagon. He laughed out loud. "You boys sure enough picked the wrong wagon to pester. You didn't bother his little girl, did you?"

"No, sir," the cowboy on the ground moaned. "We never said an unkind word to the youngster."

"Well, that's a blessing anyhow," Morgan said. "Mr. Ikard, go on and give these squirts a peek at what you had for 'em if their bad manners would have spilled over to that sweet little child of yours."

"Love to," the black man grunted, glaring hard at the cowboys. He shifted the green wool coat across his lap to reveal a double-barreled shotgun sawed off to ten inches. Both hammers were back and his finger rested on the trigger.

"What'd I tell you?" Frank watched the remaining color seep out of the boys' faces. "Where you from?"

"Ft. Worth," they all said in unison.

"What brings you whelps all the way across the county line to try and get yourselves killed?"

"The boss gave us the day off," the cowboy who cowered on the ground in front of Dog said in a quivering voice. "Would you please call off this wolf of yours? I swear I'll not move a muscle."

Frank whistled at the cur. It padded off to sit at the edge of the group, but licked its chops and kept a wary eye on the cowboys.

"You still didn't answer my question." Morgan looked down at the same cowboy and motioned with his gun barrel for him to get to his feet. "Why would you come spend your day off in Parker County? Haven't you got enough whores and saloons over in Ft. Worth?"

"We was supposed to come over and stir things up a little," the cowboy said.

"Shut up, Boomer," the cowboy with the cocky hat spit. "These saddle tramps got no right to be privy to our business."

"Saddle tramps?" Morgan shot an amused look at Beaumont, then at Ikard.

The black man shrugged. "I guess they don't know who you are, Frank. They about to stir things up, I reckon. That's what they wanted to do in the first place."

Boomer cocked a frightened eye at Morgan. His face fell even lower than it was. "Who are you?"

"It don't matter if he's Jesse James," the cocky cowboy said. "We ain't tellin' him our business."

"Walt, use your head," Boomer said. "Jesse James has been dead a long time. I think this is . . ."

The cowboy named Walt jerked his pistol. Morgan's Colt barked once and the boy slumped in his saddle, holding a hand across his bleeding shoulder. His gun thudded to the ground.

Ikard's daughter held her hands over her ears and shut her eyes.

Morgan glanced at Bose. "I apologize for scaring the girl."

The black man held up a hand. "Think nothing of it. Only did what you had to. She'll be fine."

Walt looked at Morgan, dumbfounded. "You just shot me, you son of a bitch, and now you're worried about scaring some stupid little nigger girl?"

"Shut up your own self, Walt," Boomer said. "I was just about to tell you that this here is none other than Frank Morgan. I recognize him from a drawing on one of them dime-novel books: *Frank Morgan and the Deadly Ambush*."

Morgan grinned and looked over at Beaumont. He'd never heard of that one—and they were drawing pictures of him now? He had no idea where the writers of that garbage came up with such titles. It's a wonder anyone ever read them.

"The boss sent us over to stir things up," Boomer said. "We're supposed to make everyone in Parker County know what a bad idea it would be to have our types running around if the railroad puts the stockyards over here."

"I see." Morgan lowered his gun to his thigh, but he didn't put it away. "Well, I got a proposition for you. We can either settle this now, just among us friends, or you can dump your guns in the back of Mr. Ikard's wagon and scamper your little behinds back across the county line before you bite off more than you care to chew."

"I already dumped mine," Walt nodded at his pistol on the ground at his horse's feet.

"Dump our guns?" Boomer sat wide-eyed in his saddle.

"Don't want you to get up the hill a little ways and decide to start taking potshots at us." Morgan motioned toward the wagon with his Colt. "Take it easy now. Nice and slow."

"I'll leave 'em at the Ranger office over in Palo Pinto County," Beaumont said. "If you want 'em back you can ride over and get 'em in a week or two."

"Palo Pinto's sixty mile away from Ft. Worth!" Walt protested.

"I said we could handle this now," Morgan said. "If that's what you're of a mind to do."

The cowboys put their rifles and side arms in the back of the wagon under the watchful eyes of the three hard-looking men.

Boomer took out a horn-handled bowie knife and tossed it in beside his rifle.

"You can keep your knife, son." Frank chuckled. "From the looks of your pal Walt there, you might need it to amputate his arm."

The cowboys looked back and forth at each other for a moment, then turned and rode away with tails tucked low. Even Walt kept his head bowed, the reality that he knew he'd almost been killed by Frank Morgan finally sinking in. The boy who'd fallen in the prickly-pear patch stood in his stirrups as they left. Morgan could hear him cussing long after the group was out of sight.

"What brings you back to Parker County?" Ikard watched the chastised cowboys ride over the rise before lowering the hammers on his double-barrel. "You always told me you were gonna steer clear of this place."

Frank let out a deep sigh. "I know I did, but a friend called me about all the problems ya'll are having with the stockyard decision."

"Mercy?"

Frank nodded.

"I see." Ikard silently mouthed the words, as if it was all so clear to him now.

Morgan needed to change the subject. "Bose, I want you to meet another friend of mine: Texas Ranger Tyler Beaumont."

Beaumont was about even with the wagon seat on his short horse. He reached straight across to shake hands.

"Rangers looking in on this, eh?" Ikard said. He put his arm around his daughter's shoulders and drew her to him to make sure she was all right. "It is some bad goin's-on in these parts, that's for certain. Now someone's gone and kidnapped the good judge."

"Your place is out this way, Bose," Frank said. "You know anything about the Crowders?"

"I know they got a passel of no-account sons. Tom, the youngest of 'em, is in jail right now for mistreatin' a young gal from town. I expect he'll likely hang for it."

Morgan needed to stretch his back, and stepped down from Stormy. He checked the animal's feet for stones while he spoke. "You hear any scuttlebutt about the judge?"

Ikard laughed and slapped his knee. His little girl smiled beside him. "It beats all how some folks go on and on talkin' around a black man like he don't hear nothin' at all. Crowder's got somethin' to do with it, that's for certain. I heard his boys laughin' it up about something. Whitehead, he knows better, though. He's too smart to let 'em babble on in front of me like they was. I didn't hear enough to do you much good."

"So Sheriff Whitehead *is* in cahoots with Crowder?" Beaumont nodded slowly.

"Clean up to his eyeballs," Ikard said. "Ol' Man Crowder is for the stockyards so the sheriff, he's for the stockyards too."

"I suppose I should ask you what your opinion is on the matter," Morgan said.

Ikard chuckled again, shaking his head. "You should know better than that, Morgan. I'm a black man in Texas. The war may have freed me and my kind, but it didn't give me a right to no opinion. If these folks want me to have a particular view, they'll let me know what it's supposed to be. I tell you what I think, though. I think you should have a word with young Tom Crowder over in the jailhouse. Them Crowder boys is tight. He's bound to know something and he's just dumb enough to make a slipup—if the sheriff will let you in to see him, that is."

Beaumont's face brightened. "I saw Whitehead riding out of town a half hour before we left."

"With any luck, he's still gone then," Morgan said, lifting Stormy's reins. "I hate to run off on you, Bose."

Ikard shrugged. "I'll run into you again, I reckon. Much obliged for you keeping me from havin' to kill those boys."

24

Old Man Crowder kept the group waiting while he made water behind a huge cedar tree on the bank of Cottonwood Creek. He was steaming and they all knew it. Pony and Pete both stayed well out of his way, and the handful of his hired men kept their eyes pointed at the ground.

Purnell had never seen Crowder angry before, but he'd heard the old man had a tendency to chomp his teeth like a nervous horse when he got ready to kill somebody. Right now, there was way too much chomping going on for the lawyer's comfort. Even Sheriff Whitehead kept quiet.

"It's a good thing your dear mother can't fathom what a couple of absolute dumb asses she whelped," Crowder spewed after he pulled up his suspenders and rejoined the group. "And you, Purnell, you stupid bastard. You ought to have more sense than to let 'em take the judge—with all your schoolin'." A purple vein bulged on the old man's forehead. He moved his whiskered jaw in and out and side to side as if he couldn't keep it still. His one eye darted around the group. "What were you boys thinkin'?"

"Pa . . ." Pony offered.

His father wheeled on him. "You shut your gob.

You *weren't* thinkin'. That's just the problem. I ought to kill every damned one of you."

"Mr. Crowder," Purnell tried to whisper. His voice came out of his throat more like a moaning croak.

"Speak, lawyer man," Crowder shouted loud enough to make him jump back a foot. "Tell me why this happened."

"He saw us. If he identified us, he would have tied this back to you."

"You were supposed to wear masks," Crowder screamed. His eye glowed red. The purple vein on his forehead looked as if it might burst.

"Sir, we had to take care of Pete," Purnell said. "That girl almost knocked his head off. The judge came in and surprised us. It was either kill him or bring him with us." He wanted to scream that it was all that idiot Pony's idea, but that seemed weak. Purnell felt weak enough already.

Crowder clamped his mouth shut and breathed through his nose while he stared from man to man and thought. No one looked up to meet his glaring eye.

"I want the old fool to change his mind. I want my boy to be set free by the judge."

Whitehead took off his hat and studied the inside of the crown. "Why don't you let me spring him? You say the word and one of my deputies will die, letting the boy escape. I've already got one I'd pick for the job."

Crowder spit. "I don't want him to escape. Then he'd have to be on the run for the rest of his life. I want him released—all legal and tidylike."

The sheriff continued to stare into his hat. It scared Purnell to death to see a man as mean as

Rance Whitehead cowing to anyone. "I'm afraid the horse is already out of the barn on that account, Mr. Crowder," said the sheriff.

"The hell it is. Those charges are all trumped up against the boy anyhow. That Smoot girl led him on to trap him and make us look bad—to turn the vote her father's way." Crowder hooked a thumb toward the rough log cabin fifty yards away. A hired man Purnell had never seen sat on a wooden bench smoking a cigarette in front of a heavy slat door. He had a rifle across his lap. Purnell considered the man lucky for not having to take part in the tongue-lashing from the old man.

"The judge is half loopy from the beating Pony gave him," the old man said. "He may come around to our way of thinkin' yet."

"Judge Monfore doesn't seem like the kind of man to change his mind because of a beating," Purnell heard himself say. He immediately wished he hadn't, and wanted to melt into the dark tree line at the edge of the clearing.

Crowder let his red eye rest on the trembling lawyer while he ruminated on his options. His mouth began to work back and forth again as if he had a bit of food caught between his back teeth and wanted to get it out with his tongue. He was chomping again.

"Maybe he won't take well to threats on himself, but we still got his daughter to use as ammunition if we need to." Crowder's eyes narrowed and he seemed to be plowing through a new concept in his head. "For that matter, we still got his wife we could use."

"With all due respect, Mr. Crowder," Whitehead

said. "What good would it do to take the women if we already have the judge? I think he knows you mean business by now."

"No, no, no," Crowder said, pounding his fist against the palm of his other hand. "He knows we can hurt him, but he doesn't know how deep our resolve goes—how badly we want this, what we are willing to do. If there's anything I've learned over these years, it's how mighty a man can be if he has the courage to do whatever has to be done."

The old man's eye had gone glassy and he swayed a little where he stood.

"So you want us to go get his women?" Pete asked, his voice slow and halting. Purnell felt the way Pete sounded.

"That's exactly what I want you to do. We'll drag his womenfolk out here and tell His Highness how far we are prepared to go to see this through. There's nowhere he can hide, nowhere his family can hide to steer clear of us. I foresee him coming around to my way of thinkin'. It's a destiny for this county he cannot stop. The pompous old fool must be shown."

A gust of breeze blew in and tugged at the edges of Crowder's white whiskers. With his windswept beard and the wild commitment in his eye, he looked to Purnell like some sort of Old Testament prophet ranting about doom and destruction that would surely come to pass—only this time the destruction would come at his hand.

Except for the rustle of wind through the tall cottonwoods and bushy cedars, the shadowed little glade fell silent. The men looked at one another, taking care to avoid the old man's zealous gaze.

Whitehead opened his mouth to speak, but closed it again before Crowder saw him.

Ronald Purnell wondered how the hangman's noose would feel around his neck. He'd gained weight over the years and he'd heard that heavy men sometimes lost their heads in their quick drop and sudden stop from the gallows. Bile rose in the back of his throat at the thought.

The pallid lawyer felt as if he were being swept along by a force he couldn't control. If he said anything against Crowder now, he'd be dead in less than a heartbeat. If he followed along with this ludicrous plan, he was sure to die at the end of a rope or from a lawman's bullet; they all were. If they would just kill the judge and be done with it, there might still be a chance to get away, maybe start a new life somewhere away from all this madness.

Purnell licked the beads of sweat off his upper lip and fought to keep his breakfast down in his stomach. Given the choice, he decided to put off his death for as long as he could. But he stopped fooling himself; there was no way out of this. He would never see the true heat of summer.

Sheriff Whitehead interrupted the lawyer's inner turmoil.

"There's still Morgan and that Ranger to worry about. They're doggin' around all over the county trying to see what they can find out."

"Thought you were going to arrest that son of a wily bastard." Crowder frowned. "He could be a real fly in the ointment, that one."

Whitehead put his hat back on. "I ran into a young fella who has it in for Morgan pretty bad. I just gave him a little nudge to go ahead and do what he needs to do. If he kills Morgan, our problems are solved. If Morgan kills him, I'll have a new charge to arrest him on." The sheriff's dark eyes narrowed. "And I can guarantee you. Mr. Morgan won't survive the night in jail."

"Provided he don't blow your head off when you go to bring him in," Crowder said, a wry smile of challenge hanging on the corners of his whiskered lips.

Whitehead scoffed. "He's good, but he's not that good."

The old man waved off the subject and turned his attention to his son Pete.

"Mrs. Monfore should be easy enough to take. She always struck me as a flighty sort of little hummingbird when I saw her at church. I think if somebody would just go and bark at her just right, she'd pass out and you could throw her across a horse. Slam-bam, that's all there is to it." Crowder clapped his hands together. He studied Pete's face.

"On the other hand," Crowder went on, "that girl—she could be a little bit of a problem. I only got so many sons, and the ones I got only got so many fingers. We can't afford to have 'em get all broken and butchered by some whelp of a girl."

Whitehead chuckled. "Don't you worry about her. She trusts my son, Reed. He'll take her somewhere where she can pitch whatever-sized fit she wants to. It won't make any difference at all."

25

No matter what Bob Grant did, he just didn't look like a lawman. If he bent over, squatted to put wood in the stove, or just reached up to scratch his ear, the long tail on his homespun shirt came untucked and covered half his pistol. His hat blew off constantly, even in the lightest wind, and his thinning hair stuck out in all directions.

Morgan stood beside Stormy, a block down the street from the sheriff's office, and watched the portly deputy leave to meet his wife at a small café across the street.

Morgan kept his distance.

A deputy he didn't recognize had come to relieve Grant at the jail. Morgan hoped it was just for a supper break. He didn't think any of the other deputies would be so accommodating as Grant and let him talk to the Crowder boy.

"What say we go get a big pot of coffee and some pie till our man Grant gets back?" he said to Beaumont.

"I could eat," Beaumont said, rubbing his belly. "I eat more pie than any man I've ever laid eyes on, but apart from having to let my belt out a notch, I reckon it ain't hurt me too bad. Charlene's down the street yonder is supposed to make a fine roast chicken."

Charlene's was a narrowly built "shotgun"-style building wedged in between a hardware store and boot shop; as if it was built after the fact on a whim of the landowner, who didn't want to waste one square foot of property. Though over a hundred feet deep, the building was no more than fifteen feet wide. The tables zigzagged down the length of the place to make the most use of available space. While the establishment served alcohol, there was no room for a bar. Patrons got to sit at tables to do their eating or drinking. A haggard woman with long red hair piled up in a loose beehive held together with a wooden pencil took orders and served drinks. She wore a frilly costume of white and black lace that accentuated and exposed a good deal of her full figure—and advertised her other duties besides waitressing. The place might not have had a proper bar, but it had everything else a saloon had to offer, plus a stellar reputation for fried chicken.

It was a little past supper time, and there were only a few other patrons scattered among the tables. Frank chose a chair about halfway back, facing the door. He sat a little sideways so Beaumont could also have a gunfighter's view.

Two older men in faded overalls sat two tables over playing checkers. They looked up at Frank and eyed him warily.

"Well, if it ain't the Parker County prodigal," the one pushing red checkers grumbled. There was no love lost in his voice.

Frank studied the men for a moment and realized he knew both of them. The Murphy brothers had been hired hands around the county for as long as Morgan could remember. They picked melons, herded cattle, and were not above busting someone's head for you if you paid them enough. Both had been passable gunmen in their day, and likely had chalked up a handful of killings between them. They had at times been the terror of the county. One of them, Frank couldn't remember which, had done some time in prison.

Morgan wondered if he'd ever live to retire and play checkers in a pair of bib overalls. Somehow, he doubted he'd want to.

"You know them?" Beaumont asked, wiping his face with a bandana he took from inside his hat.

Frank rested both arms on the table and leaned forward. "I guess I know most of the town either by name or reputation." He dipped his head toward the redheaded waitress. "Cordell Patterson was a good friend of mine. Hilda there was his kid sister. She used to run around in her underwear while we were picking peaches."

Beaumont studied her lacy outfit. "Well, she's not changed her ways much in that regard."

The cowbell chime on the doorknob clanged and took Morgan's attention away from his reminiscing. The day was bright enough to silhouette the new arrival, but Frank recognized him instantly. His chair clattered on the wooden floor while he got to his feet.

Beaumont looked puzzled and followed suit.

A hulking man with a bushy brow and a salt-and-pepper beard strode over and gave Morgan's hand a hearty, pump-handle shake.

Morgan couldn't keep from smiling. This was

more than he'd hoped for: first running into Bose, and now this.

"Ranger Beaumont, I'd like you to meet another friend of mine."

"Charles Goodnight," the big man said, giving the ranger's hand the same vigorous shake.

Beaumont motioned to the table. "Please join us."

"I'd love to. This place has the best fried chicken east of the Panhandle." Goodnight pulled up another chair and plopped himself down in it with a tired groan. "You here because of this Monfore business?"

"News travels fast." Morgan raised an eyebrow.

"It's a damned shame about the good judge. He's a stubborn old coot, but I can't help but like him."

"If he's alive, we'll get him back," Morgan said.

"It's a pleasure to meet you, Mr. Goodnight," Beaumont said. "I heard you spent some time in the Ranger companies."

The man grinned and shot a glance at Morgan. "I've done a bit of Rangering in my day. Back before the war, though, when we were still shootin' cap-and-ball. None of this new fancy stuff like you youngsters have today. We had to supply our own horses and cartridges."

"Not much better now," Beaumont agreed. "Sometimes I think I'm a volunteer rather than an employee of the state. . . ."

The cowbell jingled again, and all three men looked up in time to watch a thin, pockmarked man in a black hat stride through the door. He walked with a purpose and surveyed the clientele over his hooked nose as if he was looking for someone in particular. He wore no badge, but he moved with the swagger of a lawman.

"You know him?" Beaumont whispered under his breath.

Morgan shook his head and pulled the makings for a cigarette out of his vest pocket. "Never seen him before."

He offered the tobacco to Goodnight.

"No, thanks." The cattleman pounded a fist on his chest. "Spring cold. I'm afraid the smoke would aggravate it. You go right ahead, though." He looked over at the newcomer. "I don't recognize him either."

As the man moved away from the backlight of the door, Morgan could see he wore a single pistol on his left side. The holster was tied down to his thigh. He walked past Morgan and glared with a toss of his ruddy head.

He took a seat a few tables toward the back and tipped his chair against the wall. "You don't know me do you, Morgan?"

Frank threw down his cigarette and crushed it out with the sole of his boot. This one looked like he knew one end of his pistol from the other; it was best to keep both hands free.

"Sorry, partner, can't say as I do. Have we met?"

"It cuts me to the bone that you don't remember me, Frankie. A body would think you'd remember Jim Powers."

"Big Jim Powers was the biggest, meanest, ugliest kid in the county. You got one of those qualities, but it would take three of you to make up one of Big Jim."

The thin man snorted. "Spent some time in Elmira Prison during the war."

That explained the pockmarks on the man's weathered face. Morgan had heard of the nasty, overcrowded conditions at the Union Prison camp in Elmira. Horribly overcrowded, with filthy excuses for quarters, it was the Union version of Andersonville.

"Found me the Lord there," Powers continued.

"Looks like you found someone to eat your food for you," Morgan said. "The Jim Powers I knew weighed as much as a small horse."

"Prison and disease has a way of takin' the weight off a man."

"Finding the Lord make you any less ornery?" Frank asked. He already saw the answer in Powers's sunken eyes and the hollows in his pock-scarred cheeks. The last time they'd met, the big man had sworn to kill him.

"I say a little prayer over the bodies of the men I kill now."

Morgan pushed away from the table and motioned Beaumont and Goodnight to back away. Both men complied, but the Ranger scowled like he felt cheated out of a fight.

"Listen, Powers." Frank moved his head back and forth slowly to pop his neck. "I'm prepared to let bygones be bygones. I buried any grudge against you a long time ago."

"The only thing gonna be buried around here is you, Morgan. You know, I nearly couldn't bring myself to fight for the South on account-a I knew I'd be fightin' on the same side as you."

Morgan sighed. "That's a gutful of hate."

"You always were a cocky sort of braggart, Frankie." Powers let his chair tip forward and got to his feet. He never took his eyes off Morgan. "You know what stuck in my craw the most about you?"

"I can't wait to hear it." Frank rose to face his adversary. The two men playing checkers cleared well out of the way, and Hilda, the bloomer-wearing redhead, hugged the far wall by the kitchen door.

"You were every bit as mean as I was, but they all overlooked it in you. If you hurt somebody, it was all well and good—just Frankie Morgan lookin' out for the underdog, just good ol' Frank takin' care of the weak. You make me sick."

"You said it yourself, Powers." Frank narrowed his gaze. "I'm every bit as mean as you. Just simmer down and you can ride away from this."

Pure hatred glowed in the puckered scars on the thin man's face. The nostrils on his hooked nose flared and his left hand hovered over the butt of his gun. Bony fingers flexed and stretched.

Powers was quick, but Morgan's Colt boomed first and rocked the narrow room. The thin man's shot blasted a hole in the floor and his pistol spun on his hand, the trigger guard dangling from the knuckle before it fell harmlessly to the ground. He tottered, caught himself with the flat of his hand on the table, and breathed a ragged breath at Morgan.

"This don't make me like you any more," he said with a chuckle.

"Yeah, well . . ." Morgan nodded, keeping his gun trained on the dying man. "I didn't think it would do much good that way."

"Truth is . . ." A thin trickle of blood came from the corner of Powers's mouth. "People like me and you . . ." He coughed. "We been dead for years. Just takes us a while to find it out." He collapsed to his knees with a hollow crash, then pitched headlong on his face, dead before he hit the ground.

Frank shook his head and holstered the Peacemaker.

"Pitiful," one of the checker players said under his breath as he resumed his seat. "That's a piss-poor way to leave the earth after makin' it through a stint in that damned Union prison." He spit on the floor at Morgan's feet. "I hope you're proud of yourself."

Morgan shrugged off the man's attitude. Everybody always thought they could have done it better.

A tall Chinese man wearing a white smock and with a long braid down his back came out of the kitchen carrying a pan of fried chicken and looked down at the body. He shook his head and looked at Morgan, as if he knew instinctively who was responsible for the killing. He muttered something in Chinese under his breath, and set the fried chicken down on a nearby table so he could drag the dead man out into the street.

"You know, I brought Loving back from New Mexico after he got the blood poisoning and died. Buried him over at Greenwood Cemetery," Goodnight said as he came up alongside Morgan. "I suppose I can carry you over and plant you right beside him when your time comes. The way things are goin', I don't believe it will be a long trip."

"I reckon I'll be just as happy to be planted wherever I drop," Frank said. "And to tell you the honest truth, I hope it's a long way from here."

"Parker County changed that much since you been gone, Frank?" Beaumont asked.

"Nope," Morgan said. "I have."

26

Chas Ferguson recognized the first man out of Charlene's as Charles Goodnight, the famous trail driver. He let the cattleman walk past and kept the bead on the front sight of his Winchester trained on the door.

A few seconds earlier a tall Chinaman had dumped Powers's body unceremoniously on the street in front of the wooden boardwalk before stomping off toward the center of town, presumably to get the sheriff.

Beaumont came out a few seconds after Goodnight, and the two men talked in the street beside the body.

Ferguson took his finger off the trigger and stretched it. The roof of the little hardware store made a perfect hiding spot for an ambush. It had a built-in ladder off the back wall and a big wooden water tank on top to cover his retreat. A two-foot parapet ran the length of the flat roof in front with six-inch drainage holes every three feet. One of the holes lined up perfectly with the front door of the saloon.

If he did the job with one shot, there would be so much echo off the buildings up and down the street, no one would even know where the noise came from.

Ferguson had never really believed Powers would be able to take a man like Morgan. The skinny gunman was too consumed by hate to think clearly—too torn up by the past. Powers was fast all right. Ferguson had watched him shoot against a half-breed Apache that very morning over toward Lipan. But somehow, he knew there would never be any contest against the Drifter.

Ferguson had his hat off, on the roof beside him, so he wasn't spotted from below. The day was on the cool side, but he could feel a line of sweat down his back. When the wind hit it, a chill ran up his spine and made him shudder.

It would be an easy shot—no more than thirty yards—and the sun was at his back.

Morgan finally breasted the door, cocksure and arrogant, like someone who'd just taken another man's life. He looked up and down the street, then to Ferguson's horror looked directly across the street at the hardware store, studying the roofline.

The young dandy froze, not even blinking an eye for fear of causing visible movement through the tiny drain hole. He didn't relax until Morgan turned away and said something to the Ranger.

Ferguson moved the rifle barrel a scant inch so the front bead was over Frank Morgan's ear. The gunfighter stood, lean and relaxed, resting his elbow against a porch post in front of the saloon.

He was completely unaware of the lead slug only yards away that could so easily end his life.

It was the perfect opportunity for a killing shot.

Ferguson's finger tightened around the trigger.

His hands trembled slightly, and he willed himself to calm his breathing and relax. The more he tried, the more wound up he became. He felt as if all the life was welling up against a dam inside him.

He felt as if he were about to shoot himself.

The familiar queasiness returned and he relaxed his finger for a moment. He'd spent the better part of his twenty-five years learning the way of the gun. When he'd read his first book about Frank Morgan at fourteen, he knew even then that one day they'd meet. At first he idolized the famous gunman. In some way it was likely he still did; but over time, idolization gave way to jealousy and the jealousy turned into resentment.

As the years went by, Ferguson developed such a blood lust for Morgan that he found himself picturing the famous gunfighter whenever he shot. When he faced a man anywhere, it was Frank Morgan in his mind.

He lowered the hammer on the Winchester and scooted away from the roofline. He could still make out the gunfighter through the small hole in the metal roof.

One of them would be dead soon. That was a certainty. But he'd not spent these years of practice to shoot someone in the back. He pressed his face against the tar and gavel roof.

If he did that, he might as well be dead himself.

27

Deputy Grant let Morgan and Beaumont in to see Tommy Crowder with no problem. The lawman had likely heard of the gunfight at Charlene's, and didn't appear to want any part of such an adventure on his watch. He didn't even ask to take their guns when he ushered them back into the narrow cell block.

Morgan stood with his back to the wall after Grant left them alone, and turned up his nose at the smell. Jail was the one place where Morgan felt truly uneasy. He felt closed in and unable to breath. If he needed anything, it was the freedom to move around at will. Of course, he'd spent time in jails before, but when he did, he felt like a wolf with his leg caught in a trap. He'd just as soon gnaw his own foot off as spend time trapped like that again.

He took his surly mood out on Tom Crowder.

"Maybe I ought to let you out of there so we can have a little talk about what your family's been up to lately," Morgan said. His arms folded across his chest.

"You Frank Morgan?" The prisoner hung from the riveted flat-iron bars that covered the top of his cage. He swung back and forth while he talked.

"I am, and this is Texas Ranger Beaumont."

Crowder cocked his head and gave a wild laugh. "You ain't nothin' like I thought you would be." He shook his head. "I thought you'd be some sure-enough giant the way people go on and on about you."

Morgan shrugged. "I'm a free man and that's more than I can say for you. We know your family kidnapped Judge Monfore. It'll go a lot better for you if you tell us where they took him."

"I don't know what you're talkin' about." Crowder pulled himself up and touched his toes to the top bars, grunting under the strain of his exercise and ignoring his visitors. When he finally dropped back to the floor, he walked up and leaned against the cell door. He spit at Frank's feet.

"You don't scare me, Mr. Frank Gunfighter Morgan. What can you do to me anyhow? I'm already in jail just for tryin' to get a little sweetness from that fool girl."

The last comment touched something in Beaumont, and he sprang toward the bars. "You sorry bastard. I got a friend who's a Lipan Apache. He's got a lot of interesting ways to help you remember the information we need."

"Well, bring him on then." Crowder rolled his wild eyes. "I ain't ever got to kill myself an Apache. Most of 'em was already killed or runned off by the time I was old enough."

"He doesn't know anything." Morgan changed his tactics. "His pa probably doesn't trust him enough to let him in on the important plans."

"I know plenty you'd like to know." Crowder smirked. "But my lawyer said to keep my yap shut, so that's what I'm doin'." The prisoner's eyes narrowed and he pressed his face up against the bars so his cheeks stuck through. "You know what, Morgan, you skinny old goat? You better hope I don't get out of here. 'Cause if I do, I think I'll kick you ass."

Frank's right hand shot out and connected with the tender end of Crowder's nose, knocking him back into the cell and onto his rump. His hands covered his face and blood poured from between his fingers.

"No need to wait until you're out." Frank pushed his own face up against the iron cage. "I'm right here if you want me."

Crowder didn't move.

Frank stepped back and shook his head. "That's what I thought. Long on bark and short on bite."

Morgan let Stormy have his head as they trotted along the rocky road toward the Flying C. The Crowder boy either hadn't known much or was too smart to tell them anything of any use. Frank figured it was the former; none of the Crowders he'd met or heard about had too much going for them in the way of brains.

If Tom Crowder wouldn't talk to him, he'd speak with the whole family one by one. They'd either talk or get mad and fight. Either way, he'd find out what he needed to know.

While some men might figure it was better to use a little more stealth in this sort of matter—taking more time to gather useful information without tipping too much of their hand—Morgan preferred to handle things in a more direct manner. If he suspected someone of a misdeed, he'd much rather confront them about their behavior than sneak around hoping they would repent.

He sought information the same way he entered a battle; ride in shooting on pure gut instinct and sort out the particulars after the smoke cleared. Frank Morgan was about as sophisticated in that regard as a herd bull in a china shop.

The shadows were getting long by the time Frank and Tyler rode up to the Crowder homestead. A half-a-dozen outbuildings sat squat and disused in the eerie evening light.

"Did you know the Crowders when you were here before?" Beaumont asked as they neared the ranch house. A flock of half-a-dozen silver-black guinea hens came squawking out to meet them from behind a large pecan tree.

"Nope." Morgan watched for movement in the windows. With all the racket the guineas were making, someone sure had to know they were here. "They must have come in after I moved on. This place used to belong to an old German by the name of Johns. He used to let me and Luke come turkey hunting out here with my pa's old muzzle-loading scattergun."

The ranch house was a simple two-story cedar lap with a wraparound porch and awning. Harsh sun from too many summers had faded the white paint to a dull gray. Two gabled windows looked out on a weedy front yard. The window to the left was open and a yellow curtain trailed out on a slight breeze. The other one was broken.

An open window could be cause for some alarm,

but when no shot came and no movement appeared at the window or the door, Morgan relaxed. Dog plodded alongside, itching to chase the screeching guineas, but staying in place on Frank's command.

"I don't guess anyone's home," Beaumont said, as quiet as if he were in a church.

A brown and white milk cow blinked at them from a log corral beside a sun-bleached timber barn. She lowed forlornly and stood chewing her cud.

"Somebody's got to come home and milk that cow." Frank nodded toward the barn as he dismounted and tied Stormy to a cedar rail. He used a quick release "horse thief's" knot just in case he needed to beat a hasty retreat. "We'll just wait until they do."

The front door suddenly creaked open and both men turned at once, hands on their pistols.

Standing at the threshold, staring right through them as if they weren't there, was a woman about Frank's age. She had straight, straw-colored hair and a face that seemed locked in an expressionless gaze as if she were lost and trying to find some distant horizon.

Morgan tipped his hat. "Frank Morgan, ma'am. This is Tyler Beaumont, Texas Ranger. Wonder if we could talk with you a little?"

The woman continued her distant vigil without acknowledging the visitors. She had an almost indiscernible tick that made her look as if she was gently shaking her head in quiet disagreement with something. Her hands trailed down beside her blue skirt, unmoving.

"Ma'am?" Beaumont stepped up on the porch and took off his hat. "Are you all right?"

"She's fine." A young man who looked to be in his early twenties came around the corner of the house. The sleeves of his white shirt were rolled up and he carried an ax. He had blond hair like the woman, though his was more bleached from working in the sun.

"Can I help you with something?" He wore no gun, but held the ax in front of him like he might use it if pressed. His voice was not particularly confrontational, just wary. He shared the same nose as Tom Crowder, but the rest of his features looked like the woman at the door.

"Name's Morgan," Frank said. "We're looking for Mr. Crowder."

"He's not here."

Beaumont nodded at the young man. "Mind if we wait? I'm a Texas Ranger. We're lookin' into Judge Monfore's kidnapping."

The man shrugged. "Don't know when he'll be back, but you can suit yourself." He lowered the ax. "Sorry about my mother. She hasn't been right since the accident. I'm Jared Crowder."

The nose was definitely the only thing Tom and Jared had in common. Where the prisoner was snotty and indifferent, his blond-haired older brother was polite and direct. If he had anything to hide, he was doing a good job of it.

"You're welcome to come in and wait in the parlor," he said. "I need to get Mama inside and get her fed before Pa gets home. She doesn't eat as good for him." Jared gently shooed his mother away from the door and back into the house.

"Your brothers here or are you two alone?" Morgan stepped warily up on the porch.

Jared turned around to look at him over his shoulder and shook his head. "No, sir, just me and her. I was splitting wood out back when you came up. Those fool guineas are always keening on about something. Heck, a big green grasshopper can get them all riled up, so we usually pay 'em no mind.

"Go ahead and have a seat," he said, pointing to a worn leather couch and matching chair once they were inside. A single oil lamp lit the room.

"I need to finish takin' care of my ma's supper," the boy said. "She'll just sit in her chair there while I get it. She don't really like to eat in the kitchen; it upsets her. I promise she won't bother you."

Morgan put up a hand. He couldn't help but notice the drawn look of sadness in the young man's eyes. "We'll be fine, son. You do what you need to do."

Frank took a seat in one of the leather chairs across from the window and Mrs. Crowder. Her gaze drilled through him and the wall behind him as surely as a bullet. She hummed a quiet tune in soft time to the tick of her head.

Neither Morgan or Beaumont spoke. It felt rude around the woman. Frank wondered how long she'd been like this. He noticed a dirty spoon hiding among the dust under the edge of the sofa. It had likely been there quite a while.

Jared came in with a wooden tray. There was a plate of scrambled eggs, a tall glass of buttermilk, and two cups of coffee.

"Figured you'd rather have coffee instead of milk," he said. "There was only enough milk for

Mama anyhow." He set down the tray and passed out the coffee.

"You figured right on that account, Mr. Crowder." Morgan gratefully accepted the cup. "I could use a good cup of coffee."

Beaumont nodded as he took his cup. "Many thanks," he said.

"She likes eggs the best," Jared said, taking a seat beside his mother. "She can't tell us so, but she doesn't spit 'em back out like she does the mush Pa tries to feed her."

He spooned a bit of egg into the gaunt woman's mouth. She chewed methodically and swallowed. Her mouth hung open as if she wanted more. He gave her another small bite and looked up at the two men. "I put butter in it, the same way she used to fix mine. Sometimes I think I can even see her smile."

"You said she had an accident?" Morgan leaned forward and rested his elbows on his knees. He was not normally one to feel pity, but the way this young man treated his mother moved him deeply.

Jared nodded. "Rattlesnake spooked a team and it got away from my pa a little over two years ago. He couldn't stop 'em. The wagon flipped and threw 'em. Pa got his eye knocked out and the wagon rolled over Mama's head. She wandered around for two days before I tracked her down about five miles from here." He gave her another bite of eggs and wiped the corners of her mouth with a cloth he'd kept tucked in his belt.

"Pa says she'll come around any time now, but I don't think so."

Morgan scooted to the front of his seat. "You

never know about these things. I was mighty near death myself a while back." He shot a glance at Beaumont, then looked back at Jared. "Your pa mention Judge Monfore lately?"

"Not too much. I know they don't see eye to eye if that's what you mean." He finished feeding his mother and set the tray on a squat wooden table at the end of the couch. He handed the poor woman the glass of buttermilk and helped her press it to her lips, careful not to give it to her too fast.

"My pa is capable of about anything, and to tell you the honest truth, I don't think too much of him. I wouldn't even stay around here if it wasn't for my mother." He set the rest of the buttermilk on the tray and wiped her face again.

"Well, the judge has a daughter and wife who are worried sick about him right now," the Ranger piped up.

"Worried!" Mrs. Crowder screeched as loud as the guinea hens out front. Both Morgan and Beaumont jumped at the sudden outburst. Jared, apparently used to such things, held his mother's hand and stroked her arm to try and soothe her.

He looked a little sheepish. "Sometimes she mimics what folks are saying. Sorry if it startled you."

Morgan smiled and shook his head. "It's all right. We best be going now anyhow. Our work's cut out for us finding the judge. We owe it to his wife and daughter to find out what's happened."

"Worried! Judge's women!" Mrs. Crowder continued to stare into space and her face remained passive, but the words escaped her lips in intense squawks. "Women, worried. Watch women . . ."

She suddenly fell silent. Her head ticks were a little more pronounced, but everything else about her was unchanged.

"She's not mimicking anyone now," Beaumont whispered.

Jared nodded. "She must have heard Pa talking to Pete and Pony earlier. Sometimes he talks to her, not even givin' a thought that she might understand his words." The boy moved his chin back and forth slowly while he studied his mother's passive face. His eyes welled up like he was about to cry.

Morgan moved his chair closer so he could look the blank-faced woman in the eye. He gently brushed a lock of her hair out of her face and smiled. If she noticed he was there in front of her, she gave no sign of it.

"Do you want to tell us something, Mrs. Crowder?" He asked.

She sat mutely, blinking and staring into space.

Jared rose to his feet. His forehead creased in worry. "She's never done this before." He stood by his mother and caressed the top of her head. "I don't know what she's heard, but if I was you, I'd go check on those womenfolk."

Frank rose and shook the young man's hand.

"I wish you all the best with all you have to do here. You're a fine son to your mother. Sad to say, but that's a rare quality these days."

"You be careful, Mr. Morgan, Ranger Beaumont," Jared said. "I told you, my pa's capable of just about anything—and my brothers are ten times worse than he is."

28

Morgan and Beaumont sent the flock of guinea hens squawking in all directions when they left the Crowders' Flying C ranch at a gallop.

Morgan nudged Stormy over so he was stirrup to stirrup with Beaumont's bay. He kept his horse at a steady, ground-eating lope while he leaned over to speak.

"Tyler, I want you to do me a favor," he yelled into the wind.

The Ranger nodded, but stared straight ahead as they rode. "I know what you're gonna say. If you ever get like that pitiful woman, you want me to shoot you."

"You didn't miss by much," Morgan said, bending his head so his hat blocked out more of the breeze brought on by the speed of Stormy's gait. "I'd hate for you to have to live with having shot me. I was thinking you could stuff my vest pockets with bacon and send me out into the Rocky Mountains so I could make my peace with the grizzlies and panthers. They could do all the dirty work for you."

Beaumont turned in the saddle and slowed his horse a bit. "Grizzly bears?"

"Be a damned sight better than livin' like her."

Morgan kept up his speed so Beaumont would follow.

"I'll do it on one condition," Beaumont said, looking forward again.

"What's that?"

"If the situation is reversed, I'd just as soon you shot me. I'm not too partial to bein' ate up by grizzly bears."

Morgan mused the thought over for a minute before spurring his horse faster. "Glad to, kid. We got us a deal," he said over his shoulder. Stormy broke into a gallop again and they headed for Weatherford.

It was nearing sunset by the time they had the clock tower of the courthouse in view. Frank's gut was knotted with worry. He wanted to get to Mercy and Victoria before it got too dark. There were too many folks in town for a kidnapping to be successful during the daylight hours—but once the sun went down, it would be an easy matter, particularly if the sheriff could be counted on to look the other way.

Beaumont kept his stout bay pointed toward the center of town. It was easy to see the tough little Ranger was sweet on Victoria. He wasn't about to let anything happen to her.

They slowed the horses to a trot down the long hill coming into town from the north. Beaumont pulled his bay to a sliding stop in front of Harwood's blacksmith shop. Morgan followed suit and shot him a questioning look.

The Ranger nodded at a piebald paint mare with flop ears and a huge hammer head that was tied to a trough next to the smoky building. The mare had a rear leg cocked up and it looked like she'd thrown a shoe.

"Deputy Grant's horse," Beaumont said.

The rotund deputy came out the open double doors a moment later. He was gnawing on a chunk of hot bread the size of his fist and melted butter dripped down his series of chins. His face fell when he saw Morgan, and his mouth hung open.

"Hey, Frank." He tried to smile, and gave a weak wave with his bread-free hand. "My horse needs a new shoe." He pointed as if he needed some sort of reason to be there. "I had to beg Jesse to stay late and fix it."

"Grant." Morgan nodded as he dismounted. "Have you seen the sheriff around today?"

The deputy shook his head. "Not too much." His face was so free of guile and mischief, he didn't seem capable of telling a lie—not even a little one. "Danged old Jesse's upped the price of a shoein' by twenty-five cents. He gave me some fool story about how the price of shoein' is pegged to five times the price of a haircut, and since the barber on Main just went up a nickel, he's gotta go up too. I was pretty honked, I don't mind tellin' you. I expect he gave me this here piece of hot bread to shut me up."

"Fancy that," Beaumont said under his breath.

"Bob, listen here. I need to know when you last saw Rance Whitehead." Morgan's voice was pointed and hard as flint. It shut the deputy down a lot faster than a piece of hot bread.

"He's been away a lot lately," Grant said. "I saw him for just a minute about an hour ago. He asked me to go by and check on the Monfores and make certain they were home and safe."

"Are they?" Beaumont asked.

Grant began to relax when he realized Morgan didn't intend to shoot him on the spot. He took another bite of bread. "Mercy was there. She says she doesn't plan to go anywhere else this evening."

"Does the sheriff know that?" Morgan was already back on his horse.

"Told him so myself," Grant said between chews.

"What about Victoria?" Beaumont asked from the back of his jigging bay. The Ranger was full of nervous energy and the animal could sense it.

"Her mama said she was out for an evening buggy ride with Reed Whitehead, the sheriff's boy."

"Did she say where they were going?" Morgan eyed the man carefully to let him know this was important information.

Grant looked panic-stricken while he racked his feeble brain. After a mighty struggle, he smiled and let out a long sigh of relief. "Diamond Creek—they were headin' out of town a ways toward Diamond Creek. Don't seem proper, them bein' alone and all, but I reckon she ain't a spring chicken and he is the sheriff's son."

Morgan and Beaumont left Deputy Grant to finish his hunk of buttered bread, and rode on toward the center of town. The sun was just below the brushy line of oaks toward Palo Pinto and a cool wind was beginning to blow.

"Diamond Creek is southwest of town toward the river," Frank said when they got to the courthouse.

He pointed up Lamar Street with the tail of his leather reins. "Mercy's house is that way. I'm the kind of man who likes to do things myself, that's certain. But I don't see how we can get this done without splitting up."

Beaumont nodded, touching the butt of his pistol. "Me neither."

Stormy was beginning to jig and prance as much as the little bay, and Frank had to spin him on his haunches so he could look Beaumont in the eye as he spoke.

"I haven't been able to figure out for certain if she's my own flesh and blood, but the odds are damn sure in favor of it."

The Ranger started to say something, but Morgan put up his hand to stop him.

"I've got a son, and I suppose that's more than some men ever get. But the thought of having a daughter sobers me down to my boot soles. There's nobody I'd trust more than you to make sure she's safe."

"I'll do my best," Beaumont nodded.

"Do what it takes, Tyler. That's what I'm expecting of you," Morgan said. "Just do what it takes and bring her back." He spurred Stormy up the street without another word.

29

Diamond Creek was a tiny, spring-fed stream that joined the Brazos River. Where the river was a slow, tepid thing, full of sand and red clay, Diamond Creek bubbled along over a polished bed of gravel making it one of the few clear-water streams in north Texas. Bordered on both sides by a row of towering pecan trees, so tall their canopies touched across the water in a sort of an arch, the creek ran through a shadowed tunnel.

In summer, when thc pecans were covered in leaves, it was a favored spot for young couples to slip away and spend some time out from under the watchful eye of the nosey but well-intentioned parents and clergy of Parker County.

Victoria had been surprised when Reed had asked her to accompany him to such a place. He'd shown up dressed more like a cowboy than someone reading law. She'd never seen him in any other kind of hat but a bowler, and the broad-brimmed Stetson made her smile when she saw it.

He'd been nervous and behaving strangely, stepping on his words and glancing up and down the road as if he didn't want anyone to see him doing the asking. She was too flattered to say no. No matter what her father thought of him, Reed Whitehead had always been nice enough.

She was afraid, though, that he thought of her in a way far different than she felt about him. A week ago she might have settled for a life with Reed. He wanted to be an attorney, and was reading law with one of the Hansen brothers. His future in Parker County was set.

Then Tyler Beaumont had ridden in with her mother's old flame. She'd taken one look at the Texas Ranger's broad shoulders and pale eyes and decided that that was the man she wanted to spend her life beside. Beaumont appeared to share her feelings. Though he'd not said as much, a woman could tell such things.

Sitting on the bouncing buggy beside a humming Reed Whitehead, she decided it was an incredible mistake to lead him on by going with him to Diamond Creek. She had to tell him how she really felt before they got there.

Reed clucked at the grey mare and jingled the reins to keep her speed up. When he turned to look at her, his eyes had a funny glow she'd not noticed before. He'd grown quieter, hardly ever looking in her direction. It was almost as if she wasn't there with him at all. *Perhaps he sensed she was about to give him some hard news.*

The sun was dipping below the horizon, and a cool wind whispered through the cedars and live oaks along the winding wagon road that led out of town toward the Brazos River. Victoria pulled her cream-colored woolen shawl up around her shoulders. This was her favorite time of day. The fresh scent of the green grass and succulent plants that grew along the spring-fed creek drifted up on the evening breeze. They were close.

"Reed." She cleared her throat and tried to sit up straighter. The wagon seat was narrow and it was difficult not to appear that she was trying to sit close. "I have something I need to talk to you about."

Whitehead glanced at her, then turned back to the gray mare. "Don't worry, sweetheart. I've got something I need to say to you too."

Sweetheart? He'd never called her anything but Victoria before. "Really, Reed, I think you should just pull over."

"You do, do you?" He continued to stare ahead, a wry smile twisting on the corners of his lips. "Why's that?"

He'd never acted this cold. It was a good thing Beaumont came along when he did, or she might have made a terrible mistake.

"I told you. I need to talk to you and I want your full attention."

He clucked again at the horse and the buggy sped up.

"Reed, I'm asking you to stop the horse now."

"Can't," he said. "I've got a surprise for you up here in the trees."

"Oh, Reed, listen to me." This was what she'd feared. "Really, I don't want to hurt you, but I think you need to let me talk to you before we go any further."

Whitehead leaned back against the heavy leather reins to slow the gray mare. The buggy seat was on leaf springs, and rocked back and forth for a few seconds even after the wagon came to a standstill. He turned abruptly in the seat to face her.

"Let me tell *you* something." His eyes blazed and his words came out from between his clenched teeth like a cruel hiss.

Victoria shook her head and tried to speak, but he cut her off.

"You think this, you think that. I'll save us all some trouble and tell you what *I* think." He stared at her and drew air slowly through his nose like he always did when he came to some decision. "I think you should shut the hell up."

Victoria gasped. "Reed . . ."

Whitehead sent a heavy right fist crashing against the side of her face. Her eyes slammed shut and a thousand pinpoints of yellow light exploded inside her head. She'd never in her life felt such searing pain. For a moment she thought she might throw up, then everything went black.

She never even had time to scream.

The jingle of bit and harness as the gray mare nosed at the green buds on a pecan branch jarred Victoria out of a sickening unconsciousness.

She was on the ground, leaning against a buggy wheel. Her left ear felt like it was on fire. When she tried to move her jaw, she thought she might understand what it would feel like to be shot in the head.

Male voices drifted over from the other side of the buggy, nearest the gurgling creek. One of the voices belonged to Reed Whitehead; she couldn't place the others, but she thought she'd heard at least one of them before.

She cast her eyes back and forth without moving her head, partially so no one would know she was awake, but mostly because moving hurt so badly. She considered trying to make a run for it; she could outmaneuver the gray mare towing the buggy through the thick tangle of trees. But she heard other horses snorting and pawing over by the voices. With her head pounding like it was, she wasn't sure she'd even be able to walk, let alone outrun a man on horseback.

This whole situation was beyond her imagination. She racked her brain trying to figure out what had caused Reed to go so crazy. She didn't have to wonder about it long.

"I see you're still among the living." Whitehead snickered as he knelt down beside her. His voice was almost gentle—almost like it was before.

Victoria wanted to plead for an explanation, but she had never been the pleading type. Instead, she just sat and looked at him through blurry, bloodshot eyes.

"I'll say this for you," Reed said, shaking his head. "You're a tough little princess. Most women I know would have been boo-hooing their guts out by now."

Victoria realized she was too mad to cry.

Reed went on talking behind his crazed grin. "It's only a matter of time, though. I suppose that before long you'll be shedding a tear or two. Ol' Pete here says he's got a little score to settle with you."

A dark, oafish man with an ugly purple bruise over an equally ugly face stood over her and held up a bandaged hand. It was missing two of its fingers.

"You remember me, Little Princess?" The man leered at her. "You and I need to have a little talk about the way you treated me the last time we met."

Victoria held back a gasp when she recognized him as one of the men who took her father. Instead, she railed back at them.

"What have you done with my father?" She struggled to get to her feet. The fact that a man she once trusted had something to do with the kidnapping of her father filled her veins with renewed fire. "What have you got to do with all this, Reed Whitehead?"

"You know." He stood in front of her, his arms folded, looking smug. "Over the last two years you and I have spent a lot of time together. All the while I listened to everything you wanted to talk about. All the while I did the things you wanted to do. I thought you would at least have the decency to see it through to the end." He was raging now. "My father said you were just leading me on. He told me about the damned Ranger runt you're so sweet on lately."

Victoria opened her mouth to protest. She shook her head, but stopped because it made her dizzy. "You don't know what you're talking about. . . ."

"My father said you were nothing but a worthless little tease, just like your mother used to be. First I didn't believe him, but I know now."

"You watch your mouth, Reed." Now she did gasp. "I've never treated you anything but proper. And up till now you've always returned the favor. I don't understand what's gotten into you to get involved with men like this. They have my father, for heaven's sake."

His fist caught her low in the gut and drove the wind from her lungs. Reed grabbed at her shoulder with his left hand while he hit her again with his right. She fell to her knees and fought for air, opening her mouth like a fish flopped up on the bank. The sleeve and half her blouse had ripped away, leaving her exposed, but too stunned and weak to do anything about it.

When she caught her breath, she tried to cover herself with her arms. She looked up to see him holding the torn remnant of white cloth to his nose, smelling it.

Pete Crowder and another man with a long red beard and a soot-smudged face stood to the side of Whitehead.

"Give us a minute or two alone, boys. I have a few important matters to finish up with our little princess here."

All the men chuckled. Victoria's blood ran cold.

"Suit yourself," Pete rasped. "My pa said to bring her; he didn't say not to touch her on the way. I don't mind waitin' my turn." He looked to his redheaded companion. "That okay with you, Kelly?"

The man grunted and leered down at her, showing a crooked row of yellow brown teeth. "I ain't the particular sort," he said.

The other two men stepped back a few paces, laughing and elbowing each other as they went—they wanted to see the show.

Reed laughed. "Pete said you were dangerous. He said he had to bring Kelly along so you wouldn't kill us all."

He gave her a swift boot in the ribs that flipped her over and sent her into a gasping, coughing fit. She felt his presence as he knelt down beside her, even doubled her fist to hit him, but couldn't get enough air to move her arms.

Cruel hands grabbed her shoulders, pushing, pinning her to the ground. Reed laughed low in his throat, hollow and coarse, like he was inside a well. She gave up trying to keep her chest covered, and put all her efforts into the struggle. In the end, he was too strong for her and banged her head against an exposed root to calm her down.

With the other men standing by and waiting their turn, she knew it was foolish to fight. She could not win. But that really didn't matter. She didn't have it inside her to give up. Reed Whitehead and the others might have their way with her dead body, but that would be all they would get.

He tugged at the hem of her skirt, ripping the outer layer away. She pushed at his hand and sank her teeth into the flesh along his upper arm, tasting blood. He fumed, jerking back to hit her in the face again.

She fell back, unable to see clearly enough to know what was going on around her anymore. She could feel the cool breeze on her exposed skin, but her arms wouldn't work anymore. She vomited on the ground beside her, and heard the men laugh at her pain. She saw a shadow looming over her, and knew it was Reed.

Then, the pounding in her head turned into hoofbeats and the world around her erupted in a volley of gunfire.

30

Pete Crowder turned from his cheering to catch a .44 slug straight through the bridge of his nose. The red-bearded outlaw spun in time to see Tyler Beaumont shoot his partner. He clawed for his gun, but the Ranger shot him twice in the chest.

Men who would stand by and cheer while anyone treated a woman like this didn't deserve more warning that the click of a hammer coming back on the pistol.

The Ranger breasted the rise on the near side of the creek, and splashed his horse across it without pausing to watch the dead men hit the ground. He slid off the bay before it came to a complete stop, landing only a few feet from a dismayed Reed Whitehead, who knelt over a badly injured Victoria.

The sight of what they'd done to her—and what they were about to do—sent a lightning bolt of fury through the young lawman's body. He'd never in his life felt as ready to kill as he did at that very moment.

Two quick strides brought the lawman close enough to administer a brutal kick to the kneeling man's ribs. The blow sent him flying off the beleaguered girl and nearly caused Beaumont to loose his footing. The wind left Whitehead with a grunting woof and several ribs snapped from the impact of the Ranger's boot.

Whitehead was no slouch when it came to fighting. His father had seen to that. He pushed himself to his feet, cursing.

"Beaumont, you son of a bitch. You've ruined everything!"

Victoria looked up, tears in her eyes. She was dazed and frightened, like a wounded child. Beaumont's anger burned as she tried to cover herself where half her clothing was ripped away.

The pitiful look sent a shock of rage through the Ranger's veins. Whitehead threw a strong right, but Beaumont deflected it, letting it slide off his jaw without much effect. It didn't matter what the man did now; nothing was going to stop Tyler Beaumont from what he was about to do. Justice had to be done.

Whitehead groped for the pistol at his side. Before he could bring it up, Beaumont knocked it to the ground.

"Uh-uh," the Ranger panted. "You're not gonna get off that easy. I coulda shot you when I rode up." Beaumont drew Whitehead to him and gave him a fierce head-butt to the nose with his forehead. "No, sir. What you need is an ass-whippin'." Beaumont's right fist slammed into Whitehead's already shattered nose. "I'm just proud to be the one to give it to you."

Beaumont walked past another feeble punch and grabbed Whitehead by the collar. Yanking him forward, he drove a powerful knee into the other man's groin, then again into his stomach. When Whitehead collapsed to his knees, Beaumont grabbed him by the back of his shirt and began to bash his face into the thick oak hub on the buggy wheel.

"I thought you were going to be my real competition for her," the little Ranger muttered long after the lolling man had turned into a limp bloody mess of bone and torn flesh.

Whitehead moaned. His pistol lay on the ground in front of him, only inches from his shredded face.

"Shootin's too quick for you," Beaumont spit and planted a boot on Whitehead's blood-covered cheek.

The Ranger picked up the revolver and stuck it in his waistband. He shrugged off his jacket and knelt down to cover Victoria. She tried to look around, but he gently turned her face away from her dead attackers and the wounded Whitehead.

She shook her head and looked anyway. Her fine mouth was set in a grim line. "I'll be fine. I'd have gladly killed them myself if I could have." She began to sob, for the first time since the ordeal began, and buried her head against Beaumont's chest. "Do you think he'll live?" She nodded toward Whitehead.

"I'm sorry to say it, but I believe he will for the time being. He won't be boundin' around hurting any more women, though. I aim to see him hang for this . . . and anything else he might have done." The Ranger put a calloused hand against her hair and drew her tight against him. She smelled of soap and damp earth.

She had tears in her eyes. "He never . . . I mean you stopped him before . . . Oh, Tyler."

"You're one tough lady. You know that?" He put his arm around her bare shoulder and rocked her back and forth to comfort her.

She didn't pull away. Her voice caught on heavy sobs as she spoke. "You think so?"

"That I do," he said. "You're the spittin' image of your father." Beaumont flinched as soon as the words escaped his lips. He waited to see if she'd heard him.

Now she pulled away, hitching the jacket around her arms. "You didn't get here until after my father was kidnapped." She eyed him carefully through her tears. "Have you met him before?"

Beaumont wondered if she even had an inkling Frank Morgan could be her papa. They sure enough looked alike, but Mercy shared Morgan's dark features as well, the same deep sadness in her eyes. Victoria had spunk, though. She'd beaten back her would-be kidnappers and chopped off Pete Crowder's fingers in the process. She was still struggling mightily when Beaumont had come up and kicked the sheriff's son off her. *Quit* wasn't in her vocabulary when it came to fighting. If that wasn't something she inherited from Morgan, he didn't know what was.

Still, the only thing certain was that if she didn't know, it wasn't up to Beaumont to tell her.

"Well, did you—meet him before?"

He smiled and shook his head, trying to look more relaxed than he really was. "Your papa's a famous judge, darlin'. I'm a Texas Ranger. I know him by reputation, that's all—and he's got a reputation for being one tough customer."

Victoria's gaze softened again. She appeared to buy his story. Before he could relax, she asked another hard question.

"When you were fighting, I heard you say you

thought Reed might be your competition. What did you mean by that?"

Beaumont pulled her to him again and caressed her hair so she couldn't see his face. "Let's get you home, Miss. Monfore." He smiled as he felt her nod her head against his chest.

It was completely dark now. Half a moon hung in the night sky, but the bodies of Pete Crowder and his red-bearded companion were barely visible in the shadows of the huge pecan trees. Beaumont helped her up into the buggy and handed her the reins.

"I need to get some rope from my saddle and tie up Whitehead. Then I'll put my horse behind us and drive you back to town. Frank's there now lookin' after your mama."

A light of understanding twinkled in her eyes with the moonlight. "They were sweet on each other years ago, weren't they?"

Beaumont braced himself for a question about her parents he hoped she wouldn't ask. "I suppose that's true, but it was a long time back."

Victoria looked down at him for a long moment, then reached out to touch his face with her long, sure fingers. "I know more than you think I do," she said.

He swallowed hard. "Is that a fact?"

She nodded, letting her hand slip slowly off his whiskered cheek. "You go ahead and take care of Reed and your horse. I'll tell you this much, Tyler Beaumont—he was never any competition for you."

31

Morgan slowed Stormy to a trot about a quarter mile from the Monfore house. His gut told him to hurry, but his brain told him to take things slowly and ease his way in. It wouldn't do Mercy any good if he rushed into her house and saved her from outlaws inside while gunmen in the shadows killed them both. Frank vowed not to let anything like that happen again.

The streets were dim and deserted, with most of the town folks inside eating an honest supper. Lights gleamed through windows up and down the street. In some of the houses, the curtains were drawn and only a sliver got through. Other places, people moved about inside their cozy homes, serving dinner, arguing, and otherwise carrying on family business seemingly oblivious to the fact that anyone on the dark street could stand and watch their every move.

Mercy lived on the southwest side of town—the area where the well-to-do landed gentry had decided to build their fancy two- and three-story homes. It was only proper that a powerful judge should have an estate in such an area.

Morgan had no doubt that he could have afforded

to live in such a place. With the wealth he had socked away from his first wife, he could have easily bought any of the houses several times over. As well appointed as the houses were, with all their spacious rooms and sprawling porches, he couldn't help but feel hemmed in amid such crowded conditions. Each lot was no more than an acre, and although most places had several outbuildings, including a coach house, to a person used to the wide-open expanses of prairie, the whole mess seemed crowded far too close together.

Once, when Frank was hunting antelope out in New Mexico, he'd spent the better part of a late afternoon hunkered below a rise next to a water hole, watching a mound of red ants. He studied the way they scurried around crawling over one another while they went about their ant-business, and came away thinking that that was why he didn't like living in any sort of town, not even a small one. He couldn't abide crawling over someone else just to get where he wanted to go.

The fact that Parker County, a place that used to be the jumping-off point for the frontier, was now joining the ranks of all the crowded places to the east, gave Morgan a pang of sadness deep in his gut.

A hound howled mournfully up the street behind him, and he heard a woman's voice instantly tell it to hush. Frank shook his head and looked down at Dog.

"I'd not live in a place where you couldn't howl a bit if you got it in your mind to sing."

Dog cocked his ear and looked up, whining softly at the attention.

A moment later, Stormy stopped in his tracks. He gave a low snort, both ears pinned back. Dog rumbled a growl and looked off into a dark alley across the street.

Morgan froze in the saddle. He strained his senses to try and figure out what his animals had noticed. Their instincts had saved his life on more than one occasion. Suddenly, Dog tore off in a barking frenzy toward the alley.

Stormy continued to shuffle uneasily.

"Let's go, boy," Morgan whispered to his horse. "We got places to be. The dog is a fair hand at takin' care of himself."

Ten steps down the road, Stormy stopped again. The big Appaloosa nickered and threw its head back and forth, jingling the bits.

A shiver went up Morgan's spine as he saw the thin gleam of a lariat rope stretched out, head-high, across the street in front of him. He gave his horse a pat on the neck. Someone was in the shadows. He could feel them.

He heard the click of a hammer coming back.

"Step down," a voice from the darkness whispered. Morgan didn't recognize it.

Frank raised his hands slightly and took stock of his situation. He'd already tucked his jacket behind his pistol so he could get to it fast if he needed to, but his target was in the shadows. Dog had gone off to take care of something or someone across the street, and there could be more than one hiding on this side.

"I told you to step down!" The voice had a little edge to it now, as if the speaker wasn't quite sure of himself.

"Glad to, friend," Morgan said. "I just don't want to get shot in the process."

"I'll shoot you when it's time and not before. Now clamber down off that horse."

Frank gave a slow nod. "All right then. I just wanted to get the shooting thing settled." He stood in the stirrups and put his left hand on the saddle horn, preparing to dismount.

"You better slow it down, mister, or I'll blow you from here to Jehosephat."

Saddle leather creaked as Morgan climbed down slowly, keeping the Appaloosa between him and the shadowed gunman. There was a good moon, and Frank knew he was an easy target in the middle of the street.

"Don't think you're hiding from me behind that big spotted horse of yours. I'll easily shoot your legs out from under you, kill him, then come back and finish you off."

"Kind of figured that's what you aimed to do anyhow," Morgan said.

Dog barked and snarled in the alley across the street. He was having troubles of his own.

"Not unless you make me. We . . . I . . . got other plans for you."

Morgan gave Stormy a swat on the rump so he stepped past the neck line stretched across the street. The voice was right. If he was going to shoot, he would have done it already.

"I'm getting mighty tired of talkin' to someone who won't come out in the light and show himself. If you're not planning to kill me, then let's get on with whatever it is you got in mind." Morgan's hand hovered above his pistol. His eyes sought any movement in the shadows.

"You got an awful big yap for someone who's about to meet his maker."

"So you do plan to gun me down in the street then?"

"Oh," the voice said, "you're gonna die all right, but I won't gun you down like a dog unless you make me. Anybody could do that. It'll be a fair fight, man to man."

Frank had had enough talk. "Come on out and let's get at it then. I got no stomach for cowards who hide in the dark." There was movement in the shadows, a rustling of leaves and shuffling of heavy branches. Mercy's house was less than four blocks away. Frank could feel in his bones: she was in grave danger.

He didn't have time for this foolishness.

32

Mercy dipped her pen in the marble inkwell on her polished cherry-wood desk and held it poised over a clean sheet of paper. She thought writing a short letter to her cousin in Georgia might help take her mind off things, but she found she couldn't concentrate long enough to think of even one word.

A drip of ink fell from the pen in her trembling hands like a black tear, and splattered against the stark whiteness of the paper. This was her third attempt. Crumpling the paper, she dropped it in the wicker wastebasket at her feet and gave up.

Any other time, she would have cooked to calm her nerves. Isaiah loved to eat and she loved to cook for him. Now, with him gone, she didn't know what to do with herself. Frank would get him back if anyone could. But even he might not be able to. Sometimes things just happened and there was no stopping them. Mercy, of all people, knew the truth in that.

Even the chiming of her grandmother's wall clock could set her teeth on edge lately. She worried for the safety of her husband, she worried for Victoria—and she worried about the way she felt about Frank Morgan.

She could vividly recall the day Frank had fought Orville Muncy when he had called her names. Though Muncy stood a head taller, Frank was not the type to abide such conduct—even at the age of ten. He'd climbed on top of the larger boy and given him the thrashing of his life, bloodying his nose and boxing his ears until Orville pleaded for him to stop.

The violence of it all had frightened her so much back then that Mercy had hardly been able to speak. But she knew from that day on she would love Frank Morgan for the rest of her life. She loved her husband and wanted him home more than anything—but even that couldn't dispel the feelings she would always harbor for the handsome Drifter.

The bird dog stretched on a blanket in front of the fire, groaning against the white linen bandage that encircled his belly. He looked up at Mercy with pitiful brown eyes and whined, as if to ask when his master was coming home.

"It's all right, Gallows," she whispered, more to calm herself than the dog. "He'll be all right, I think." Her voice caught and she choked back a sob.

A loud knock at the door caused her and the dog both to jump. She stooped to calm the animal, and he laid his head back against the blanket. The knock came again. It pounded the door hard enough to shake the china cups in the hall cabinet.

"Who's there?" She couldn't control her tremulous voice. She winced when she heard how frightened she sounded, and wished she had more of Victoria's courage.

"It's Ronald Purnell, Mrs. Monfore. I need to speak with you. It's about the judge." The voice sounded almost as brittle as hers.

She'd met Purnell; he was a lawyer in town who practiced in her husband's court. Peeking out the window to make certain he was alone, she turned the bolt and let him in.

The lawyer rushed past her as if he was running from something, barely giving her a quick nod. Inside, he wrung his hands and chewed on his bottom lip. He was dressed in riding clothes, a fact Mercy found curious. She'd never even seen the man on a horse. She knew her husband had little respect for his ability as a lawyer, and she'd always found Purnell a little odd.

"What can I do for you, Mr. Purnell?" She motioned him into the sitting room and toward a chair. She wished the man would get to the point. "You say you have information about my husband."

The lawyer took a tentative step toward the chair, but didn't sit down. He paced back and forth in front of it, clutching and tugging at the mousy brown hat in both hands behind his back.

Gallows lifted his head from his spot in front of the fireplace and sniffed the air. He sprang to his feet and broke into a fit of snarls and growls when he saw Purnell.

The lawyer put his hand on his gun, but Mercy calmed the dog and sent him into the other room.

Purnell's eyes were bloodshot and wild, as if he'd been crying. "Mrs. Monfore. I don't know any other way to say this, so I'll just say it right out—I know where your husband is."

Mercy felt like someone had just thrown her a

hundred-pound grain sack. Her whole body felt heavy. She should have been happy at the news, but the way Purnell presented it seemed full of danger. Instead of happiness, she was filled with a sudden sense of foreboding and dread.

"Where?" She stood, putting a hand on her chest to try and control her breath. "Who has him?"

"Ma'am, it's not as simple as all that. If I could just have your word that you would cooperate, no one else has to get hurt."

Mercy wanted to scream, but she let her breath out slowly and bit her bottom lip before trying to speak. "Where is my husband? Is he hurt? Mr. Purnell, if you had something to do with this . . ."

"Oh, he has plenty to do with it." A husky voice pierced the shadows from the hallway. "He's in this clean up to his nose hairs. Ain't you, Purnell?" A dirty man with a lolling head and drooling mouth came in and grinned at her. She recognized him as one of the Crowder brothers. A huge oaf with greasy blond hair down to his massive shoulders followed him in. "He's in the middle of it all right. He just can't get to the point."

"In the middle of what?" Mercy felt dizzy. She half-sat, half-fell back into her chair. "Mr. Purnell, what is he talking about?"

"She's finer than you said she was," the greasy-haired giant said. He licked his lips and looked through half-shut eyes at Mercy, the way a starving man looked at a cooking piece of meat.

Mercy shuddered. "So help me, my husband will see you all hang for . . ."

Pony Crowder threw back his head and laughed an open-mouthed laugh. He stared at her, all the humor draining from his puffy, unshaven face. "Listen to me, lady. The last time I saw your husband he was bleedin' out his ears. I don't reckon he's gonna see us do a damned thing except put a bullet in his head." She tried to look away, but he leaned forward and took her face in his rough hand, squeezing her cheeks against her teeth and forcing her to face him while he spoke. "Not a damned thing. *Comprende?*"

Mercy nodded slowly against the pressure of his hand. She could feel tears pressing out through clenched lashes and running down her cheeks. Crying wouldn't help against such men, and she was furious at herself for doing it.

"Now, you need to put on some riding clothes 'cause we're goin' on a little trip." Pony let go of her and stood back.

The giant leered. "That's a good idea. Have her put on some ridin' clothes."

"Where? What kind of trip?" Mercy rubbed her eyes and dabbed at her nose with the back of her sleeve.

"To see your husband, little lady," Pony said. "My pa seems to think you'll be able to convince the old fool to let my brother out of jail. I ain't the brightest star in the sky, but even I know that ain't likely. Still, I gotta do what my pa says or there'll be hell to pay. *Comprende?*"

"Very well." She stood and tugged at the belt of her robe. "I'll go put on a skirt."

The giant grinned and licked his lips again. "I'll help you get changed, pretty lady."

Mercy cringed and held her breath. There was no way to fight off such a man. He was just too big.

Pony raised his hand and laughed. "Hang on there, you ol' dog. Pa didn't say anything about taking advantage of the lady." He turned to Mercy and winked. "I'm the onliest thing keeping this galoot off of you, so you better treat me with some respect. *Comprende?*"

Mercy nodded, letting out a ragged sigh.

"I don't see what he sees in you. You're old and wrinkled as a raisin. Old enough to be his ma, I reckon." Pony cocked his head to one side and stared at her as if in thought. "Oh what the hell," he said at length. "Go on ahead, R.D. Pa never said *not* to take advantage of her."

"Now wait just a minute!" Purnell said from the doorway. It looked to Mercy like he'd been trying to slip out. "What are you boys thinking? If you do this there'll be no turning back. The judge won't listen to a word your father says, not if you harm his wife."

Pony smirked. "He ain't gonna listen to my pa anyhow. You know that and I know that. We passed the turning back point a long time ago. The old man just ain't owned up to it yet. Now you shut your face before I shut it for you." Crowder turned back to Mercy and shrugged. He looked at his greasy companion. "R.D., do what you gotta do and let's get on our way."

The giant took off his filthy hat and put it on Mercy's chair behind her. He put a heavy arm around her shoulders and leaned down to smell her hair. "So, you only got a little while left. Might as well enjoy yourself while you still can."

Mercy closed her eyes and willed herself not to

give these men the satisfaction of seeing her shed even one more tear.

Purnell took a step into the middle of the room, committing himself.

"Listen," he said. "If your pa thinks you messed this up on account of going after the woman, there'll be hell to pay."

Pony put a hand to his chin. R.D. kept his arm around Mercy but looked to the Crowder boy, waiting for a decision.

"He'll shoot someone," Purnell reasoned. "You know he will. If his plan doesn't work, you'll still have the woman."

Mercy cringed as R.D. bent to sniff her ear. "You smell good," he said under his stinking breath.

Pony scratched his chest and sighed while he considered what Purnell had said. His head tipped to one side as if one ear weighed more than the other. Drool dripped from the corner of his sagging lips.

Mercy closed her eyes. She didn't want to think that her immediate future was in the hands of a person as utterly vile as Pony Crowder.

33

"I ain't no coward," the voice snapped from the darkness. It was a voice Morgan had heard before. It was tight and had an edge to it. The man was stalling for time, waiting for something else to happen. Some other part of a plan to fall in place.

"A coward wouldn't be able to get the drop on the famous Frank Morgan."

"Who says you got the drop on me?"

"Really funny, mister. You keep them hands up high and I'll show you how much of a coward I am." The voice trailed off as if the speaker was trying to convince himself. "No funny business now. I'm coming out."

Morgan let both arms rest across the crown of his hat. It kept them relaxed and would allow him to move with lightning speed.

There was more shuffling in the shadows and a dark figure stepped out into view. The long barrel of a shotgun caught the moonlight and appeared to glow.

It was Tom Crowder.

"Got ourselves a little furlough, did we?" Morgan kept his hands still. The boy's face twitched. He kept cutting his eyes across the street in the direction Dog had run off to.

"Sheriff himself let me out," Tom said. "Told me it was all gonna be worked out after tonight."

Frank dipped his head. "That right? What's happening tonight?"

Crowder snickered. "You would be interested in that, wouldn't you."

Morgan sighed. He knew Mercy was in danger and that was all he needed to know.

"Listen, Tom," he said. "I got an important engagement. If you want to fight me, then let's get it over with so I can be on my way." He stared hard at the other man in the moonlight—hard enough to make him take a step back. "If you don't aim to fight me fair, then go ahead and take your shot now, 'cause I'm gettin' mighty tired of hearing you yammer on." Morgan's voice grew cold as ice. "I'll warn you, though; you'd best make that first one count."

Crowder shot a quick glance up and down the street. The same hound dog howled again, and the boy looked away for an instant. Morgan counted to three while the dog continued its mournful song.

He knew what would happen next.

When the woman yelled at the animal to quiet it, Tom looked away again, and Morgan shot him in the chest.

The shotgun slid harmlessly from the boy's hands and he dropped to his knees in the moonlight.

All hell broke loose up and down the street. Windows lit up as people peeked out from behind their curtains. Front doors yawned open and dogs began to bark and howl in earnest.

"What's goin' on out there?" a fat woman with a lantern said from her front porch two houses down. The moon was bright enough that she'd have been able to see if she hadn't had the lantern to blind her.

"Texas Rangers," Frank lied. He couldn't afford to be caught up in any more feuds until he looked in on Mercy. "Had a little jailbreak, but everything's fine now. Please go back inside, ma'am."

Apparently satisfied, the woman threw a rock at her neighbor's dog, took her lantern, and waddled back inside, slamming the door behind her.

Morgan knelt beside the dying boy. "Tell me what's happening tonight, Tom. Who was supposed to meet you here?"

"Furg . . . Fur . . ." the boy gurgled. A thin line of blood trickled from the corner of his twisted mouth.

"Slow down, son, and try to get a little breath." Morgan gently lifted the dying boy's head. "Were you on your way to the Monfore place?"

Tom shook his head. "Pony and R.D.," he groaned. "There now . . ." Tom's eyes suddenly cleared. He looked up, shook his head slowly, and chuckled.

"Damn, Morgan. I think you killed me." His body went suddenly rigid, then slack. Morgan lowered him to the street.

"Mr. Morgan?" Another voice called from across the street.

Frank rolled into the shadows.

"Mr. Frank Morgan," the voice called again. "It's me, Jasper. I . . . I work for Mr. Perkins."

Frank relaxed a notch. "Jasper, what are you doin' out pokin' around in the night like this?"

"Mr. Perkins sent us to check in on you. I'm comin' out, don't shoot me."

Luke's baby-faced cowhand stepped timidly into the moonlight. He was wearing a gun on his hip, but his hands were up. "Mr. Perkins said he woulda come his own self but the missus is in the middle of havin' her baby."

"Where's Chance? I've never seen one of you without the other." Morgan hadn't lived so long by trusting things at face value.

"There was another bugger hiding in the dark over yonder in that alley. Chance gave him a conk on the back of the head when we came up. Looked like he was waiting to ambush you. Tough bird, though. When we heard the shot, we looked this way, when we turned back around, he was gone."

Satisfied, Morgan motioned with the barrel of his gun. "Go ahead and put your hands down, son. What did this other fellow look like?"

"He's a young feller, about my age." Jasper shrugged. "Had long curly hair like a girl a-peekin' out from under a fancy hat. Chance took out after him, but I thought I better come check on you after I heard the shot."

Morgan nodded and drew the razor-sharp skinning knife from his belt. "I think I know who it was. I've noticed him ghostin' around behind me ever since I left Amarillo. Been wondering when he was going to get up the nerve to make a play. Some nerve, ambushing me in the dark."

Frank cut the rope that was strung across the

street and climbed back aboard Stormy, who waited patiently a few yards away.

"You best go back and check on Chance. That man he's after is a hell of a shot and if he's cornered, it'll take a lot more than a clunk on the head to put him down. Can you shoot?"

Jasper nodded, touching his pistol. "Yessir, passable at it if I do say so myself."

"Good. This man's name is Chas Ferguson. And he's every bit as fast as me. He's just a little short when it comes to courage. If you catch up to him, don't wait for him to draw. Shoot him where he stands, because he'd do the same to you and that's certain. He showed us his true colors tonight."

"Will do." Jasper nodded and turned immediately to go. It was easy to see why Luke would send someone like him on this kind of errand.

Morgan wheeled the stout Appaloosa, then turned back to the young cowboy. "I'm much obliged to the both of you. I've got to go check on Mrs. Monfore. You go look after your friend so I can thank him as well. You mind what I told you now. Shoot Mr. Ferguson where he stands."

Frank tied Stormy to a sycamore tree three houses down from the Monfore place. The big horse, used to such treatment, let out a long sigh and cocked up a hind foot to rest it.

"When Dog gets back," Morgan whispered to his horse, "tell him I won't be long."

He crouched, drew his Peacemaker, and moved up the street.

All the curtains were drawn, but when he got

closer, Morgan could hear voices inside. It was just as he'd feared, they'd beaten him here. He checked around back and counted four horses tied to the rail beside the coach house. If they planned to kidnap Mercy, that left three inside. Frank holstered his gun and took out the knife. He moved quietly in case they'd posted a guard.

They had.

In the shadows by the back door, Morgan caught a whiff of cigarette smoke on the evening breeze. He froze and watched a tiny orange ash glow as the guard inhaled.

Morgan sank into the shadows by the corner of the coach house and cursed the bright moon. He needed to get in the house quickly, but couldn't chance spooking the guard and alerting the others. Men on guard were usually jumpy, unable to work off any of their jitters like the ones actually pulling off the job. Morgan decided to play on the jumpiness.

He took up a handful of stones and pitched one at the group of horses. He hit a big brown in the rump, but the horse seemed unbothered by it. He threw another and the horse drew up a hind leg, kicking at the small annoyance. Another stone brought a nicker and some shuffling of hooves. He had the whole string spooked now. Frank continued to throw rocks at each of the horses until they milled back and forth and tugged at their tie ropes, stomping their feet in the gravel.

The guard finally came to investigate. Morgan couldn't make out his face, but he sounded gruff, like he'd been kicked in the throat.

"What's got into you critters?" The guard walked

to the horses and looked up and down the deserted alley. When he seemed convinced there was no one around, he petted the big brown on the neck. It was likely his horse. "You animules simmer down now. They'll be out in a minute, I'm a-thinkin'."

Frank moved up next to the house while the guard was busy with the horses. He met the surprised man head on as he stepped back into shadows.

"What in hell . . . ?" the guard was able to rasp before Frank's sharp blade slid in and took the wind out of his pipes. Frank caught him as he slumped forward into the knife and lowered him silently to the ground.

Wiping his blade clean on the front of his pants, Morgan twisted the kitchen doorknob and found it turned easily. He eased it open and stepped inside. Two gaslights burned along the wall making the gleaming kitchen with its polished oak table look as bright as noonday. Frank took a moment to get his eyes used to the light.

Voices trailed in from the front room. He could hear men arguing. He wondered what they'd done with Mercy, and felt a fire growing deep in his belly.

"Look at this silver," a low voice said. "And all these fancy books."

"Forget the fancy stuff," another voice said, this one with a higher pitch—like the wind across a fence wire. "He's a damned filthy-rich judge. There's bound to be a load of money around here somewhere. That's what I'm after."

Frank stood still, listening intently. He strained to hear Mercy's voice. It sounded like he'd arrived in the middle of a burglary. He didn't have time to wait around.

"What the . . . ?" the man with the squeaky voice squealed when Morgan kicked open the door that led into the living room.

"Hello, boys," he said, pointing his Peacemaker back and forth at the two startled burglars. "I noticed all your horses were wearing the Flying C brand."

"Where's Abe?" a skinny cowboy with a moth-eaten wool vest asked, looking at the window toward the horses.

"Was that his name?" Morgan threw them both a look that was as cruel as he felt. "He's not doing so good since I sent him to Hell."

"Are you Frank Morgan?" Squeaky asked. There was a look of dread across his face.

"I am," Frank said. "And I need one of you to tell me where Mrs. Monfore is." He thumbed back the hammer on his Colt. "And I should warn you. My patience ran out about an hour ago."

Both outlaws had their hands up. Squeaky pointed at his own chest with a hooked thumb. His voice had gone up even an octave higher. "Mr. Morgan, I ain't no good at all with a gun."

"Glad to hear it," Morgan said. "Just makes my job easier.

The man in the ragged vest took a chance and made his play while his high-voiced friend was talking. It was a deadly mistake.

Morgan's Colt barked twice as the skinny outlaw tried to draw. The mortally wounded man fell back against the writing table, knocking off an inkwell before he crashed to the ground. He coughed, the rattling cough of a man who was dead but didn't know it yet.

Squeaky bent low, trying to make himself as small a target as possible. He'd kept his hands raised throughout the shooting. He was a coward, but at least he was alive and Morgan needed him alive.

"It's up to you now, mister." Morgan brought the pistol to bear on the trembling cowboy. "Where is Mrs. Monfore?"

"He'll kill me," the man shrilled.

Morgan let out an exasperated sigh. "You oughta look at your options here."

Squeaky clenched his eyes, pressing out tears. "I can't, Mr. Morgan. I ain't kiddin' you. Mr. Crowder's mean as the devil his own self. He'd kill me if I told you anything at all."

Frank didn't have time for this. He thumbed back his pistol and pressed the barrel against the trembling outlaw's pursed lips. The room began to smell like fresh urine.

"That woman is very dear to me and I aim to find out where she is, even if I have to kill you to do it. Now listen up. I'm gonna count to one; then I'm gonna blow your fool head off."

The outlaw's eyes shot open. "One?" he peeped.

"I don't have time to go any higher."

He thumbed the hammer back with a resounding click.

"Cottonwood Creek. Mr. Crowder has a line cabin there he uses to check on his stock. It's about five miles out near the salt hills." The outlaw let the words pour out of him as if Morgan had knocked open a spigot. "They took her there. I swear she was alive when she left here."

"Cottonwood Creek?" Morgan prodded with the gun muzzle to be certain.

Squeaky moved his head up and down quickly. His eyes were shut tight. A squinting grimace crossed his face as if he still expected to be shot.

Morgan thought about it. He was sure this man would have been just as cruel to Mercy as the rest if given the chance.

He brought the Colt down sharply on top of Squeaky's head, sending him to the floor in a rumpled pile. Morgan had hit him hard enough that the wound could have been fatal, but he couldn't let the outlaw go. If Squeaky died, that was his problem.

Hoofbeats sounded outside in the darkness. Morgan slid two fresh rounds in his Colt and snapped the loading gate shut.

Coach wheels crunched in the gravel. Frank relaxed a notch when he heard Tyler Beaumont's familiar voice.

"Morgan?"

"In here," Frank shouted. "She's gone."

The Ranger came through the door with Victoria in his arms. Her face was bleeding and purple with bruises. A bare arm trailed from underneath Beaumont's jacket.

Morgan's breath quickened when he saw her.

"She'll be okay," Beaumont said as he set her gently on the couch. She was fast asleep and snoring softly.

"The Whitehead boy do this?" Morgan shut his eyes in an effort to calm himself.

"He did," Beaumont whispered. "But if you want a piece of him, you'll have to go over to the jail. Take a shovel if you go because I poured what's left of him all over the floor in one of the cells. He may yet live to hang. I cheated the hangman on two others."

"Many thanks, Tyler." Morgan looked at the young woman who could very well be his own flesh and blood. He was flooded with relief that she was all right. "Many thanks," he whispered again.

Jasper and Chance came clomping up on the front steps a few minutes later. Jasper agreed to take charge of the unconscious outlaw while Chance stood guard on Victoria while she slept.

Morgan and Beaumont had serious business to attend to at Cottonwood Creek.

34

"What are we gonna tell the poor girl if we find both her parents murdered?" Beaumont asked a mile away from the Cottonwood Creek cabin. They moved slowly, picking their way through dense stands of poplar, briar, and trailing grapevine along the creek bed.

"We'll tell her we did our best." Morgan's voice was stretched tight. He always ran through the possible outcomes in his head before a confrontation if there was time. Things rarely turned out anything near what he'd envisioned. "That's all we can tell her."

"It makes no sense, Frank. Why kidnap the judge and his wife and daughter? Who would be fool enough to do something like that? There's no money in it. You gotta leave someone behind to pay the ransom."

Morgan kept Stormy pointed straight ahead into the dark night. "What we're dealin' with here is not about a ransom," he whispered against a quiet breeze. "It's got more to do with one party sayin' to the other: 'Here now, you look and take notice at how strong I am. I can whip your ass anytime I please.' These are bad men, Tyler. Bad as they come, I guess."

"You think they're already dead?"

Morgan shrugged. "No tellin'. Mercy's a friend of mine. We were very close at one time. I'd like to think I'd be able to sense it if she was gone."

"And you don't feel any such thing, right?"

Morgan was silent for a time. Only breathing horses and the groaning creak of saddle leather could be heard above the rustling brush. He wanted to think he'd feel something if Mercy had been killed. He wanted to have hope that she was still alive so he wouldn't have to tell her daughter—maybe his own daughter—that he'd only been able to do his best and that just wasn't good enough.

"No," he said at length. "I feel like she's probably still alive. I fear for her safety with men like these. And I fear for her honor, but I think she's likely still alive."

"You got a plan?"

Morgan turned to him in the mottled moonlight. He pulled a thick black vine, the size of his wrist, to one side so Stormy could squeeze through.

"These boys have already shown they have no regard for human life. They were willing to stand by while another of their lot abused an innocent young woman. They've taken a judge and his wife prisoner in such a way that they're bound to have to kill them eventually. What else can you do with vermin like that but stomp 'em out before they stomp on you."

"I believe you're right in that respect," Beaumont said, following through the same hole in the underbrush.

"All right then." Morgan reined up and looked the Ranger square in the eye. "As long as we're of one mind, let's us agree on this plan. I say we burst in and shoot anyone who's not Mercy or the judge."

Beaumont tensed and sucked in air through his teeth. They showed white in the moonlight. "El Deguello," he said, referring to the march General Antonio Lopez de Santa Anna's men played when he attacked the Texan holdouts in the Alamo.

Morgan pounded the edge of his fist on the top of his saddle horn. "Deguello."

The old Spanish tune signified there would be no mercy. No quarter.

The bright half-moon blazed down through the purple night and made approaching the cabin without being seen almost impossible. Dried oak and cottonwood leaves covered the ground providing for an instant alarm if anyone tried to make an approach on foot.

Morgan and Beaumont hid below the lip of the deep creek bed, just out of sight of the back door and less than twenty yards away. They'd tied their horses in a small clearing a quarter mile away on the opposite side of the creek.

"You smell coffee?" Morgan whispered, wrinkling his nose on the brisk night air.

"I think so."

"Sure makes me wish for a good cup before we start this little hurrah." He shrugged. "After we're done I'll help myself to some of theirs. Outlaw coffee. Likely taste like horse leavin's."

He took his hat off and inched up even with the

dirt ledge. He held onto an exposed cottonwood root to keep from sliding backward. Horses stomped in the dark trees nearby, but he couldn't see them. As he suspected, there was a guard posted by the back door. The man stood back in the shadows, under the heavy eaves, and it was impossible to see him clearly.

Morgan let himself slip down a foot so he was next to Beaumont again. They were inches apart. "Unless I miss my guess, there's a guard at the front door as well as the back. Can you give a whippoorwill cry?"

"Not hardly." Beaumont smirked in the darkness. "They'd know right off it wasn't a bird as soon as I tried. That's for certain. I can do a passable redbird or a bobwhite."

"We need some sort of night bird. Both of those are day birds." Morgan hung his hat on the root and scratched his head. "Can you hoot?"

The Ranger shrugged. "I reckon I can hoot as well as the next man."

"All right, a hoot it is then. It's important we take both guards at the same time." Morgan dipped his bare head toward the far side of the cabin. "I'll work my way up here while you move around through that stand of cedars to the front door. When you feel like you're in position, give me the best hoot owl you can. We'll both make our moves then."

Morgan drew the long knife from the scabbard on his belt. "This is touchy, son. No guns if you can help it. Once we bust in the door, we'll make enough noise to bring down the devil. Until then, it's quiet as a Papago—otherwise, those poor souls inside haven't got a chance in hell."

"Understood," Beaumont said quietly, taking out his own knife. There was a look of grim determination on his boyish face, as if he wanted to be certain he didn't let his mentor down. He hung his hat on the root beside Morgan's. "Quiet as a church mouse."

A moment later, the Ranger faded into the dark shadows at the edge of the creek bed. Morgan took a deep breath and heaved himself silently onto the level ground behind the cabin.

He figured it would take Beaumont less than ten minutes to move around and get in position, and he wanted to be ready when the signal came.

The guard at the back door had a habit of walking out a few steps every minute or so. He'd venture out into the open and peer at the shadowed tree line along the creek long enough to make him feel like he was doing something, then retreat back to the safety of the cabin wall where he'd wait to start the whole process over again.

Each time the guard moved out toward the creek, each time the sound of gurgling dark water below helped to cover any noise, Morgan inched across the ground. He held the knife in his teeth and used his hands to drag himself forward just a few scant feet at each opportunity. It was tediously slow going, knowing Mercy was inside, but he didn't have far to go.

By the time ten minutes had passed, Frank was tucked safely in the shadows at the near end of the cabin. The guard was not fifteen feet away. Morgan was close enough to hear the little nonsense tune the man hummed to himself. Close enough to smell him.

He was an older man, maybe in his fifties, probably taking the little walks to keep his legs from getting stiff. He held a short-barreled Winchester carbine across his chest as he hummed and walked, completely oblivious to the gunfighter's presence.

Beaumont's timing was perfect even if the birdcall wasn't. The clear "whoo, whowhoo" rattled the quiet darkness just as the back guard took a step out from under the cabin eaves.

The man stopped, straining his ears to make certain the mournful sound he'd heard was really an owl.

Morgan slipped up behind him in three noiseless strides. "Passable," he said under his breath.

The guard spun at the sound of Morgan's voice. "Wha . . . ?" he grunted, his eyes showing like two white saucers in the moonlight.

"I said, that was a passable hoot owl," Morgan whispered as he plunged his blade into the astonished outlaw's belly, drawing it upward to sever his diaphragm before the dying man could draw another breath to cry out. Morgan kept cutting.

The old outlaw slumped forward, still clutching the rifle. His lips muttered breathless words of surprise that carried no sound. Morgan caught him in his free arm and lowered him carefully to the ground.

The back door remained closed.

A moment later, Beaumont eased around the corner. He held his own blood-covered knife in an equally blood-soaked hand. There was a wild look about him and he blinked as though he had something caught in his eyes.

"You all right?" Morgan put away his knife.

"It wasn't quite like I thought it would be." Beaumont stared down at the dead outlaw at Morgan's feet. "It took mine a bit longer to go down than I thought it would. Kind of frazzled me, that's all." The young Ranger shook his head to clear it.

"Not the kind of thing I hope you have to ever do again," Frank whispered, resting a hand on the Ranger's shoulder. "But you gotta put it out of your mind right now—you hear me?"

Beaumont nodded. "I'm fine, really."

"Good, 'cause we got a ways to go before we're out of the woods on this one." He drew his pistol. "Now you see why I want you to let the grizzlies do all the work when I get old and senile. No killing ever ought to come easy, but some kinds come a little harder than others."

Beaumont gave a resolute nod. His face was still pale, but Morgan had seen him in action before. He couldn't think of anyone else he'd rather have with him at this particular time. Beaumont's mettle had been tested before against Ephraim Swan. He would come through this scrape all right. Frank was certain of that.

Morgan took up a position on the far side of the split-wood door while the Ranger stood at the other. Muffled voices spilled out on thin shafts of light from long cracks in the planking.

"Ready?" Morgan put his hand on the wooden lever that acted as a latch.

"Deguello," Beaumont hissed. His back was to the wall, his pistol in hand. The color had come back to the young Ranger's face and he was all business.

It was time.

* * *

R.D. Horne stuck his filthy hat on a rusty nail behind the woodstove and brushed a lock of oily hair out of his equally greasy face. Purnell shuddered when the giant approached Mercy and knelt beside her, leering. He pushed her skirts up slowly and put a hand on the pale flesh of her exposed knee.

Isaiah Monfore, who was bound with stiff leather cords to the stout wooden chair next to her, growled in anger when the grubby outlaw touched his wife. "Keep your damned hands off her!"

Horne growled right back at him and gave him a stiff backhanded slap for good measure.

"You shut your gob hole, old man," the outlaw said, gazing lustfully back at Mercy. "Don't you try and bully me around when it comes to pretty women." He turned his attention back to Judge Monfore and poked roughly at his chest with a sausage-sized finger. "I'm the king of bullies round here. This ain't your almighty courtroom. You hear me?"

Horne drew back to strike the judge in the face again, but Whitehead stopped him.

"For hell's sake, R.D., you got a woman right there in front of you and you spend all your time slappin' on her husband. What's wrong with you? You caused the pompous fool more hurt every time you touched her damned knee than you could ever do whippin' his sorry hide."

R.D. paused, blinking slowly as he let the words sink in.

Purnell stood with his back to the wall, next to the front door. He wanted to sink into it, to disappear and leave all this craziness behind. He felt his stomach churn at the horrible truth the sheriff had just taught the greasy hulk of a man. He'd never met anyone as cruel and soulless as Rance Whitehead.

"Why?" Mercy sobbed. "Why are you doing this?" She sat still and gray as stone in the chair beside her husband. Her hands were pulled back behind her and tied with the same leather cord. Tears streaked her face and dripped off the end of her nose. Her red eyes were almost swollen shut.

"See there." Whitehead nodded toward the weeping woman. "You got 'em both goin' now." He winked at Horne, who now grinned from ear to cauliflower ear. "Stolen kisses are all the sweeter if you're stealin' 'em right under a husband's nose. Ain't that right?"

Past the point of despair, Mercy tugged at her bonds and railed. Her face glowed and spit flew with the ragged scream of her words. "Will someone please quit talking about me and start talking to me?"

Pony Crowder sat on the edge of a bunk across the room playing a not-so-friendly game of poker with two brooding hired hands named Carlos and Miguel Fernandez. Between the two of them the brothers shared almost a full head of jet black hair and a doubly large dose of sour disposition. Carlos was the eldest and sported a full beard to make up for his thinning scalp. He took his poker playing seriously and glared at Mercy for her outburst. His younger brother tapped the handle of the fancy nickel pistol at his belt and raised an eyebrow at Pony. He spit something in Spanish.

Pony nodded and looked up from his cards and winced like his ears were hurt. His eyes locked on Horne.

"R.D., I wish to hell you'd go ahead and do what you gotta do. Jeeze o' Pete, I feel like I'm with a bunch of yippin' pups or something. Maybe if you'd get down to business, it'd shut the coyote bitch up for a minute so we could get some peace around here. I'm gonna get up and cut her loose in a minute if you don't. That way you gotta deal with her one way or another. *Comprende?*"

Horne put his hand back on Mercy's knee and licked his lips. The woman's head lolled to one side and she looked sadly at her husband.

Whitehead suddenly stood and grabbed his hat from the back of his chair. He walked over to stand directly in front of Mercy and the judge. "As much as I'd like to sit around and chat with you nice folks, I got a county to look after."

That brought a round of chuckles and laughs from the others in the room—all except Purnell, who had to fight to keep his supper down. The sheriff continued.

"Don't know if I'll be seeing either of you again, but Judge, I want you to know I'll take care of things when you're gone. Parker County and that pretty little daughter of yours will be in good hands, so don't you worry."

Monfore groaned, low in his belly. The sound built slowly until it became a full growl. "Whitehead, you worthless . . . I'll see you hang for this." The judge yanked against the leather bonds and let his full wrath pour out into the confines of the small cabin. His broad face reddened from exertion and his chair bounced impotently with his struggles.

Across the bunk from Pony Crowder, a circumspect Carlos spread out a straight flush and glanced up to chuckle softly at the judge's attempted tirade. Miguel folded, but joined his brother in the laugh.

Pony threw his own cards down on the blanket and glared at everyone in the room as if it was their fault he was a poor poker player.

Whitehead put on his hat. He ran a slow forefinger across his broad mustache. "Monfore, I'd shut my fool mouth if I were you. The only thing you're gonna see is R.D. here slobberin' all over your wife. I reckon it's gonna hurt you a hell of a lot more than it does her."

Whitehead turned to go. "I'll be back tomorrow, boys. Don't kill anyone while I'm gone if you can help it."

"Go ahead and git if you aim to go," Pony sneered from his card game. "You're as loud as the damned woman."

The sheriff gave a soft chuckle and tipped his hat to Purnell as he went out the door. "Watch these rowdies," he whispered. "They're animals."

Purnell jumped when the door slammed shut. He cringed despite himself and swallowed hard. He didn't like being this close to a man like the sheriff. The Crowder boys were bad, but Whitehead was a rabid dog. It was hard to believe anyone could have that much of a mean streak.

"I'll do my best," Purnell said weakly. He wanted to run, but couldn't bring himself to move. Instead, he stayed next to the door.

"Holy hell," Pony spit, suddenly rising from the

bunk and drawing his knife. Horne jumped at the suddenness of it and jerked back his hand. "You're gonna take all night just to get started and I won't get any peace."

The Fernandez brothers laughed out loud.

Pony strode over to Mercy and walked behind her, brandishing the knife. "Feelin' a little bloody right now." He bent low, his drooling jaw next to Mercy's ear. He held the blade in front of her, only inches from her nose. It caught a glint of yellow lantern light and threw it around the room while he worked the knife in his hand. "I think I'll cut both their damned throats right here and now—just for the grins of it."

35

The sound of Mercy's scream nearly tore the wooden door off its hinges. Morgan helped it along with a stout shove from his shoulder.

Inside, two Mexican men by a cot stood and reached for their pistols at the sound of intruders. Morgan and Beaumont each took one and they collapsed in a flurry of smoke, blood, and playing cards. A hulk of a man with thin greasy hair huddled behind the judge for protection, both hands straight up in the air in a sign of surrender.

Two quick shots came from over Morgan's shoulder, and he knew Beaumont was taking care of business behind him.

A door slammed as someone ran out the front.

"You best drop that gun, mister." Pony Crowder stooped behind Mercy. A long-bladed knife glinted under her chin. His face drew back in a hissing snarl, like a cornered wolf. His teeth gleamed yellow in the lantern light. "I could cut through her soft little throat like a hot knife through butter, so you best mind your p's and q's. *Comprende?*"

"I'm right behind you, Morgan," Beaumont's voice came from Frank's right.

Morgan let his pistol swing back and forth from Pony to the big outlaw. Mercy's eyes were wide and her shoulders shook. The judge moaned softly, his head collapsed against his chest. Dark, thick blood ran from his nose and left ear.

"You watch the big ugly one," Morgan said over his shoulder. "I'll take care of the little ugly one. I'm thinking this is Pony."

"Damned right I'm Pony," Crowder spit. "And I'll tell you what else. Me and R.D. are gonna slide right outta here or else the little lady's blood covers the floor. *Comprende?*" His words rattled with penned-up energy.

"I got it," Morgan whispered. The outlaw only left a few inches of his face exposed as he peeked around Mercy's face. "Pony, you need to calm down a little and think this through. You can give it up and get out of this alive, or you can keep on this trail you're on and be dead in the next half minute."

"If I'm dead, she's dead. You got that?"

Morgan kept his Peacemaker pointed at the edge of Pony's face. He could have easily shot the boy's ear off, even put a bullet in the side of his cheek. But he'd seen too many bandits put up a hellacious fight after they'd been shot in what should have been a lethal spot. Morgan knew he couldn't afford to just wound with the knife so close to Mercy's throat. He had to do the trick in one shot, an instant kill, no mistakes. Morgan needed a better target. He had to draw Pony out.

"Your move," the outlaw said.

The razor-sharp blade bit into the tender flesh at Mercy's throat and a thin trickle of blood ran down her neck, pooling at the collar of her soiled white blouse. The sight of it pressed like a fist at Morgan's gut.

His voice grew quiet and cold.

"I want you to listen to me, you ignorant son of a bitch. You got five seconds to drop that knife or I'll start carving off little pieces of you until I get to something that does the trick."

Mercy clenched her eyes shut, pressing tears through the lashes.

"I'll kill her." Pony's voice rose half an octave in pitch. "I got nothin' to lose here. *Comprende?*"

"One . . ."

"Morgan, listen to me." The voice was brittle now, as if it would shatter at every word.

"Two . . ."

"I'll do it. I'm dead serious."

"Three," Morgan said. His voice was calm-smooth, his eyes hard enough to pierce steel. He shook his head slowly in disgust. "You idiot bastard, you're dead and don't even know it."

"No one calls me an idiot," Pony railed, and leaned just a little too far to the left.

Morgan's shot took the outlaw in the eye and sprayed the room behind him with blood and gore.

Pony listed sideways. His remaining eye stared in disbelief. The knife slid out of his hand, hit Mercy's lap, and clattered harmlessly to the floor only a second before Pony's lifeless body joined it.

Mercy's body pitched forward against her bonds and her chin lolled on her chest. Blood covered the front of her blouse, and for a moment Frank worried Pony had been able to make good on his promise. The soft rise and fall of her shoulders told him she'd merely fainted.

Morgan took a step back so he stood shoulder to shoulder with Beaumont, and trained his pistol toward the boulder-sized giant behind Judge Monfore.

"What now?" the hulking outlaw asked.

"Get to your feet," Morgan hissed.

The big man kept his hands high. He stood taking a step away from the judge.

"You the one they call R.D.?"

He nodded, a little too defiantly for Frank's taste. This one didn't look like he'd truly given up.

"That's right. R.D. Horne. I work for Old Man Crowder. He sent me along to look after his boy."

Morgan motioned the outlaw away from the judge with the barrel of his pistol. "Well, I'd say you did a hell of a job of it. I'll tell you what, Horne, you any good with that pistol?"

"Good enough, I reckon." R.D. sneered and let his hands lower a few inches.

"Uh-uh, you try to touch the rafters or I'll plant you here and now."

Horne lifted his hands higher, but not as high as they had been. "The great Frank Morgan, huh? I expected more from the stories I heard. They say you're pretty damned hot with that Colt." He eyed the gun in Frank's steady hand.

"Hot enough, I reckon," Morgan mimicked.

Horne's eyes played around the room and landed back on Frank. "If I go back with you, they're sure to hang me."

Morgan shrugged. "That's up for a jury to decide." He saw what was coming.

"I don't think I could bear the thought of hangin'. As big as I am, the drop would likely rip my head plumb off." Horne was quiet, but matter-of-fact, as if he'd thought this through a few times before.

"You are a heavy man," Morgan agreed. "It might at that."

"How about we settle this between you and me right here?" Horne's hand dropped to the gun at his hip. He hadn't even touched it before Morgan and Beaumont each sent a volley of bullets crashing into the outlaw's chest.

A big man can soak up a lot of lead, and R.D. Horne was about as big as they come. It took five rounds between them to finally put him down. He teetered where he stood and blinked, wide-eyed, at Morgan and the Ranger.

"It's better this way," he moaned as he dropped to his knees. "I really didn't fancy my head bein' torn off." He pitched headlong onto the dirt floor with a giant whoosh of wind that flickered the lantern flames.

Morgan kicked at the body before holstering his pistol. "It is better this way. He saved us some time and the county about twenty feet of good hemp rope."

"One of 'em slipped out the front door while we were takin' care of the Mexicans." Beaumont reloaded as he spoke.

"That would be Ronald Purnell," Mercy said. She was awake now and shivering like she'd just been dunked in a freezing lake. "He's a local lawyer, but he's in the middle of all this." Her teeth chattered as she spoke.

Morgan knelt beside her and used Pony's knife to cut her hands and feet free.

"You're in a bad way. We need to get you to a doctor." He took out his bandanna and touched it to her neck, dabbing at the blood.

She brushed his hand away, holding it for just a moment. "I'm fine. Isaiah's the one who's hurt. They beat him something awful and made me watch." A sob caught in her throat and she stared down at the fallen R.D. Horne. "He was about to . . ." She choked back the tears so she could speak. Morgan let her talk it out. It was better than bottling it all up inside.

"They were . . . touching me before you came in." Her eyes blazed with a fury only a woman could possess. "They touched me in front of my own husband—made him sit there and watch it—then got mad and beat him when he called them cowards."

She suddenly turned, her eyes glowing in terror. "The sheriff was here a little while ago. He's a part of all this as well. Victoria went for a ride with his son tonight!"

Morgan touched her shoulder in spite of himself. He never could bear to see her in pain. That's why he'd never been able to say good-bye. "She's fine, Mercy. Ranger Beaumont here rescued her and made a corned-beef hash out of the sheriff's boy."

She turned her gaze to Beaumont. "Did they . . . ? I mean to say, is she all right?"

The Ranger nodded. "They hurt her, but that's all. I got there before anything else could happen."

Mercy buried her face in both hands and sobbed, this time with relief. "Thank you. Thank you both."

The judge stirred, lifting up his head. He slowly tried to look around. He moved his jaw from side to side, touched it, and realized his hands were free. He tried to rise, but Beaumont stopped him.

"Cowards, the whole lot of you," he railed, coughing up blood as he spoke.

Mercy immediately forgot her own wounds and knelt beside her husband, stroking his cheek in an effort to calm him. It was such a tender, private moment, Frank felt uncomfortable and looked away.

"It's all right now, Isaiah," he heard Mercy say. "These men are here to help us. Texas Rangers."

Frank noticed she didn't mention his name. He wondered how much the judge knew about their past—about him.

His wife's gentle touch made the judge more lucid by the moment. Mercy used Frank's bandanna and a bowl of fresh creek water to clean his wounds. The beating had rendered him unable to walk, but after a few moments he began barking orders, and it was obvious there was nothing wrong with his mind.

"What day is it?" Monfore opened and shut his eyes trying to focus in the dim light of the cabin.

"It's Tuesday night, sir, about midnight," Beaumont answered.

"Tuesday, well, that's good then," the judge said. He winced as Mercy touched a particularly tender spot on his high forehead. "The stockyard vote is Thursday. I was afraid those scoundrels had caused me to miss it." He looked up at Morgan through swollen eyes. "You there, what's your name?"

"Frank Morgan."

The judge nodded and took a deep breath. "I thought as much. You fit the description I had in my head—a bit thinner than I'd envisioned you, but you definitely fit the description." He opened his mouth as if to say something else, then thought better of it and patted the back of Mercy's hand. "Is Whitehead among these bodies?"

"I'm afraid he left before we came in," Morgan said. "Him and Purnell both. Three of the Crowder brothers are dead, as well as a good many of their hired gunmen. Whitehead's boy is in bad shape, but he'll likely live to see prison or a rope."

"Your Honor, I'm assuming you'll issue a bench warrant for us to bring them in," Beaumont said as he handed Mercy a clean bowl of water.

The judge rubbed a bruised hand across his jowly face and nodded. "Yes, yes of course. Consider warrants outstanding for anyone involved in this treachery." He looked at his wife. "Is Victoria safe?"

She filled him in on Beaumont's rescue.

"That's a blessing in any case. Purnell is weak—not much of a threat by himself," Monfore mused. "He's like a common garden slug. The biggest danger is that you might get some of his slime on you. There'll be hell to pay with Silas Crowder over his sons, but he's nothing more than a sad old man when you cut to the core of things." The judge sat up straighter and looked Morgan in the eye. "But Rance Whitehead, he's a different story altogether. I've never seen a man so fast and deadly accurate with a gun. It's not just his accuracy that makes him dangerous. I believe he enjoys the killing—swaggers around with his chest puffed up for days after he shoots someone. He fairly revels in it. The man is as mean as a cottonmouth and every bit as quick. Facing him won't be any picnic."

Morgan looked at Mercy and the angry gash along her fragile neck. He smiled at the judge. "Maybe so, sir, but it's something I'm looking forward to just the same."

36

Rance Whitehead heard gunfire as soon as he cleared the trees across Cottonwood Creek. Fearing a company of Texas Rangers, he kept to the shadows and watched. He watched Purnell slip out the front and dash to his horse with his tail between his legs. More shots came from inside the cabin.

Whitehead's horse, a tall gruella with a lot of white in his eye, pranced in place, tugging against the bits. He listened intently, straining against the darkness for any sign of a voice or clue as to what was happening across the creek.

For a time it was quiet, and he knew another man had died. Deep in his gut, Whitehead knew Frank Morgan was behind all this. He clenched his teeth and wheeled the big gruella horse. Without knowing how many men Morgan had with him, it would be foolish to face him tonight. But his day would come, Whitehead promised himself that. With the judge alive, there was no longer any reason to pretend. No fancy writ or paper was going to save Frank Morgan now.

* * *

It was nearly two by the time Whitehead made it back into Weatherford. The streets were completely deserted. A few boisterous voices carried out the swinging doors of the Peachtree Saloon on the still night air, but no one ventured outside.

On the ride home, Whitehead had taken some time to reflect on his situation. He knew now he needed to get out of town for a little while. He'd socked away a sizable amount of money over the years, and kept it hidden away in his safe over at the jail. Even his wife didn't know about that.

Gretchen was a steady enough woman, but he couldn't trust her with anything involving his business ventures. She was too much of a churchgoer for that. Oh, she was more than happy to spend his money—much more money than he could have possibly ever made as a lowly county sheriff. She never thought to ask where he got it, and he never thought to tell her. Up until that damned Frank Morgan showed up, it had been a pretty good arrangement.

There was a light on in the jail window. Whitehead looked over his shoulder and shivered in spite of himself. Morgan and the others were a good hour behind him. He felt sure of that, but there was no time to lose.

He couldn't remember who was working Tuesday nights, but hoped it was that fool Grant. Whitehead felt the desperate need to shoot someone, and it might as well be the idiot who'd let Morgan live the moment he came into town. He'd just flipped the horse's reins around the hitch rail when he caught a flicker of movement to his right. He froze.

"I wouldn't go in there if I were you." A coarse

whisper pierced the night and sent a shiver up the sheriff's spine.

"Who's there?" The night was too still to speak in anything but a whisper.

Slowly, like a ghostly apparition with a gun in his hand, Chas Ferguson stepped out of the shadows. "It's me, come to save your life."

"Why the pistol then?" Whitehead stood completely still behind his horse.

Ferguson holstered the weapon. "I didn't know what you'd do when I came up on you like this. You got a reputation for sorting things out after the smoke clears." The dandy shot a worried look over his shoulder at the door to the jail. "We need to *vamanos*. It's not safe here—for either of us."

Whitehead shrugged him off and started for the jail. He had to get his money.

"There's three armed Texas Rangers forted up just behind that door. The doctor's in there with 'em," Ferguson hissed. "I'm sure they'd love it if you just waltzed in there to them. Keep them from havin' to hunt you down, that's for sure."

Whitehead stopped in his tracks. "What's the doctor got to do with anything?"

The dandy's face fell. "You best come with me before someone hears us or you decide to do something foolish. We both need to make tracks while we still can. I got a room at a widow woman's house north of town. We should be safe there for a few hours."

Ferguson disappeared again into the shadows. Whitehead could hear leather creak as the dandy mounted his horse in the nearby alley that ran alongside the jail. He looked again at the lighted window and thought of all the money he had in the safe. With three armed Rangers inside, it would have to wait. He had no choice but to follow.

The sheriff caught up with Ferguson at the north edge of town before they cut west on the Poolville road. He reined up his tired gelding and fell in next to the young gunman's sorrel.

"Now, tell me what business the doctor had doin' inside my jail. Did they hurt the Crowder boy?" Whitehead kept to Ferguson's left so he would have a straight shot, but the dandy would have to shoot across himself, if they got in a scrape with each other. He was still a long way from trusting the pompous kid.

Ferguson stared straight ahead into the moonlight night. "I'll tell you, but you won't like it."

Whitehead fumed. "Listen, if you know what's . . ."

"It's your boy." Ferguson stopped his horse and turned so he was facing the sheriff on the road. "That sawed-off little Ranger beat him pretty good. I doubt you'd even recognize him."

"Did he kill the Monfore girl?"

Ferguson shook his head. "He likely would have from what I hear. Didn't have much of a chance, though. Seems the daring Ranger Beaumont swept in and shot Pete Crowder right between his peepers. Killed every mother's son there except for your son. Thrashed him to within an inch of his life."

Angry bile welled up in the back of Whitehead's throat, and he had to choke it back down to keep from vomiting. "Will he live?"

Ferguson urged his sorrel forward again with a

cluck of his tongue. "Everyone at the saloon is sayin' he'll live long enough to hang." He looked across at Whitehead. "Sorry to be the one to have to break all this to you, Sheriff."

Night birds called in the distance. Dark shadows of oak and cedar lined the edges of the glowing ribbon of road in front of them.

"I'm not the runnin' type," Whitehead said as they rode along in the blue-shadowed moonlight. He suddenly felt trapped and he didn't like the feeling. He couldn't trust anyone, least of all this dandy puke who was riding next to him. He'd watched the man's total disregard for life. For all Whitehead knew, the cocky bastard was leading him into an ambush right then and there. He pulled his horse to a stop.

Ferguson stopped a few feet ahead and turned around. "What is it?" he asked.

The sheriff shook his head. "Oh, nothing really. I'm just a man who likes to weigh all my options. I don't see you in any of 'em. This is as far as I go with you."

The dandy took off his hat and ran a hand through his blonde curls. "Fine by me. I was just thinking you and me could go after Morgan—tend to a little unfinished business, so to speak."

"The only reason it's unfinished is because you didn't finish it," Whitehead spit, poking his finger at the cocksure upstart.

"That's all the thanks I get for savin' you from those Rangers back there?"

"Yeah, well, thanks for nothin'. I ought to blow you off that bag of bones for all the good you ever did me."

A serene smile fell across the young gunman's face. He returned the fancy hat to his head and drew a deep breath. "That wouldn't do either of us any good at all." His eyes narrowed. Saddle leather creaked as he leaned forward in the stirrups. "You can draw on me if you feel like you have to, but the best thing you can hope for is that we shoot each other."

Whitehead could see the dandy was right. There wasn't any money in a fight right now. He needed to save himself for Morgan. His head spun. He needed time to get his mind together. He wondered if his wife, Gretchen, knew about their son, knew about him and what he'd been up to with Old Man Crowder. When she found out, it wouldn't matter how much of a churchgoer she was. She would never forgive him.

Ferguson sat steady as a rock in the saddle, staring at him in the moonlight. "What's it gonna be, Sheriff? I won't be an easy man to kill."

Whitehead took up his reins. "Neither will I."

Ferguson relaxed and turned his horse back down the Poolville road. "Sheriff, that's exactly what I'm counting on."

37

Jared Crowder opened the door and gave Purnell a drawn look. The whole damned family had that same pitiful, used-up look, Purnell thought, but especially this one.

"Yes?" The boy sighed as if he expected bad news was always waiting just outside his door.

Purnell was out of breath from a hard ride and he found it hard to speak. "I need to talk to your father. It's urgent."

"He's in the kitchen with my mama." The boy looked tired, as if he hadn't slept in weeks. Purnell knew how he felt. Jared stepped back and motioned him into the parlor. "I'll tell him you're here."

The lawyer took a seat in the chair across from the tattered sofa. There was a small writing desk next to him with a dusty coal-oil lamp and a pile of papers. He turned the knob on the lamp to add a little light to the otherwise dreary room. The rows of photographs along the wall took on a frightening appearance in the long shadows cast by the smoky glass chimney.

Purnell wondered how he was going to break the news to the old man that most of his family was dead. Three boys in one night. He'd watched Frank

Morgan put a bullet in Pony's head, and he'd seen Tom's body as he fled the Monfore house. He could only guess what had happened to Pete, but he'd heard the Ranger brought the girl back and the only live prisoner was Reed Whitehead.

Silas Crowder came out of the kitchen drying his hands on a frayed dishrag made from an old pair of red flannels.

"Have you got 'em both?" His white beard flowed back around his round face. In the flickering yellow light he almost looked like he was smiling—until Purnell opened his mouth to speak.

"I . . . uh . . . There's been a new development. . . ."

"I don't want to hear about any damned developments," Crowder fumed. "You get your ass back out there and bring in those women. I want my boy out of jail. . . ." Anything that ever resembled good nature fled from Crowder's face. He glared down at Purnell.

The lawyer hung his head and stared at his lap. Out of the corner of his eye, he searched for an avenue of escape.

"What?" Crowder bellowed. He threw the rag on the floor and stomped up. "You sniveling little bastard. What is your important development?"

Purnell blurted it all out like a penned-up sickness. He wanted to purge himself of all the news at once.

"Someone let Tom out of jail earlier tonight, Mr. Crowder. It wasn't part of your plan, but somebody let him out and now he's dead. A man named Frank Morgan killed him. The same man killed Pony and R.D. We were there to take Mrs. Monfore, but he showed up and killed them both before we could finish. I only just escaped with my own life."

"But you did—escape." Crowder's face was as flat and expressionless as one of the yellowed photographs on the wall behind him. "And Pony's dead?"

Purnell could only nod. "I'm not sure what happened to Pete." He was certainly dead, but the lawyer saw no reason in telling the old man now.

Just then, Jared came in from the kitchen with his mother. She was wearing the same yellow dress she'd had on the last time Purnell saw her.

"Everything all right, Pa?"

Crowder helped his wife take a seat on the sofa. He swayed a little on his feet, then took the spot beside her. "Jared, Mr. Purnell here says Tom and Pony went and got their fool selves killed tonight. For all he knows, Pete's done in as well. I need you to hitch up the wagon and go into town and fetch the bodies for me."

"Yessir," Jared sighed as if he had known all along this was going to happen and the recovery duty would one day fall to him. He took his hat from a peg on the wall and went out the door without looking back.

"It was a tricky plan to begin with," Purnell said, putting his hands on his knees to stand.

Crowder motioned for him to stay seated. "I'm obliged to you for comin' all the way out here to tell us about our boys." His face had become blank—like his wife's.

"I'm really sorry about this, Mr. Crowder."

The man shook his head slowly back and forth. His eyes peered right through Purnell as if he wasn't even there. "Keep your seat if you don't mind. I got some legal papers I need you to take a look at." Crowder rose, patting his wife's shoulder. "I keep 'em in a box in the other room. With the boys gone, I need to change my will so Jared will get it all." He muttered as he half-shuffled out of the parlor, more to himself than to Purnell. "Got to settle our accounts. I have to make certain Rebecca is taken care of."

Purnell knew he should get up and run right then and there. There was no reason to stay. Crowder owed him money, that was a fact, but in his present mental state, the old man was more likely wanting to kill him than pay him.

The lawyer felt for the pistol at his side and gave it a reassuring pat on the wooden grip. He'd not fired the gun in years. When he had, it had only been to scare some cows out of the middle of the road so he could pass with his buggy. He knew he could have never taken Frank Morgan, but an old man like Crowder, that was a different story. Without his sons around to do all his dirty work, what was he anyway? Nothing more than a pitiful old man with a crazy wife.

Alone with the blank-faced Mrs. Crowder, Purnell couldn't keep from staring. She sat no more than ten feet away. It was impossible not to see the thin trickle of clear drool that ran down her chin. Her hands were relaxed in her lap, but she rocked back and forth slowly in time with the tick of her head.

Purnell wondered if she was aware of anything around her—if she'd somehow understood when he'd told her husband three of her sons were dead.

He jumped when he heard the creak of Crowder's footsteps as he came back in to the parlor. Any of the bravado he'd conjured up fled as the steps drew closer.

The old man was no more animated than when he left, and hardly took time to look at him when he dropped a pile of crumpled and yellow papers on the small desk next to the lamp.

"My will's in there somewhere," Crowder grunted. "Look it over and then you and I can settle up."

Purnell took a pair of wire-rimmed reading glasses out of his vest pocket and took up the papers. Most were yellowed by time; some were so brittle they fell apart in his hands when he touched them. The top few pages appeared to be handwritten letters from Crowder's wife. Love letters written in a different time, when the two were young and vibrant.

"Mr. Crowder, I think you may have given me the wrong set of papers. . . ." He glanced up over the rim of his glasses and gasped. "Wh . . . what are you doing?"

Crowder sat next to his wife, a wan look of fatigue crossing his ashen face. The long-barreled black pistol in his steady hand was pointed directly at Purnell.

"Don't be fooled by this rusty old horse pistol," the old man said. "Still shoots as good as it did when I was makin' my grubstake with it."

"Mr. Crowder." Purnell licked his lips and tried to think of something to say. He thought of the pistol at his own side, but it seemed foolishness to think he could outdraw someone who already had a pistol pointed at him. "Please, let's think all this through."

"Please?" Crowder bellowed. It was the first emotion he'd shown since his outburst right after Purnell had delivered the news. "Is that all you can say is *please*? If you'd at least show a hint of backbone, I'd . . ."

"You'd what?" Purnell stammered.

"I'd nothin'," the old man spit and fired the pistol.

The gun barked with a deafening roar and sulfurous smoke filled the small parlor. Purnell felt a terrible blow as if he'd been stomped by a mule. He instinctively put a hand to his belly. When he brought it up again it was covered in dark, almost black blood.

The horrible realization that he'd been shot washed over him slowly. Oddly enough he felt no pain, but when he tried to get to his feet, he found he had no feeling at all below his waist.

"This thing's a brute," Crowder said, waving the gun around in front of him to help clear away the smoke. "Big ol' chunk of lead likely tore your whole spine out."

Purnell couldn't speak, and he had to fight to keep his eyes open. The old man fired again. Purnell flinched, but heard the crash of glass and realized it was the lamp and not him that received the second round.

Coal oil from the lamp's reservoir covered the pile of papers on the desk and flames jumped up immediately, spreading to the carpet and across the floor.

Crowder sat beside his wife and gazed into the

flames. "Everythin' I worked for has done and gone. Jared ain't got no head for business and no stomach for the gritty work. He can sell the land. That ought to be enough for him alone." His voice was low, almost a whisper.

Purnell could see that his pants legs were on fire, could smell the odor of his own burning flesh, but he couldn't feel a thing.

"No one's left who's tough enough to take care of my Rebecca," Crowder droned on. "I'm sorry, sweetheart, but the boys are dead and they'll surely put me in prison or worse."

Mrs. Crowder continued to rock slowly, oblivious to the flames at her feet. Purnell looked on in horror as Silas Crowder kissed his wife gently on the cheek, then shot her in the head. The old man turned before he could see what he'd done to his poor wife. He saluted with the smoking horse pistol before putting it to his own gray temple.

"I'll see you in Hell," he said and pulled the trigger.

Purnell gasped to keep from crying at his situation. He wondered if Jared would see the smoke, but decided the boy was likely long gone. The old man had given him plenty of time to get down the road. By the time he got back, the dry old house would be nothing but ashes, and him along with it.

The lawyer blinked his eyes to look through the smoke, and tried to make out the slumped bodies of Mr. and Mrs. Crowder. Flames already licked at the blood-soaked couch.

He hadn't thought he'd go out like this. He'd always believed he might have been hung for his crimes, but he didn't think he'd burn to death. At least this way he wouldn't have to face the condemning eyes of the judge.

He thought again of the pistol at his side. The flames moved up his chair and scorched his arms and face. He wished he had the guts to put the gun to use the way Crowder had.

Purnell's hand rested on the wooden grip and he began to sob. He just couldn't do it. The smoke was so thick he couldn't see anyway. It wouldn't be long.

38

Judge Monfore was as tough as a fighting rooster and, though he still had trouble walking, refused to miss the county vote on the stockyard proposition the following Thursday. His head remained bandaged and his right eye was swollen shut. He had to lean on Mercy to cast his vote at the post office on Spring Street.

Rance Whitehead had not been seen in town since the rescue, so Morgan and Beaumont both stayed nearby and kept a watchful eye on the Monfore family. Stories and rumors about Whitehead ran through the area like a stampeding herd after his wife came covered with blood and bruises driving into town in her buggy. The battered woman refused to talk to anyone about what happened except the Reverend Armstrong, and he was one of the few in the county who could keep a confidence.

Some folks said Whitehead had left the area to go back to Galveston, where he was from. Others swore they'd seen him sleeping in this barn or that, acting mad as a cow on loco weed.

Morgan could believe the man had gone crazy. It wasn't too big a leap to think any man who'd lost everything was only one short step from losing his mind as well. Frank knew that all too well. But he couldn't bring himself to believe Whitehead had gone very far. No, he had a score to settle, and if Frank knew any thing about human nature, Rance Whitehead was not the kind of man to let a job like that go unfinished just because he went insane.

"Mr. Morgan," the judge said as he stepped down from the post office steps. "Would you do us the honor of allowing me to buy you and your friend a decent lunch? I have a small proposition I'd like to pose to you."

Monfore blinked his open eye and rested against his wife's shoulder, smiling a sincere smile. Frank wondered if the man had any idea of the things that had gone on between him and Mercy all those years ago.

"Come, Frank, you simply must accompany us to lunch." Mercy smiled, her voice dripping with Southern charm. She looked up at her husband. "He is a judge, you know. I'm not certain you're allowed to turn him down on a request like this."

"We'd be honored," Beaumont piped up from behind them. He was hand in hand with Victoria. In the hours after the rescue, the two had hardly spent a minute apart.

This is going to be one hell of an uncomfortable lunch, Morgan thought to himself, but he couldn't think of any way around it.

"You know," the judge said a short time later over a bowl of noodle soup, "of course I have my views, but I'm not so much concerned about the outcome of this vote as I was about the dialogue that led up to it."

"You could have fooled me two weeks ago, Papa." Victoria sat across the table between Morgan and Beaumont. "You were . . ."

"Victoria!" Mercy lowered her eyes to get as menacing a look as she could muster—which wasn't very menacing at all. "Your father has been through a great strain. Why don't we keep the conversation light for a change?"

The girl opened her mouth to speak, but thought better of it. She smiled softly and put her hand on Beaumont's, which rested on top of the table beside his soup bowl. It was an extremely forward move, but no one—least of all Beaumont—said anything in protest.

"Morgan." Judge Monfore pointed with an empty soup spoon. "I need to be honest with you. When I learned my wife sent for you I had grave reservations to be sure. I've heard stories about you that would curdle a decent man's blood."

"I don't doubt it," Morgan said.

The judge put down his spoon. "Now you let me finish. We judges aren't used to being interrupted. I heard you were a hard killer with a quick temper and ruthless personality."

"Sorry to interrupt again, sir, but all those things are true to a degree," Frank said. He wasn't upset, but he wasn't about to be ordered around by a judge anywhere but a courtroom.

"Well, that's just the point, man." Isaiah Monfore pounded the table hard enough to make Mercy jump. "I didn't realize it at the time, but those are the qualities we need around here, provided they reside in the heart of an otherwise honest and law-abiding man."

The judge felt around inside the breast pocket of his frock coat and pulled out a silver six-pointed star. He set the badge on the table between them. "Morgan, what would you say if I offered you a job? Now that Whitehead has stuck his foot in the sty, so to speak, we are in need of a capable sheriff."

"I appreciate this vote of confidence, Your Honor." Frank was already shaking his head. "But I'm not interested. I don't really need a job."

"Damn it, man." The judge pounded the table again. The badge and all the soup bowls bounced in unison. It was easy to see the man wished he had his gavel in hand the way he kept banging on things. "Parker County was your home once. Don't you ever think about settling down and giving something back?"

Morgan shrugged. "You said it yourself, Judge. I'm a hard man—but I am honest—and to be honest, I'm just not interested. You got good men aplenty around here who would make you a fine sheriff." He chanced another glance at Mercy, and caught her looking sadly at him. She, of all people, knew what he was going to say. "The fact is, I was planning to move on this afternoon."

Monfore nudged the silver star forward an inch with his knuckle. His voice grew quiet and sincere. "I'm asking you to reconsider. The people around here could use a man like . . ."

He was interrupted by a commotion out in the street. Beaumont was first out of his chair and to the front window in the café.

"It's Whitehead," the Ranger said over his shoulder. "And he's buzzin' like a stomped rattler."

Rance Whitehead looked like he'd been dragged through a mud bank along the Brazos River by a runaway horse. A jagged purple gash, crusted with dried blood, creased his right cheek from the corner of his mouth to his ear. His dark hair was matted and filthy across a furrowed brow as he stood hatless in the bright noonday sun.

"You reckon his wife did that to him?" Beaumont whispered into the glass.

"Morgan!" Whitehead's voice was a hoarse screech that held the jagged edge of broken glass. It sounded as though he'd been yelling at the top of his lungs for hours. "Frank Morgan!" he said again as he stalked down the empty street. Everyone with any sense at all had long since found somewhere else to be. "Morgan, you stinkin' bastard. I know you're in there somewhere. Are you gonna get out here so I can square with you?" The sheriff's eyes raged with the predatory fury of a wolf on the hunt.

Beaumont watched him from the window. "He's been through the mill, that one has. Look at that. His shirt's about ripped to shreds. I reckon those stories folks are tellin' about his wife and him having a knock-down-drag-out are true enough."

"Frank Morgan!" Whitehead croaked again. He was less than a half a block away now. "Mooooorgan! I'm gonna start taking heads off everybody I lay eyes on until you get your worthless ass out in this street!"

The Ranger hitched up his gun belt and released

a deep breath. "Well," he said matter-of-factly. "I reckon I better get out there and take care of this."

Frank watched lines of fear streak across Victoria's face as Beaumont drew his Colt and calmly checked the cylinder. The gun clicked quietly as he turned to see that each chamber was loaded. He showed no sign of apprehension.

Outside, Whitehead stood alone under the blazing sun and continued to rant and rail into the windless air.

"Tyler, please," Victoria pleaded. Her chest heaved with rapid, shallow breaths. "You don't know what Sheriff Whitehead is capable of. Some say he's the fastest man alive today."

"Ranger Beaumont." Morgan came up behind the young man and put a gentle hand on his shoulder. "I appreciate what you're about to do, but this is a county matter." He held up the silver badge the judge had left lying on the table. "I believe that duty falls to me. No need for the state to get involved."

"Frank," Tyler protested. "You're not even over your last fight. I saw how hard it was on you out at the cabin. I'd be an awful poor excuse for a friend if I don't take care of this. Whitehead is bad medicine, but I can take him. I know I can. I got right on my side."

"Wrong men kill right men every day of the week." Morgan gave a resigned sigh. "Anyhow, he doesn't want you. He wants me. Listen to him out there. If I allow you to do this when it's my duty, and something happened to you, I'd never be able to forgive myself." He glanced up and caught Mercy's eye, then smiled softly at Victoria. "And the

Good Lord knows I got a wagon load of things to feel guilty about already."

"Don't worry so much, Frank. I can do this."

"I don't doubt your skill at arms, son. You know that." He began to check his own pistol. "You ever seen two buffalo bulls when they fight?"

Beaumont shrugged. "I don't believe I have."

"Well let me tell you, there's a lot of huffin' and bellerin' to begin with. But, after it's all said and done, one of those bulls is torn up and injured so bad he can't be helped." Morgan paused and slipped the Peacemaker back into his holster. He looked Beaumont square in the eye. "And the other bull—well, that other bull is dead. Get out of my way, Tyler. You got plenty of days left to fight your fights."

Mercy suddenly tore away from her husband and threw her arms around Frank. The judge stood still, watching. If his wife's behavior upset him, he didn't show it.

"Don't do this, Frank," she whispered. Her voice was breathy, almost too soft to hear. "I'm afraid he'll kill you. I don't think I could bear losing you all over again. I got you into all this with that foolish telegram. This isn't even your fight."

Morgan gently pushed her away with both hands. He smiled and settled his hat squarely on his head. "I got a handful of fights left in me—but this one here is surely mine."

39

The sun was high when Morgan breasted the door and stepped out on the street to face Sheriff Reed Whitehead. The buildings around the open courthouse square cast squat shadows in the dust. It was close enough to noon that neither man would have to contend with light in his eyes.

"Well, looky here," Whitehead said when Morgan stopped to face him. His voice was raw rough as a saw blade. "I figured you were busy slinkin' out the back door—or hiding behind that slut girlfriend of yours. Oh, don't think we didn't know about the two of you. The whole town knows you had a thing goin' before you ran away."

Morgan stood still, watching for the telltale movement that would signify Whitehead was about to draw. He let the harsh words about Mercy slide off his back without comment or second thought. Insults before a fight, particularly insults about an innocent woman, would not be tolerated. During a fight, Morgan kept his temper in check. A quick temper clouded the mind and wrecked the concentration. It was more than likely to get a man killed. There was no need to get upset when a reckoning was already so close at hand.

"I owe you a good thrashing," Whitehead growled. "For what you did to me and my family."

"Suit yourself," Morgan said. "Throw down your gun and I'll face you in a fistfight."

The sheriff shook his head. He winced slightly as if the action hurt him. His eyes were narrow bloodshot slits. "No, Frank Morgan needs to die in a gunfight."

"You got no way out of this, Whitehead. Even if you managed to take me, this town will never let you just ride away."

"I know that. I'm a dead man. But that's what makes this so easy. Men who know they're dead anyhow don't have a lot to fret about."

The sheriff's hand hung motionless above the butt of his pistol. If he had a telltale, he wasn't showing it. There was something in his face, something in the way he stood, that Frank couldn't quite make out.

At first he chalked it up to swagger, or maybe just false confidence. When he hit on the answer, it stunned him as much as a slap. Whitehead had a complete lack of fear. There was a quiet calm about the gunman that said he'd plowed this ground many times before and he was ready to go at it again.

It was a look Morgan had seen thousands of times—every time he looked in a mirror at his own reflection.

Rance Whitehead was not going to be an easy adversary.

Both men stood completely still, looking at each other, searching for a weakness in their opponent. Finding none, they kept looking. They were less than ten yards apart.

"When I'm done with you," Whitehead said, "I'll have time to take care of the judge and your girlfriend before I'm finished."

"You gonna get down to business, or you just gonna stand there and talk trash all day?"

"Maybe I'll have time to finish what my boy started with that little whore."

Whitehead's breathing had been relaxed and slow. When he stopped and held his breath for an instant, Morgan knew he was a hairbreadth away from drawing.

Tyler Beaumont would later say he never saw either man draw.

Their guns appeared in their hands simultaneously. Smoke and fire flashed from both barrels at the same moment. When the smoke cleared, both men stood, still facing each other. Onlookers held their breath, waiting to see what would happen next. Then, Whitehead's gun spun on his finger and fell to the dust. The tall man swayed, blinking unbelieving eyes before he pitched forward into the deserted street.

Beaumont was first out the door. He kicked Whitehead's pistol out of reach and rolled him over. He looked up at Frank. "You shot him in the mouth." The Ranger took off his hat and scratched his head. "Straight through the damned mouth. Who shoots anybody through the mouth?"

"That's what I was aimin' for. I got sick of listenin' to his trash." Morgan reloaded his Colt and slid it back in the holster. "Don't think I could have put up with another word of it."

Beaumont stood when Frank came up next to the body. He noticed a long rip in the gunman's shirt, just under his right armpit.

"You hurt?"

Morgan followed Beaumont's eyes to the spot and reached up to touch it with his left hand. "I don't believe I am."

He fingered the torn cloth. "Looks like he grazed my shirt," he mused. "Luke's wife, Carolyn, is mighty handing with a needle and thread; maybe she'll sew it up for me."

"You were half an inch from taking another bullet. Inches away from dyin' and it don't seem to bother you."

Morgan shrugged. "I reckon none of us are that far off from dyin' one way or another."

"Whatever you say, Frank," Beaumont scoffed, and gave his friend a good-natured slap on the back. "Some of us are closer than others."

40

"Are you certain you won't reconsider?" Judge Monfore leaned against his cane with a beefy hand and gave Morgan a sidelong look.

"Nope," Morgan said. "I don't believe I will." He had a long list of reasons why he shouldn't take the job as sheriff of Parker County, but excuses appeared flimsy as corn silk when said out loud. It was best to just decline.

"Your Honor, this county is chock full of capable men. I know; I grew up with some of 'em." Morgan gave Judge Monfore back the silver badge and shook his hand. "You'll find someone who'll fill the bill much better than I would."

Mercy was misty-eyed, but her face showed relief that he was not going to stay around and complicate her life. "Where will you go from here?" she asked.

"Well, I got a few things I need to catch up on. First, I intend to stop by and see Luke and Carolyn Perkins. They got 'em a new baby son." Morgan took off his hat and smoothed back his hair. "They're namin' the poor little cuss Frank of all things. It's a damn poor thing to do to a child if you ask me."

He reached out to shake Victoria's hand. She

took it, but smirked and tugged him to her. "You'd think I was a little girl and you were about to pat me on the head. Give me a proper good-bye, Mr. Morgan." She wrapped her arms around his waist and squeezed, hugging him hard, and gave him a surprising kiss on the cheek.

"I'd leave too, if I thought you'd say good-bye like that," Beaumont joked.

"Well, now," Morgan said, a little dazed from the sudden outpouring of emotion. "Since you're not a little girl, I reckon you should dispense with the Mr. Morgan business and go on and call me Frank."

"I'll do that, Frank," Victoria said. There was a tear in her eye, but her lips smiled brightly. "Come by and see us more often."

When Frank returned his hat to his head and tipped it like he was ready to go, Mercy suddenly broke away from her husband. Victoria stepped over so the judge could lean against her.

"May I walk alongside you to your horse?" Mercy's voice was soft and sweet as honey.

Morgan glanced up at the judge. Monfore gave him a smiling nod. There was no animosity in it. Frank wondered if *he'd* be such a generous man if the situation was reversed.

"Give us a minute, Tyler, and then meet me over by the livery," Frank said as Mercy took his arm. "I need to talk to you before I go."

"You got it," Beaumont said.

"I'd given up hope of ever seeing you again," Mercy said when they were out of earshot of the group.

"I figured a man like me was pretty easy to get over."

"Hardly." Mercy turned to face him when they got to the horses. "Frank . . ."

Morgan held his breath, almost afraid she'd confirm what he already felt was true. He had a dozen questions he wanted to ask, but he intended to keep his promise.

"Frank," she continued. "It really doesn't matter who's daughter she is, does it?"

He shook his head. "I suppose not."

"All right then. Don't let it keep you away." She tiptoed up to kiss him softly. Her lips trembled. "Now, I'm a happily married woman. That's the last time that will ever happen," she said as she smoothed the front of her dress with both hands. "But I hope this isn't the last time we see you. You can be a drifter if you want to, Frank Morgan, but don't let that make you a stranger."

"You beat all I ever saw, Mercy Monfore," Frank whispered. "You sure do."

Beaumont walked along with Morgan as he led Stormy and the new palomino packhorse north out of town toward the Double Diamond Ranch. The shadows were long and orange. There was only about an hour of daylight left, but Frank felt the need to be on the move—at least as far as Luke's.

"This is a fine-looking mare you got yourself here." The Ranger ran a hand down the packhorse's broad rump. "I have to say, though, I never figured you for a man to ride a yellow horse."

"I don't intend to ride her. She's a packhorse."

Frank grinned and waved over his shoulder at Mercy and the others. He tipped his head and took on a conspiratorial tone. "To tell you the truth, I've had my hands full of dark-headed women for the last little bit. I believe I'll go with a blonde for a while."

"Speakin' of dark-headed women," Beaumont said. He took off his hat. "I wonder if I could get your permission to court Victoria more seriously."

Morgan stopped in his tracks. He shrugged. "It's not up to me. I reckon you should be going to the judge with that petition. Doesn't matter what happened in the past. He's her father."

"I know that, and I already checked it out with him. He said he wouldn't stand in our way."

"Well, there you go then," Morgan said, ready to dismiss any further talk on the matter. He reached to turn a stirrup toward him and speared it with his boot.

"You know what Miss Vicky said? She said I still had to ask your permission."

Morgan took his foot out of the stirrup and turned around. "She did, did she?"

The Ranger nodded. "She did."

Morgan was taken aback a little. He climbed into the saddle with a groan and reached down to shake the lawman's hand. "You have my blessing then, Tyler Beaumont. Just do me a favor and treat her better than I did her mama. Settle down and base your Rangering out of here."

"Where shall we wire if she decides to take me up on a proposal—down the road a little?" Beaumont bounced in his boots and seemed about ready to bust with boyish enthusiasm.

Morgan gathered up Stormy's reins and thought for a minute. The horse's ears perked and he pawed the ground with a forefoot. "I'll wire you in a week or two. Maybe you'll know which way is up by then." Morgan prodded Beaumont with his toe. "You're so bum-fuzzled right now, you'd likely give me the wrong date and time. If there is to be a wedding, you can feel free to tell Miss Vicky I'll be pleased to come back for it. That's certain."

Morgan paused and looked down at the tough little Texas Ranger who'd become like a son to him over the past few months. "You remember that sad little excuse for a window in my room back in Amarillo?"

Beaumont shrugged. "I guess so. Wasn't much of a window."

"No, it wasn't. The fact is, you taught me a lesson then, when I was lookin' out at the tumbleweeds and all poutylike. Likely as not, you thought it was the shootin' contest that got through to me—or the telegram from Mrs. Monfore here." The Gunfighter dipped his head toward Mercy. "Truth is, it was you and your little lecture about the window."

"No foolin'? I don't remember sayin' anything profound."

"The fact is, kid, I never was meant to be inside lookin' *out* any window. The Good Lord made me to be outside rollin' along with the tumbleweeds and cottonwood fluff." Morgan kept his eyes on Mercy as he spoke. She stood with clenched hands beside her husband. He leaned on her—probably more than either of them realized.

"I can ride by someone else's window every once

in a blue moon and see 'em all warm and snug by their fire. For a minute, I think I'd like to be in there where it's cozy and all, lookin' out the other way—but that ain't the life I'm cut out for."

Morgan twisted and dug through his saddlebags behind him. "I almost forgot." When he turned around again he held the nickel-plated revolver he'd won in Amarillo. He grabbed it by the barrel and offered it butt-first down to Beaumont.

"I didn't win this, you did," Beaumont stammered. He licked his lips when he saw the beautiful handgun again.

"Just take the damned thing." Morgan took the reins in his hands and grinned. "Consider it an early wedding present."

"You think really she'll take me up on my offer when I ask her?"

Morgan wheeled Stormy around in a complete circle and tipped his hat to Mercy and the judge. He nodded at Victoria and took the packhorse lead from Beaumont.

"Well," he said as he put the spurs to Stormy, "if she doesn't she's no kin of mine."

Epilogue

The good people of Parker County, Texas, decided it would be best if the railroad took their stockyard and put it somewhere else—namely Ft. Worth, which was already gaining a reputation as being a rowdy cow town with all the attendant vice and violence.

Morgan spent two days with Luke Perkins and his large extended family. He looked in on his namesake, and spent some time teaching Jasper and Chance to shoot down by an old clay bank where the noise wouldn't scare the baby or the milk cows.

Both boys had talent, but they had a tendency to rush their shots. Frank suspected they were each showing off for their respective Fossman twin. Each of the girls stood a few feet behind them with hands over her ears.

High on a limestone mesa, unbeknownst to Morgan and the others, or even to the scruffy cur dog that lazed in the sun, oblivious to the noise, a lone figure knelt in the cedar brush and watched through a brass spyglass. He was careful not to let it catch the sunlight and give away his position.

Watching Morgan shoot made Chas Ferguson feel light-headed. He collapsed the spyglass and returned it to its leather case before rolling over on his back to look up into the cloudless sky. A cool wind brushed the thin blond beard on his boyish face.

Ferguson had watched from the hotel across the street while Morgan shot Rance Whitehead in the mouth. He'd jumped like a surprised dog when he heard the shot. Later, he looked at the body and saw the way the teeth had all been broken or torn away. As he looked, a deadly calm overcame his body. It was at that moment he realized that it didn't matter if the same fate lay in store for him. He had to play the cards that were dealt. One way or another he had to face Morgan. There was no getting around it.

Ferguson backed away from the edge of the mesa before he stood and brushed off the front of his fancy striped britches and returned the Stetson to his curly head.

Maybe Frank Morgan would shoot out all his teeth—maybe he would kill Frank Morgan. None of that really mattered anymore. Some things were worse than dying. As long as the Gunfighter went on living, Ferguson knew he would never truly be alive himself.

The dandy climbed into his saddle and listened to thc pop and crack of the shots over the ledge behind him. They didn't make him flinch anymore. He wheeled his horse and smiled to himself.

"Frank Morgan," he whispered into the wind. "I do believe I'm ready."

AFTERWORD:

NOTES FROM THE OLD WEST

In the small town where I grew up, there were two movie theaters. The Pavilion was one of those old-timey movie show palaces, built in the heyday of the Mary Pickford and Charlie Chaplin silent era of the 1920s. By the 1950s, when I was a kid, the Pavilion was a little worn around the edges, but it was still the premier theater in town. They played all those big Technicolor biblical Cecil B. DeMille epics and corny MGM musicals. In Cinemascope, of course.

On the other side of town was the Gem, a somewhat shabby and rundown grindhouse with sticky floors and torn seats. Admission was a quarter. The Gem booked low-budget B pictures (remember the Bowery Boys?), war movies, horror flicks, and westerns. I liked the westerns best. I could usually be found every Saturday at the Gem, along with my best friend Newton Trout, watching Westerns from 10 AM until my father came looking for me around suppertime. (Sometimes Newton's dad was dispatched to come fetch us.) One time, my dad came to get me, right in the middle of *Abilene Trail,* which featured the now-forgotten Whip Wilson. My father became so engrossed in the action he sat down and watched the rest of it with us. We didn't get home until after dark, and my mother's meatloaf was a pan of gray ashes by the time we did. Though my father and I were both in the doghouse the next day, this remains one of my fondest childhood memories.

There was Wild Bill Elliot, and Gene Autry, and Roy Rogers, and Tim Holt and, a little later, Rod Cameron and Audie Murphy. Of these newcomers, I never missed an Audie Murphy western, because was Audie was sort of an anti-hero. Sure, he stood for law and order and was an honest man, but sometimes he had to go around the law to uphold it. If he didn't play fair, it was only because he felt hamstrung by the laws of the land. Whatever it took to get the bad guys, Audie did it. There were no finer points of law, no splitting of legal hairs. It was instant justice, devoid of long-winded lawyers, bored or biased jurors, or black-robed, often corrupt judges.

Steal a man's horse and you were the guest of honor at a necktie party.

Molest a good woman and you got a bullet in the heart or a rope around the gullet. Or at the very least, you got the crap beat out of you.

Rob a bank and face a hail of bullets or the hangman's noose.

Saved a lot of time and money, did frontier justice.

That's all gone now, I'm sad to say. Now you hear, "Oh, but he had a bad childhood" or "His mother didn't give him enough love" or "The homecoming queen wouldn't give him a second look and he has an inferiority complex." Or cultural rage, as the politically correct bright boys refer to it. How many times have you heard some self-important defense attorney moan, "The poor kids were only venting their hostilities toward an uncaring society"?

Mule fritters, I say. Nowadays, you can't even call a punk a punk anymore. But don't get me started.

It was "howdy, ma'am" time, too. The good guys, antihero or not, were always respectful to the ladies. They might shoot a bad guy five seconds after tipping their hat to a woman, but the code of the West demanded you be respectful to a lady.

Lots of things have changed since the heyday of the Wild West, haven't they? Some for the good, some for the bad.

I didn't have any idea at the time that I would someday write about the West. I just knew that I was captivated by the Old West.

When I first got the itch to write, back in the early 1970s, I didn't write westerns. I started by writing horror and action adventure novels. After more than two dozen novels, I began thinking about developing a western character. From those initial musings came the novel *The Last Mountain Man: Smoke Jensen*. That was followed by *Preacher: The First Mountain Man*. A few years later, I began developing the Last Gunfighter series. Frank Morgan is a legend in his own time, the fastest gun west of the Mississippi . . . a title and a reputation he never wanted, but can't get rid of.

The Gunfighter series is set in the waning days of the Wild West. Frank Morgan is out of time and place, but still, he is pursued by men who want to earn a reputation as the man who killed the legendary gunfighter. All Frank wants to do is live in peace. But he knows in his heart that dream will always be just that: a dream, fog and smoke and mirrors, something elusive that will never really come to fruition. He will be forced to wander the West, alone, until one day his luck runs out.

For me, and for thousands—probably millions—of other people (although many will never publicly admit it), the old Wild West will always be a magic, mysterious place: a place we love to visit through the pages of books; characters we would like to know . . . from a safe distance; events we would love to take part in, again, from a safe distance. For the old Wild West was not a place for the faint of heart. It was a hard, tough, physically demanding time. There were no police to call if one faced adversity. One faced trouble alone, and handled it alone. It was rugged individualism: something that appeals to many of us.

I am certain that is something that appeals to most readers of westerns.

I still do on-site research (whenever possible) before starting a western novel. I have wandered over much of the West, prowling what is left of ghost towns. Stand in the midst of the ruins of these old towns, use a little bit of imagination, and one can conjure up life as it used to be in the Wild West. The rowdy Saturday nights, the tinkling of a piano in a saloon, the laughter of cowboys and miners letting off steam after a week of hard work. Use a little more imagination and one can envision two men standing in the street, facing one another, seconds before the hook and draw of a gunfight. A moment later, one is dead and the other rides away.

The old wild untamed West.

There are still some ghost towns to visit, but they are rapidly vanishing as time and the elements take their toll. If you want to see them, make plans to do so as soon as possible, for in a few years, they will all be gone.

And so will we.

Stand in what is left of the Big Thicket country of east Texas and try to imagine how in the world the pioneers managed to get through that wild tangle. I have wondered that many times and marveled at the courage of the men and women who slowly pushed westward, facing dangers that we can only imagine.

Let me touch briefly on a subject that is very close to me: firearms. There are some so-called historians who are now claiming that firearms played only a very insignificant part in the settlers' live. They claim that only a few were armed. What utter, stupid nonsense! What do these so-called historians think the pioneers did for food? Do they think the early settlers rode down to the nearest supermarket and bought their meat? Or maybe they think the settlers chased down deer or buffalo on foot and beat the animals to death with a club. I have a news flash for you so-called historians: the settlers used guns to shoot their game. They used guns to defend hearth and home against Indians on the warpath. They used guns to protect themselves from outlaws. Guns are a part of Americana. And always will be.

The mountains of the West and the remains of the ghost towns that dot those areas are some of my favorite subjects to write about. I have done extensive research on the various mountain ranges of the West and go back whenever time permits. I sometimes stand surrounded by the towering mountains and wonder how in the world the pioneers ever made it through. As hard as I try and as often as I try, I simply cannot imagine the hardships those men and women endured over the hard months of their incredible journey. None of us can. It is said that on the Oregon Trail alone, there are at least two bodies in lonely unmarked graves for every mile of that journey. Some students of the West say the number of dead is at least twice that. And nobody knows the exact number of wagons that impatiently started out alone and simply vanished on the way, along with their occupants, never to be seen or heard from again.

Just vanished.

The one-hundred-and-fifty-year-old ruts of the wagon wheels can still be seen in various places along the Oregon Trail. But if you plan to visit those places, do so quickly, for they are slowly disappearing. And when they are gone, they will be lost forever, except in the words of western writers.

As long as I can peck away at a keyboard and find a company to publish my work, I will not let the old West die. That I promise you.

As the Drifter in the Last Gunfighter series, Frank Morgan has struck a responsive cord among the readers of frontier fiction. Perhaps it's because he is a human man, with all of the human frailties. He is not a super hero. He likes horses and dogs and treats them well. He has feelings and isn't afraid to show them or admit that he has them. He longs for a permanent home, a place to hang his hat and sit on the porch in the late afternoon and watch the day slowly fade into night . . . and a woman to share those simple pleasures with him.

But Frank also knows he can never relax his vigil and probably will never have that long-wished-for hearth and home. That is why he is called the Drifter. Frank Morgan knows there are men who will risk their lives to face him in a hook and draw, slap leather, and pull that big iron, in the hopes of killing the West's most famous gunfighter, so they can claim the title of the man who killed Frank Morgan, the Drifter. Frank would gladly, willingly, give them that title, but not at the expense of his own life.

So Frank Morgan must constantly drift, staying on the lonely trails, those out-of-the-way paths through the timber, the mountains, the deserts that are sometimes called the hoot-owl trail. His companions are the sighing winds, the howling of wolves, the yapping of coyotes, and a few, very few precious memories. And his six-gun. Always, his six-gun.

Frank is also pursued by something else: progress. The towns are connected by telegraph wires. Frank is recognized wherever he goes and can be tracked by telegraphers. There is no escape for him. Reporters for various newspapers are always on his trail, wanting to interview Frank Morgan, as are authors, wanting to do more books about the legendary gunfighter. Photographers want to take his picture, if possible with the body of a man Frank has just killed. Frank is disgusted by the whole thing and wants no part of it. There is no real rest for the Drifter. Frank travels on, always on the move. He tries to stay off the more heavily traveled roads, sticking to lesser-known trails, sometimes making his own route of travel, across the mountains or deserts.

Someday perhaps Frank will find some peace.

Maybe. But if he does, that is many books from now.

The West will live on as long as there are writers willing to write about it, and publishers willing to publish it. Writing about the West is wide open, just like the old Wild West. Characters abound, as plentiful as the wide-open spaces, as colorful as a sunset on the Painted desert, as restless as the ever-sighing winds. All one has to do is use a bit of imagination. Take a stroll through the cemetery at Tombstone, Arizona; read the inscriptions. Then walk the main street of that once-infamous town around midnight and you might catch a glimpse of the ghosts that still wander the town. They really do. Just ask anyone who live there. But don't be afraid of the apparitions, they won't hurt you. They're just out for a quiet stroll.

The West lives on. And as long as I am alive, it always will.

THE MOUNTAIN MAN SERIES BY
WILLIAM W. JOHNSTONE

__The Last Mountain Man	0-8217-6856-5	$5.99US/$7.99CAN
__Return of the Mountain Man	0-7860-1296-X	$5.99US/$7.99CAN
__Trail of the Mountain Man	0-7860-1297-8	$5.99US/$7.99CAN
__Revenge of the Mountain Man	0-7860-1133-1	$5.99US/$7.99CAN
__Law of the Mountain Man	0-7860-1301-X	$5.99US/$7.99CAN
__Journey of the Mountain Man	0-7860-1302-8	$5.99US/$7.99CAN
__War of the Mountain Man	0-7860-1303-6	$5.99US/$7.99CAN
__Code of the Mountain Man	0-7860-1304-4	$5.99US/$7.99CAN
__Pursuit of the Mountain Man	0-7860-1305-2	$5.99US/$7.99CAN
__Courage of the Mountain Man	0-7860-1306-0	$5.99US/$7.99CAN
__Blood of the Mountain Man	0-7860-1307-9	$5.99US/$7.99CAN
__Fury of the Mountain Man	0-7860-1308-7	$5.99US/$7.99CAN
__Rage of the Mountain Man	0-7860-1555-1	$5.99US/$7.99CAN
__Cunning of the Mountain Man	0-7860-1512-8	$5.99US/$7.99CAN
__Power of the Mountain Man	0-7860-1530-6	$5.99US/$7.99CAN
__Spirit of the Mountain Man	0-7860-1450-4	$5.99US/$7.99CAN
__Ordeal of the Mountain Man	0-7860-1533-0	$5.99US/$7.99CAN
__Triumph of the Mountain Man	0-7860-1532-2	$5.99US/$7.99CAN
__Vengeance of the Mountain Man	0-7860-1529-2	$5.99US/$7.99CAN
__Honor of the Mountain Man	0-8217-5820-9	$5.99US/$7.99CAN
__Battle of the Mountain Man	0-8217-5925-6	$5.99US/$7.99CAN
__Pride of the Mountain Man	0-8217-6057-2	$4.99US/$6.50CAN
__Creed of the Mountain Man	0-7860-1531-4	$5.99US/$7.99CAN
__Guns of the Mountain Man	0-8217-6407-1	$5.99US/$7.99CAN
__Heart of the Mountain Man	0-8217-6618-X	$5.99US/$7.99CAN
__Justice of the Mountain Man	0-7860-1298-6	$5.99US/$7.99CAN
__Valor of the Mountain Man	0-7860-1299-4	$5.99US/$7.99CAN
__Warpath of the Mountain Man	0-7860-1330-3	$5.99US/$7.99CAN
__Trek of the Mountain Man	0-7860-1331-1	$5.99US/$7.99CAN

Available Wherever Books Are Sold!

Visit our website at **www.kensingtonbooks.com**

THE FIRST MOUNTAIN MAN SERIES BY
WILLIAM W. JOHNSTONE

__**The First Mountain Man**
0-8217-5510-2 **$4.99**US/**$6.50**CAN

__**Blood on the Divide**
0-8217-5511-0 **$4.99**US/**$6.50**CAN

__**Absaroka Ambush**
0-8217-5538-2 **$4.99**US/**$6.50**CAN

__**Forty Guns West**
0-7860-1534-9 **$5.99**US/**$7.99**CAN

__**Cheyenne Challenge**
0-8217-5607-9 **$4.99**US/**$6.50**CAN

__**Preacher and the Mountain Caesar**
0-8217-6585-X **$5.99**US/**$7.99**CAN

__**Blackfoot Messiah**
0-8217-6611-2 **$5.99**US/**$7.99**CAN

__**Preacher**
0-7860-1441-5 **$5.99**US/**$7.99**CAN

__**Preacher's Peace**
0-7860-1442-3 **$5.99**US/**$7.99**CAN

Available Wherever Books Are Sold!

Visit our website at **www.kensingtonbooks.com**